A Stranger in the Night

Tammy Teigland

Copyright page

Copyright 2010 © Tammy Teigland

Printed in the United States of America

Second Print December 2014

First Published February 2010

Other Releases

Taken

7 Sons of Sin

Zephyr's Kiss

Consequences

To Contact Tammy Teigland, or to receive updates about new releases, visit her website:

www.tammyteigland.com

Acknowledgments

My thanks and appreciation goes to those who supported my ideas for this book and encouraged me to write it.

To Greg Garofalo, I couldn't have done it without you.

And special thanks to Karen; I always knew this first book could be the story it was meant to be.

Prelude

It was an unusually warm day for May in Wisconsin. Katie loved the feel of the sun and wind on her face but today she'd never even noticed; she was on a mission and it was not a pleasant one. The morning paper lay folded on the seat next to her.

According to the article, a woman had been found raped and murdered late last night, the woman was unidentified. Katie had recognized her from the sketch that accompanied the report; it was the same woman she had seen leaving the bowling alley with Derrick. She didn't want to believe that Derrick had had anything to do with it; she refused to believe he could, but why hadn't he come forward and at least identified her? Did he even know his lady friend was dead? Hurt, angry and confused, she needed to confront Derrick about the other night.

Her thoughts were swirling, chasing each other like maddened squirrels, as she drove directly to Derrick's apartment above the print shop in town. When he finally opened the door she handed him the paper, folded to show the unidentified woman's sketch. "Who is she, Derrick, and why were you even with her?"

"I have no idea what you're yelling about, I don't know her!"

"Then explain to me, Derrick, because I saw you with her leaving the bowling alley two nights ago and I'm not leaving until you tell me the truth!"

"How dare you even ask me that let alone admit that you're spying on me!" Derrick growled.

"What? Ask you why you were with a woman who was found murdered?" Katie's voice rose in a mixture of anger and rising disbelief.

Angrily she turned away from him and with that Derrick snapped.

Grabbing her arm and whirling her around, Katie saw the look of a killer in his eyes.

"Stop it! You're hurting me!" Katie shouted in protest.

Derrick threw her down to the floor, cracking her head on the coffee table as she fell.

"Ahh! Are you crazy?" She was dazed but tried to fight him off. Derrick, being much bigger and stronger than she was, sat on top of her, viciously backhanded her, and then grabbed her face hard when she tried to scream.

"Scream, go ahead nobody is going to hear you, you bitch!" He yanked her arms over her head as she fought and pinned them down. Taking hold of both wrists with one hand he squeezed her face hard again. "I'm not crazy! And just so you know she pleasured me the way you never could, but I think you're going to, I know you're going to." He leaned in and licked her face, savoring the flavor of fear.

Looking down at her with an evil smile he said, "Oh relax; you might enjoy this as much as I'm going to."

"No, don't! Please - don't," She cried.

Derrick slapped her face again. Katie cried out in pain and then gasped for air as he punched her. She tried to fight back harder; Derrick's eyes were wild. He slapped her again this time splitting her lip. His hand moved to her neck; she felt his hot murderous fingers wrapping around her throat, squeezing, choking off her screams.

As black spots danced before her eyes, she realized that the more she fought the more he was getting turned on. She knew it was far too late to try anything else; she knew she was fighting for her very life. In the haziness that filled her mind she kept asking herself "who is this man?"

Derrick released her wrists but jammed his forearm to her throat pinning her like a butterfly to the floor. Katie bucked and thrashed to free herself, her clawed fingers digging deep into his arm, but, it was no match for his maddened frenzy. He ripped open her shirt, buttons flying, and pulled at her bra, its bands dug deep into her flesh until it finally gave. He bit her left nipple and raked his teeth over her breast. The more she cried out and fought, the more Derrick enjoyed himself. He violently pried her legs apart keeping them spread open with his knees; fumbling with the front of his pants and released his obscenely swollen member. Hovering over her, he slowly licked her face again relishing the taste of her tears.

Sick with fear and trembling with horror, Katie felt his hand wrap once again around her throat, slowly applying more pressure.

Knowing she was about to die, her barely audible plea came out as whimper, "Please..."

"Oh honey you don't have to beg." With that he furiously jabbed his rock hard cock into her dry and unwilling flesh, plunging deeper and deeper inside of her. The pain was like nothing she'd ever felt before, ripping her in two. He rode her hard, working himself into an orgasmic rage. His howl of success was the last thing Katie heard.

Feeling a steady drip of water, Katie slowly opened her eyes, not knowing how long she had laid there ripped in half. Her eyes widened with terror when she saw Derrick kneeling next to her pouring a cup of water over her head. "Wakey, wakey, Sleeping Beauty. Did you enjoy that, Sweetheart? I sure did. That was your best performance yet and if you liked that you're going to love this!"

Grinning manically he rose from his knees and kicked her hard in the ribs, grabbed her hair and flipped her over on to her stomach. Katie couldn't speak, couldn't fight, believed he had done his worst, she was wrong.

Pinning her arms behind her back, Derrick pushed her face into the carpet; biting her hard on the shoulder as he force himself into that place where she'd never been invaded before. The searing pain was too much for her. She cried out as he tore her apart with his hard battering ram.

As she began to black out again she heard the door crashing in, raising her eyes she saw her best friend, and now savior, come flying through the wreckage, it was Pete.

In that moment Katie shot up, fighting to catch her breath, her heart throbbing in her chest, her entire body aching from the adrenalin coursing through her veins. Her hair was matted to her face with sweat, her head flooded with the painful images still fresh in her mind. She was reliving the horrors of that fateful day and now it was haunting her dreams. The memory forever fixed in her mind.

Sitting amid the tangled up sheets she slowly looked around her room relieved to see it was empty of Derrick. Waiting for her heart rate to return to normal she looked around her new bedroom. It wasn't much right now but she had a few ideas. This was going to be her fresh start. Derrick was now only a nightmare; something ugly from her past that she was learning to overcome every day. While mentally and physically healing, Katie remembered the long road she had traveled to get to where she was today, she fought to restore the shattered pieces of herself and make them whole again. She tried desperately to hang on to who she was so she could return only stronger and wiser than before.

This new town and this old house were exactly what she needed.

Chapter 1

Her name was Katherine McGuire, but everyone called her Katie. She had just graduated from college when she had been raped, putting all her hopes and dreams on hold. Her fresh start was in the town of Burlington, Wisconsin. It was a place where the majority of the people were either farmers, or factory workers. A small clean town that had just as many taverns as it did churches. This was a friendly place where just about everyone knew you, or knew of you. Nothing exciting ever seemed to happen in Burlington.

Shortly after coming to town Katie got lucky and found a 100-year old, two-story farmhouse in the paper and rented it from an old farmer, Mr. Warren. It was a dump needing lots of work and just the perfect thing to help her overcome her past. Whoever had lived here before, must have liked living in a cave since most of the lights only had 40-watt bulbs in them. The kitchen was large and painted a dark split-pea green, the living room was muddy-brown, and the bathroom was painted a bright orange! There were three bedrooms and they weren't much better. One bedroom downstairs was a medium ocean-blue, and the other two were upstairs one being neon-green. The Picasso who had done the painting was none too careful; the paint had been dripped carelessly onto the base boards and trim. The bedroom that she would make her own looked like they must have run out of paint halfway through because part of it was pink and the rest was a peach color. At least the house had hardwood floors. Mr. Warren told her he would replace the roof, windows and siding. He also gave her permission to do whatever she would like to fix up the inside; he would deduct the cost from her rent which sounded fair to her considering the amount of work to be done. There wasn't much of a yard belonging to the house but the backyard was open to the cow pasture which made the property look larger than it was. It was going to be a challenge, but it made her happy to think of the possibilities of painting and decorating the inside, and maybe planting some flowers around the house. Where it was located, was peaceful and quiet; except on Tuesdays when she'd wake up to a little rumbling. That's usually when they dynamited the quarry behind the house.

***

Katie was able to find a job as a cocktail waitress at a local bar called the Brick Yard, the busiest bar in town. It was not what she had spent all those years in school training for but it was a good place with mostly a younger crowd from all over the area. They had up and coming bands, comedians and once in a while even Karaoke. It was a fun place to work and the owner, Bob Donnelly, was great. He made her feel welcome and, most importantly, it paid the bills.

Katie knew if she kept busy she wouldn't have time to think about the past. The first few weeks, after moving in and finding work, she spent cleaning the farmhouse; washing windows, walls, floors and all the millwork. She ripped up the old linoleum that was filthy and torn, to reveal the beautiful hard wood floors underneath.

After work she'd come home to sleep for a few hours and spend the days patching holes and cracks in the walls. She even rented a floor sander to sand those hard wood floors. She put clear coat over the finished project. At the end of three weeks the rooms were ready for paint and paper. Katie was exhausted but happy. She left the bathroom to remodel for last; it needed the most work; a total gut job.

Chapter 2

After several weeks of back breaking remodeling and large weekend crowds at the Brick Yard, Katie realized just how tired she was. She decided to talk with Bob Donnelly, and if he approved, she would enlist the help of Billie Jo as a part-time cocktail waitress working Friday and Saturday nights, to start with. Although Billie Jo was a phenomenal photographer, Katie knew she needed the extra money to cover the bills too.

As sole proprietor, Bob, was always there making sure everyone, and everything, was taken care of; he truly cared for "his kids". The bar's bouncer, Erik Jorgensen, looked like a walking advertisement for Nordic Warriors or the Green Bay Packers front line. He was large and well built at 6' 3," 255 pounds. While most people respected his size they were too intimidated to take the time to get to know him. Katie quickly made friends with him realizing he was both kind and protective of her.

There were two female bartenders Tanya and Jessica. They were the tall model types with long straight blonde hair, perfect makeup and manicures. Both were a little uppity and would rarely give Katie or Billie the time of day. Steve Young worked the upstairs bar with Tanya, usually. *He* was a character. A playful college kid, dancing around behind the bar while he mixed drinks, grabbing Tanya to spin her around, and acted like he was auditioning for the movie "Cocktail". Steve was having fun and the patrons loved him.

The bar's manager, Jack Carter, was in his early to mid thirties and in really great shape physically. He was ruggedly handsome, but quiet and aloof. Jack was always well aware of his surroundings, constantly observing every customer and employee; he knew everything that happened in the bar. Jack was rarely seen to drink or go to the "after-hours" parties. He came in early did his time and went home. In the summer he rode a black Harley proudly displaying a POW-MIA logo on the tank with the American Flag.

Katie found out that he had moved here from New Mexico as a kid, had gone to school and graduated from Burlington High. He then joined the Marines, but would never say what he did and after that he just sort of...disappeared. She also knew his father was the Medical Examiner for Burlington and Racine County. Other than that, Jack remained a mystery and like all good mystery junkies; Billie Jo was hooked.

Some nights Billie talked endlessly about him to Katie, but Billie never had the courage to approach Jack herself. She was hoping Katie would be her "wing man" and help her out. However, Jack kept to himself and didn't really converse with Katie much either.

Billie Jo was a fun loving, silly, natural blonde everyone called BJ. She was slightly taller, but even more petite than Katie with a body that lent itself to being a total clothes horse. A fantastic photographer, a sweet girl, but she had the warped idea that men were attracted to dumb blondes, and acted accordingly.

Some nights the bar was insanely busy and it was on those nights, when Katie needed her most, that she couldn't get Billie to actually work. She was too busy dancing with the patrons and having fun; it was one big party for BJ.

***

Erik was quietly sitting at the bar trying not to be too obvious about his feelings for Jessica. He wore the same thing every day; blue jeans and a tight white T-shirt that showed off every bump and ripple of muscle. His arms were larger around than Katie's thighs, and Jessica noticed. All the women noticed.

Katie felt Tanya was over the top. She didn't like the way she would carry on and bring unnecessary and unwanted attention to Erik.

"Erik, I didn't know you had a birthday coming up!" Tanya coyly exclaimed, putting her hand on Erik's broad shoulder.

"Of course you did, Tanya!" Erik said with a sarcastic smile.

Billie and Katie listened while getting their trays ready for the bar to open. Rolling their eyes at each other and mimicking Tanya.

Jack came up from behind and slapped Erik on the back. "Hey buddy! We're all going out Tuesday night! None of us work that day and it is all set!"

"Jaaack, are you feeling alright?" Erik asked while stretching out his name in a deep questioning way.

"Nope – consider yourself hijacked! I even have a designated driver all lined up for you!"

Erik was grinning from ear to ear, "And who would that be?"

Jessica piped in, "That would be me!"

Erik raised a very interested brow, "So Jess, does that mean I can get my birthday kiss?" He beamed with pure joy on his face.

Jessica threw a bar towel at him, "We'll see!" She quipped.

Jack made his way over to the end of the bar where Billie and Katie stood listening in. "You girls are invited too ya know! Erik wouldn't want it any other way."

Billie didn't wait for her friend's response. "We would love to! Sounds like fun!"

Tanya was slightly jealous of Katie and Billie; it was obvious by how she glared in their direction anytime Jack talked to them.

"So where and when?" an overly bubbly Billie asked.

"Doug's around 7 p.m. Bob is even getting a cake accompanied by a fire extinguisher!" Jack said with an evil grin.

"We'll be there." Katie said glancing back at Tanya, making sure her barb had hit the mark.

Jack turned picking up on Tanya's disdain; he just shook his head giving her a disappointed look.

Billie was dying to find out what *that* was all about.

Chapter 3

Tuesday came and Billie showed up early at Katie's. She had a habit of just walking in without knocking, then shouting, "Hey girlie! Where ya be?"

Katie, expecting Billie, was in her room trying to decide what to wear. "I'm up stairs!" She hollered back.

Billie's cowboy boots clomped as she walked up the wooden treads and stepped into the bedroom. "So, what do you think?" She asked while admiring herself in the old-time dresser mirror.

Katie poked her head out of the closet long enough to take a quick glance. Surprised at Billie's outfit she stepped out. "WOW! Who dressed you?"

"What does that mean?"

"Well, you look nice!"

"Okay - what does *that* mean?" Billie stood with her hands on her hips, feigning a hurt look.

"Nothing, but it isn't how you usually dress. You actually look...well...you don't look like a hooker!" Katie said positively chuckling.

She stuck her tongue out at Katie. "I don't dress like a hooker!" Paused while taking a second look in the mirror, "Okay, maybe a little slutty at times." She said with a smile.

Billie had on a pair of nice fitting blue jeans that hugged her curves, not too tight, with a Kippy belt to add some bling and accentuate her small waist, a sleeveless loose fitting ruffled silk blouse tucked in, black leather motor cycle jacket in hand, and her fancy cowboy boots. Her hair and makeup were done up like she was going for a job interview instead of a party. Katie was very impressed and wondered just why Billie looked so good. Well, not really, Katie amended; she knew the attraction Billie had for Jack.

"You look really good, Billie! Now I have to figure out something to wear!"

"Just grab your button fly Levi's, put on that cute little red cotton sweater set you got from Pete and your red high heel pumps! It is a classic look for you." Billie grinned like she just solved all the world's problems.

"You're right...I love that outfit. But we're going to Doug's aren't the red heels a bit much?"

"Hell no! That's what makes the outfit!"

Billie was anxious to go and even Katie thought a night out with friends would be enjoyable. Everyone liked Erik; he was a lot of fun!

"Come on Katie! How can it take you so long to put your face on? You barely wear any makeup!"

"Sweetie, that's the idea, to look like you aren't wearing any. Besides we are less than 10-minutes from Doug's bar. We still have a half hour before we have to leave. What's the rush?"

"Oh? I guess I didn't read the time right."

"You're dying to get there, so tell me?"

Billie was about ready to burst. "Okay - so I asked Steve what was up with Jessica and Tanya and why they don't seem to like us? Well, he told me that Erik has always had a mini crush on Jess, and she has a jealous streak. And Tanya used to date Jack, but then he dumped her just like that!" She said with excitement as she snapped her fingers.

"Steve told you this?"

"Yeah, and when I asked him about Jack he didn't say much."

Katie knew Billie was dying for her to ask for more information on Jack and so, with the usual prompting tones and questions she got Billie to tell more. Sigh, "What *did* he say?"

"That Jack isn't seeing anyone right now and hasn't since Tanya, and no one really knows why, not even Tanya! But she would love to get back with Jack. Steve also said that there was this other guy that might have had something to do with it, but it was just a guess. Jack doesn't talk about it and no one dares to ask."

"Really, that explains a lot. Especially the dirty looks we get. Tanya probably thinks he's interested in one of us."

"I just hope he notices me tonight."

Katie unplugged her curling iron.

"Finally, can we go already?"

"Don't be in such a rush; don't you want to be fashionably late?"

"Whatever, let's go!" BJ said impatiently.

Katie slid on her red heels and locked the door behind her. "Billie, I would like to drive if that's alright with you?"

"Sure! I'll just leave my car where it is."

The girls climbed into Katie's Candy Apple Red 1969 Chevy Nova SS. It was a classic muscle car and Billie loved cruising in it.

Katie started her up and the beautiful car barely made a sound as it rumbled to life. You could just feel the powerful engine vibrating. Hardly touching the gas, Katie quickly pulled out onto the highway and they were gone.

It was a beautiful evening so the windows were down and the girls' hair blew in the wind.

"So much for doing our hair!" Katie joked.

Billie just smiled leaning forward and turned up the radio. AC/DC was playing, which happened to be one of their favorite groups. By the time the song "Highway to Hell" had finished they were parked at Doug's. They rolled up the windows and gently shut the doors to Katie's pride and joy.

As Katie turned back to make sure her car was locked, a beautiful orange and black 1969 Roadrunner pulled into the spot next to hers. The beefy engine pulsed through the ground, through her high heels and rumbled right up her spine. Katie froze looking at the magnificent car not noticing the silence when the car was shut off.

The Roadrunner's door opened and Katie saw a slick cowboy boot step onto the ground followed by a pair of long legs hugged in jeans. Her eyes traveled up the trim waist to the snug polo top clinging to a well muscled chest. Unable to help herself, her slow inspection continued to a strong jaw, straight nose and the most piercing grey eyes she had ever seen, the close cropped dark hair didn't even register in her mind.

For his part, the owner of the Roadrunner first noticed the car, it was obviously a labor of love, and then he couldn't help but notice the woman in the red high heels. She was cute as hell. Her auburn red hair, windswept and wild, tumbled around her shoulders and set off her hazel-green eyes. The lipstick she wore accented her plump bowed lips, that he would dearly love to kiss, and a smooth creamy complexion just waiting to be touched. She was slender and toned, standing gracefully on impossibly high heels. He knew that without the shoes she would snug up just right into his shoulder.

At that moment Bob Donnelly broke the spell surrounding the two. "Hey girls, I am glad you came. Erik is going to get the biggest kick out of this!" As the girls turned and walked over to Bob he saw Cal walking up behind them.

"Cal!" He said jovially, "I want you to meet Katie and Billie Jo. They are our two newest members at the Brick Yard. A couple of great gals."

"Girls, this is Cal Chapman, one of Burlington's finest, and a close friend of Erik's."

Reaching out a hand to both girls, "It's nice to meet you."

"You too," they answered back.

"So Katie, that's a great car you have out there."

"Thanks! She's a nice ride." She said with a smile.

"I am sure she is." Cal smiled back, skillfully hiding his real thoughts about that ride. But his smile was genuinely warm and friendly if a bit distracted.

Jack saw the girls walk in with Cal. He couldn't take his eyes off Billie, watching her long blonde wavy hair flowing down over her black leather jacket. Jack also noticed that she sure could fill out a pair of jeans. *"Damn she's hot, young, but hot. Watch it boy"* he thought to himself as he gave a nod in their direction.

Billie, not wanting to miss an opportunity, strolled over to the bar to order a drink at the place next to Jack. "Can I get a 7-up, please?"

"What? Taking it easy on your night off?"

Billie just coyly shrugged as she took a sip from the straw the bartender put in her glass.

She asked Jack, "What time is Erik supposed to be here?"

"Well, that depends on Jessica!" Jack said with a sly grin.

Cal and Katie were still talking cars when they finally made it over to the bar.

Cal shook Jack's hand, "Jack can I get you another beer?"

"Hell Cal, I won't refuse a beer from you! Thanks."

"Katie what would you like?"

"Crown Royal and Pepsi if they have it?" Katie answered.

"Crown Royal? You a whiskey girl, Kate?" Jack was surprised.

Apparently Cal was also surprised, holding up two fingers, "Make that two." He told the bartender.

"Sorry — I'm not a cheap date!" Katie said laughing.

"A date huh?" Cal flashed her, his warm smile.

She gave him a little wink doing her best to flirt. It had been a while, but this felt good to loosen up.

Bob walked over with another guy to join them. "I want you guys to meet Eddie Landers. I just hired him to help Erik out."

This was the first Jack knew about this. He usually had a hand in the hiring. He eyed Eddie up and down, taking measure.

Bob continued "Eddie, this is Jack, Billie, Katie, and Cal. Cal's a local yokel. You will get to know him real well considering some of our clientele."

Eddie, who was relatively new in town and fresh out of the Army Rangers, was about 6'2" and made of lean muscle, had a chiseled jaw line, deep set dark-brown eyes that were almost black and wore his hair in a typical military buzz cut. He was quiet and kind of standoffish, but the group included him and joked around while waiting for the rest of the party to get there.

Cal noticed that Eddie may not have said much but he couldn't keep his eyes off Kate. Who could blame him, Katie was a looker.

Erik finally came bursting through the door larger than life. He was genuinely happy to see everyone that came to wish him a happy birthday. He whisked up both Katie and Billie in his mammoth arms and spun them around, setting them back down and giving both a big kiss on their cheeks. "Thanks girls! I'm glad you're here."

Later on after a few shots of various liquors, Erik got a little braver, slapping Jessica on the rump.

Shooting him a big grin Jessica said, "Good thing it's your birthday!"

Katie sat with her back against the wall observing the party and thinking to herself; *I think she is just playing hard to get. There is something going on that they weren't ready to make public yet.*

Cal, Jack and Billie all sat at the same small table with her. Billie tried really hard not to talk too much. Katie knew Billie must really like Jack if she wasn't even doing that annoying giggle thing she does when she gets nervous.

Jack leaned into Billie so he wasn't yelling because of all the noise, or so he told himself, "Are you ready for a cocktail?"

Billie nodded yes. "Seven and Seven."

Jack motioned to Cal and Katie if they wanted another round. They shook their heads 'no'.

Billie noticed the ease with which Katie interacted with Cal. When Cal wasn't watching, she gave Katie the thumbs up.

Katie was actually enjoying Cal's company tonight, especially since that didn't make her the 3rd wheel for a change. She loved his casual coolness among other things about him - she definitely wanted to know more.

Jack returned with a couple of cocktails. Billie took a sip. "Thanks, Jack!"

Jack remained standing, observing Erik's guests. Billie, seeing another chance, tugged on his belt loop to get his attention. "Do you want to dance?"

Jack looked down at her blankly before answering. "Not really but if you want to I could twirl you around the floor." Then winked, at Cal?

Billie flashed her big blue eyes at him and took his hand.

Cal just chuckled, shaking his head.

"What's so funny, did I miss something?"

"Yeah, Jack doesn't dance and this isn't a dance bar!"

Katie got the joke, but caught the glare Tanya gave Jack, who was two stepping it with Billie, making her think Tanya wasn't as amused as the rest of them were.

"So what is the scoop with Jack and Tanya? Am I going to have to watch BJ's back?"

"I see you noticed Tanya's 'evil eye'. Jack - he's the bad boy she wanted to tame and couldn't. Funny thing, Tanya's kind of high maintenance, and most men can't be bothered. I should know since my brother dated her a couple of times. Tanya puts on a good act but she won't confront your friend. No worries there." Cal looked up to find Tanya glaring at Jack, and caught Eddie intently watching Katie.

Katie interrupted Cal's people watching, "So Jack is the bad boy? Do I need to warn Billie about him?" Katie said with a joking smile.

"Jack is one of the few you don't need to worry about. He will treat your friend right if it progresses to that. He moves fairly slow...your friend will probably lose interest before he gets around to realizing he likes her."

"And what about you?" She flirted, "Are you a bad boy?"

Cal smiled, and then shook his head in subtle denial. "Don't let the gun fool you."

"Really?" Holding his gaze with her eyes.

He observed how striking they were. Her hazel-green eyes had a dark ring around them, unusual yet incredible with that dark red hair. He always did like redheads.

"No, I'm more of a geek; computers and science. To tell you the truth after high school I went out East to Quantico. I was interested in forensic science, but ended up taking a different avenue with the FBI."

It was very noisy in the bar and trying to talk over the loud music was difficult, they leaned in closer to each other. Katie asked, "So what brought you back here? Sounds like you're over qualified to work for the Burlington P.D., there have to be better places to work."

"It's a long story...But if you really want to know more maybe we could have this conversation some other time?"

Katie agreed, "Next time?" Her smile warmed his heart.

Changing the direction of their conversation he asks about her, "Okay, your turn...tell me how you got here? A very attractive smart girl, and one who knows a thing or two about cars is slinging beers at the Brick Yard? What gives?"

Katie was having such a good time with her new friends, and especially with Cal, that she didn't want to ruin it by bringing up her past. "Well, that too is a really long story." She said with a big smile.

Cal was intrigued, "Well, then I guess we will have to do this again, because I definitely want to know more about you." He gave her a smile, genuine and warm, that showed even in his eyes.

Katie was happy to hear that, very happy indeed.

Jack twirled Billie back to the table. They were both laughing and had smiles so wide Jack almost didn't look like Jack. "Happy now, little lady?"

"Yes – I am! Thanks!"

Cal joined in with a chuckle; "Jack, sometimes you really surprise me!"

BJ was so wrapped up in her own little world of happiness she didn't see Tanya storm out. Apparently Jack didn't either, or if he did he didn't let on.

Erik appeared to be not quite drunk but a little beyond tipsy as he pulled up a chair, squeezing in at their tiny table. "Bar keep!" he barked, "A round of shots here please!"

He slapped Cal on the back, "Having a good time buddy? I see you finally found time to talk to a lady."

Erik leaned in towards Katie, but shot a look in Cal's direction. "Katie, now don't let this guy fool you. He's a lot smarter than he looks." Erik had a big contagious laugh.

Doug, the bartender, brought the shots out to the table including one for himself. Passing them out, then holding up his shot in a toast, "Erik, my good man...here's to life, happiness, and finding a good wife. And may you lose your virginity tonight! Bottoms up!"

"Hey now! Why do I have to find a wife, can't I just lose my virginity?" That made everyone laugh even more. This was a fun group of people. Katie was having a fantastic time.

Jack leaned over and said something to Billie. She nodded yes, and then leaned over to whisper in Katie's ear. "I am going for a ride with Jack. He said he would bring me back to get my car later. Okay?"

Katie nodded okay. "Be careful!"

When Billie got up to leave, her feet didn't seem to be touching the floor and Katie wished she could remember being that happy.

Katie watched out the window as Jack straddled his Harley, handed Billie a helmet to put on, then started the big bike it up. Billie got what she was hoping for tonight. Jack did notice her.

Katie stood to leave, so did Cal, rare for this day and age. "Oh, you don't need to stand on my account."

"You're taking off?"

"Well, it is getting kind of late."

"Then let me walk you out." Cal helped Katie with her jacket. As they left Doug's, Cal caught Eddie out the corner of his eye, studying Kate.

Katie opened her car door, "Thanks Cal, this was fun."

Cal reminded Katie, "Well don't forget, we both have promised to do this again?"

"Okay!" Katie said with a pleasant smile. "But you will have to let me know when."

She turned the key and the V-8 engine purred to life.

"You know there is nothing sexier than a woman driving a hotrod?"

"Is that so?" She couldn't hide the smile that was plastered on her face.

Cal took out his business card and handed it to her. "I will stop in to see you some time."

"You do that." Then she soundly shut her door.

Her '69 Nova was something to see, with the street lights reflecting off that glossy red paint. Cal watched as her tail lights disappeared with joy in his heart. He'd never been so taken by anyone before meeting Katie.

***

Jack toured around the lake with Billie holding on. Billie's heart sped up and the smile on her face grew wide. It was a warm evening, the stars were out. The breeze gently blew the tall grasses along the lake in waves.

Jack pulled off onto a path down by the edge of the lake and came to a stop, killing the engine. Billie swung her long leg off and around the back of the bike. She unfastened the helmet, pulling it off and tousling her blonde locks loose. Sliding a shim under his kickstand Jack took the helmet from her setting it on the bike seat. The only sound in the dark night was the ticking of the cooling engine.

"I didn't know you could get back here? This is cool!" Jack was enjoying Billie's enthusiasm.

He took Billie's hand leading her down to the rocky edge of the water. The moon was quite bright, and the lake looked like a giant mirror reflecting the night's treasures in the sky. Billie was quiet though she was dying to talk, but she just followed Jack's lead. He led her to an over grown path, where he held back the brush so they could sneak through. They came to a little clearing with a fallen tree. Jack guided them to a spot on the tree where they could sit down side by side.

"Jack this is spectacular! How in the world did you ever find this place?"

"Actually, this is my haven. I come here to just get away, and think about things."

Billie stared up at the night sky. Jack just smiled watching her looking out across the vast glistening canopy. She had an innocence about her that he couldn't help but be attracted to. He gently stroked the back of her hand with his thumb. Jack could tell how nervous she was and thought it was cute. He knew she couldn't keep quiet for too long and found it humorous she was trying so hard.

"Beautiful, really beautiful," he said to her.

"Yes they are."

"Billie Jo, I meant you are beautiful." Jack said.

She was stunned speechless. No one had said that to her before.

Even in the black velvet of the night he could tell she was blushing.

Jack gave a quiet little laugh and kissed her.

It wasn't a 'now I'm going to take you' kiss. This was a great kiss. This was a 'hello I want to know more about you' kiss. Billie, of course reciprocated. Jack took her face in his hands and they kissed again; long tender sweet kisses. Jack could have taken Billie right then and there, she was ripe for the taking but he also felt her bring out his protective side. Instead he put his arm around her and merely held her. They talked for hours just looking up at the beautiful night sky and out over the lake, with the stars twinkling in the small waves and the warm summer breeze whispering over them.

Chapter 4

Katie was doing her shopping at the local market when her cell phone went off. Looking at the number, she was not surprised to see that it was Billie, again. It wasn't that Katie wasn't happy things were working out for Billie; but she needed a break from the giddiness. She just ignored her phone. Katie continued walking up and down every aisle, and marking things she needed off her list as she acquired them. Every now and again the new guy, Eddie would be in the same aisle, but he didn't seem to be buying much. When she got into the checkout, she realized Eddie was right behind her in line.

She knew he was kind of quiet, so she said hello first. "Eddie right?"

He just gave a nod, peering into her with those black eyes. It gave her the creeps. She tried to be friendly. "Sorry I don't get to talk to you guys much when we're working together. So how do you like the Brick Yard so far?"

Eddie just made an "alright" motion with an upward shrug of his shoulders, and grunted.

"Well I guess I'll see you at work."

So much for trying to be friendly. Her cell went off again. Damn it, Billie!

Katie loaded up her groceries and returned her cart. She had a funny feeling that someone was watching her. She looked around, but really didn't see anybody obviously watching her. However, there was a guy wearing a dark hoody, smoking by the donation drop box. She just got into her car and drove home. As she crested the top of the bridge she could see BJ was already parked in the drive in front of the house. And Katie's cell rang a fourth time. She took a deep breath, letting it out in a long sigh.

Katie parked and went to open the door yelling over her shoulder. "Hi, Billie!"

"Haven't you gotten my messages? I've been trying to call you!"

"Sorry Billie, I was shopping" Handing BJ a couple of grocery bags. "I must have left the phone in the car."

Billie looked like she was about to start the water works. They brought all the bags in and started to unpack them. While Billie helped, she vented. "You are not going to believe this! I just don't get it. Jack hasn't called me!"

"Jack hasn't called you? ...Go on..."

"That's it."

Katie was completely confused at the urgency of Jack not calling. "Was he supposed to?"

BJ just huffed, shifting her weight from one side to the other. "Well!" She said absolutely exasperated by the lack of sympathy from Kate.

"Billie! Did I not tell you to not smother Jack? I said 'he is about 10 years older than we are and he doesn't do things the way the other guys you have dated do them.' "

"But! He..."

"Did I not?"

"Yes. I know what you said...I was just hoping there would be more to it than just one night."

"Now, tell me what the real issue here is, because it has only been a week!"

Billie continued venting while handing Katie cans and boxes of food to put away. Telling her how wonderful he was that night he took her for a ride. Then joked around with her that weekend while they worked, and how she asked him to go see a movie with her yesterday, but he declined. Now he hasn't called back and she won't see him until Friday night.

Brain numbing! Sigh. "Billie, did Jack give you any indication that you two were an item?"

"No!" she pouted.

"Did Jack say that you would have any more dates after last Tuesday?"

"No."

"Did you do something stupid and sleep with him?"

"Katie! Not that it's any of your business...but no...he didn't even make the offer."

"So really, you don't have an issue other than you expect him to dote on you and give you his complete attention until you get bored with him?"

"Yeah, I mean no! I really like Jack. I was hoping he felt the same way but he hasn't even called to ask me out again! What's so wrong with me?"

Katie smiled and said, "Where do you want me to begin?"

Billie shot back, "Yeah, ha ha!"

Katie took two wine coolers out of the fridge, opened one and handed it to Billie. "I know you have really been trying not to be a pest with him and talk too much or to act all giddy. But when I asked if you honestly want more than a couple of dates with him, to take his lead, I meant it! Don't rush him."

Chapter 5

Thursday night at the Brick Yard was packed. Katie called Billie in around 10 p.m.

"Thanks, Sweetie! I don't think we've ever been this busy on a Thursday."

"Sure. I'm glad I was able to come in." Which was Billie's way of saying she had nothing better to do, at least she could see Jack again.

Sometime into the evening a stranger started to inquire about Katie, asking Billie all kinds of questions. Unfortunately, she was all too eager to answer. It never occurred to her that she didn't know the man. She was so wrapped up in her commentary with this tall dark haired stranger that she didn't realize she was neglecting her tables or saying things she shouldn't.

Jack noticed Billie sitting down talking with this man and watched for a while. As the bar manager he was not happy with her ignoring their customers but as a man he really did not like feeling the green eyed worm of jealousy. Throwing a bar towel over his shoulder he stepped out from behind the bar. He was making his way through the crowd when the stranger saw Jack coming. "Say, I don't want to get you in any trouble, I have been keeping you." He said with a little wink, then got up and walked away.

"Billie!" Jack barked getting her attention over the loud music.

Jumping a little at the sound of her name she whirled around and saw Jack. They met each other in a few steps, and then Jack growled, "Do you know that guy?"

"Ah, no - he just started talking to me and asked me about Katie."

"So Katie knows that guy?"

"No, he was just interested in her and..."

Jack was really irritated and cut her off, "I hope you didn't tell him anything!"

"Oh, I didn't realize.." She said dejectedly her voice trailing off.

Jack glared at her for a moment. "Billie, come with me please?"

Billie followed but had the sinking feeling she just blew her job. He held open the storage room door for her, and then he followed in behind.

She panicked and started to talk a mile a minute, "Jack I am really sorry, I won't sit down on the job again. I promise. Katie got me this job and I don't want to ruin things for her. I didn't realize I was sitting there so long. And..."

"Do you ever take a breath?" Jack had a faint smile on his face when he interrupted her rambling.

Billie looked totally confused. "I'm talking too much? I'll stop now."

Jack raised an eyebrow at her, "I don't like the looks of that guy; there's something about him I just don't trust. I don't want you to discuss anyone here to anybody else. I can't stand gossip and especially about the people we work with to complete strangers. Do I make myself clear?"

"Yes...," she said looking down at her sneakers. "I said I was sorry and it won't happen again. Can I keep my job?"

Jack just shook his head, but still had that little smile. "Billie, I am not firing you, I wanted to make sure he wasn't bothering you. Okay?"

Billie nodded.

"And by the way; it's not Katie I'm interested in. Now why don't you help me with this keg? I need to change it out."

Billie's mood changed instantly. She liked Jack and this was the most he had said to her in days. Of course she would help him.

Katie made her way to the bar with a huge drink order. A table in the back by the stage had pitchers of beer coming and because Katie was the only one on the floor the patrons were starting to get impatient. There were so many people tonight Katie could barely get through the crowd to deliver her drinks. She picked up the tray with 4-pitchers of beer and some shots. Weaving across the floor, Katie had to stop where some bar hags were leaning against the center wall, flirting with a couple of guys. Of course they saw her coming with a full tray but they weren't going to move. Katie couldn't go around them and this was the best path to take to the back.

"Excuse me please!"

The hags just looked at her with annoyance.

"Excuse me, I need to get through."

"What was that? Exsqueaze you?" They said mockingly.

Yeah, like she'd never heard that one before.

Annoyed, Katie was through asking nicely. "Okay then, MOVE IT OR LOSE IT!"

"I don't think so." The busty bleach-blonde sneered.

By now there was a small audience. Jack and Billie were coming out of the storage room, just in time to witness what was happening.

Katie grabbed one of the pitchers and dumped its contents on the blonde's head.

Surprised by Katie's actions, the blonde was shocked and completely dumb-founded, her mouth opening and closing like a fish trying to scream.

Eddie, the new guy, enjoyed watching the whole event unfold, and he was quite amused. "Red sure is feisty."

Other patrons snickered, a table full of women clapped and laughed. They obviously knew the blonde.

Jack had the biggest smile sneak across his face. Billie thought she might have even heard a quiet chuckle come out.

"Oh shit!" Billie said under her breath, she knew when Katie got to the point of dumping perfectly good beer on someone he or she obviously deserved it. She also knew someone better escort the blonde out before Katie got more creative.

Just then Erik stepped between Katie and the blonde while Billie worked her way over to help her friend to the side. It was pretty easy to walk to the back now. More like Moses parting the Red Sea.

The rest of the night went pretty smoothly, no one wanted to run the risk of wearing their beer.

At closing time, Billie and Katie counted their tips and gave the house money back.

Billie commented while watching Katie count her cash. "You did great tonight considering you gave someone a beer bath."

They both chuckled at that.

"Do you mind if I follow you home?" She leaned in to whisper, "I have to talk to you." Billie looked up, catching on that Jack was paying attention to their conversation. He was washing the bar glasses but lifted an eyebrow in Billie's direction, letting her know he heard her.

Billie gave Jack a sheepish smile.

***

The two pulled in, one in front of the other. The sound of their doors closing echoed between the farm machinery dealer building and the house. It was really dark, the outside light must have burned out. Katie fidgeted with her keys and unlocked the door to the house. She flipped on the lights in the kitchen, hung up her keys and tossed her purse on an antique flour bin against the wall.

Katie really liked this old farmhouse. It made her happy, and it felt comfortable to her. She had fixed it up inside really nice. The kitchen was painted in a soft sunny yellow and had light colored curtains with butterflies on them. She didn't have much in the way of cabinets in there so she built a pantry that she stained to match the cupboards. The bathroom was finally redone; new toilet and sink with vanity, even new flooring. The bedroom that was downstairs, she had turned into her dining room. It was painted antique white, and she hung really pretty wallpaper up on one wall that had cherry blossoms all over it in shades of cream, mauves, and cherry. She had made curtains for this room as well, and the wood floors looked beautiful in here.

Billie made herself at home grabbing a wine cooler from the fridge and offering one to Katie.

"Sure! I think I need something to relax." Katie chuckled, thinking about earlier in the evening. "That was almost fun!"

They headed into the living room and put the radio on for background noise. This was the most comfortable room in the house. Katie had done it up in beiges, browns and gray. She had some antiques that she hung on the wall and mixed in nicely with some more modern things she had. She even hung an Oriental rug on the wall behind the stereo cabinet. The rug was mostly cream with burgundy and black. It was quite pretty.

They sat down on the couch; both kicked off their shoes and curled one leg underneath them.

"Okay, I know you are dying to tell me something!"

"I think he might like me!" BJ burst out with excitement.

"He...?" Katie knew who she was referring to but had to toy with her.

"Jack! He had me follow him into the storage room tonight, and I thought he was going to fire me 'cuz I was talking to that guy. Who he thought was bothering me, but he was asking questions about you, and I thought Jack was concerned because he was into you and..."

"Hold up a minute! What guy was asking about me? What did he look like?"

"Well, he was, I don't know sort'a tall, and had longish black hair and these eyes! His eyes were like...icy blue. Really chilly ya know?"

"What did he want to know? You didn't tell him anything did you?"

"Well, he was just wondering if my friend was seeing anyone. Can I get back to my story?"

"Billie, just please don't talk to anyone about me okay?"

"Yeah, sure."

Katie knew she really wasn't paying attention to her request, she was too anxious to talk about Jack.

"So anyway..." Billie continued to tell Katie all about what happened and what was said. And did Katie think that meant something. Should she get her hopes up?"

It felt like high school all over again...oye!

"I don't know Katie. He didn't make a direct move on me or even try to kiss me. But we had this moment, ya know?"

"I don't know what to tell you Billie. He's not at all like any of the guys you've been dating. Just take it easy, and stop acting like you're still in high school! If you really like him you won't push him. Just let it happen. Okay?"

Billie was a little miffed that Katie said she was acting like a high school girl, but decided to over look it. "I guess you're right. Well, it's late I suppose I should go home."

"Billie, why don't you just crash here tonight? That way I don't have to wonder if you made it home." It was easy to talk her into staying and truth be told, Katie really didn't want to be alone tonight.

"Thanks! Can I borrow something to sleep in?"

Chapter 6

Friday Billie and Katie were both exhausted from another long night at the bar.

"Billie do you plan on going home tonight or do you want to spend the night again?"

"Nah, I better head home. I think Torre misses me. I might find a coughed up hair ball in my shoes if I don't go home."

Katie smiled, "Ah, the benefits of owning a cat!"

She joked with Billie, but was disappointed that she would be alone tonight.

Once again Katie arrived home a little after 3 a.m. It was pitch black. *"I forgot to change the damn bulb!"* She thought to herself.

The crickets were chirping and other little noises of the night greeted her as she walked up to the front door. She took a deep breath and stepped into the house, a nagging feeling that something would be amiss followed her.

She went about her routine of changing out of her smoky clothes and tossing them down the cellar steps. Nothing seemed to be out of place. Katie locked the door to the basement and made sure it hooked.

Then she got a light bulb from the storage closet to replace the one by the front door. As she reached up to unscrew it, her fingers touched the bulb, it instantly blinked on. "Well, that's strange, how in the world does a light bulb unscrew its self?" She questioned as she closed the door behind her and locked it.

Now the only sound was of her bare feet padding across the kitchen floor. The cupboard door had a tiny squeak in its hinges. Taking a glass she filled it with water, and then took a sip. The cool water streaming down her throat was refreshing. Feeling very alone, and quite tired she took her glass of water to bed. The weight of her footsteps made the stairs squeak and creak and echo up the hallway ahead of her. They never seemed so loud before, but she was in this old house alone, and even the crickets were quiet now.

Setting the glass on the nightstand next to her bed Katie just fell into the turned down covers. She would surely fall asleep fast tonight.

***

Outside a stranger sits patiently in his car; waiting, watching, and thinking. The moon was high in the dark night sky, extending its pale beam like a searchlight through the blackness, onto the little white farmhouse. The stranger sees some movement to the north of the farmhouse. The shadow of a man slinks in-between the heavy farm equipment. The stranger watches him lurking around Katie's windows. Soon the front light goes out again.

The shadow jumps onto a low hanging branch and climbs the large oak out in front of the house.

"What's this guy doing?" He whispers to himself. The stranger in the parked car doesn't like this shadowy intruder. "Where did he go?" The shadow disappeared out of sight. Aggravated by this intruder, the stranger quietly leaves the sanctuary of his car, the dome lights disabled so as not to give him away. Stealthily he moves in closer to the house in search of the shadowed intruder.

From behind a Lilac bush the stranger waits as patiently hoping, no willing, the intruder to leave, *"He's been in there too long. What's he doing?"*

A soft scraping sound from the front of the house up on the roof, the stranger slowly raises his head towards the sound. Completely in shadow, the intruder climbs out of a vent and down on to a branch.

"So that's where he went! That sneaky little bastard!"

Jumping down to the ground the intruder had no clue that the stranger watched him. Waiting for him to lead the way north around the large farm implements, the stranger then followed the dark hooded intruder.

Chapter 7

The very next evening the stranger returned to watch from afar. He sat there for hours watching, and waiting; day-dreaming about *his* Katie. Her eyes, that red hair, and her feisty spirit. Though he waited for hours, the shadowy figure didn't come back. For an entire week the stranger would watch Katie's house waiting to see if the little sneak would come back.

Now he had to start all over again but this time the hooded creature came back. When he left Katie's he had a package of some kind. This made the stranger very curious. But he had to wait until the following night to find his way in to the dark cramped attic. The small area was hot, heavy and smelled vaguely familiar. He took a lighter from his pocket and flicked on the flame. "Holy shit! Look at all this weed. That little bastard has pot stashed up here."

The stranger quietly looks around to see what else might be in the attic. He's distracted by a noise and freezes where he stands. The floor boards squeaked a little and then, there in the far corner, was a slight trace of light. Silently moving closer to see what it might be, he finds a hidden panel. He hears movement on the other side of the wall. Waits, until the sound moves further away, he then taps on the panel lightly; then thumps it even harder in one corner. It swings out with the faintest squeak of its hinges. The stranger looks through the small opening, but only sees shoes on the floor and some clothes hung on a low rod. He realizes he's looking down into her clothes closet. Not sure if he will be able to fit through the opening he quietly closes the small door. Then leaves back the way he came.

**

Saturday came and went just as quickly. Once again coming home in the dark, Katie made her way to the front door fumbling with her keys. She opened up the door and switched on the kitchen light. She reached up to screw in the bulb again and found it was gone. "What the…?" She looked down on the porch, there was no broken glass. And she didn't see anything on the ground next to the edge either. "Who the hell steals light bulbs?"

She closed and locked the door behind her completely dumbfounded. That nagging feeling was still with her but she tried not to be paranoid.

Tonight she needed a hot shower. The bar was extra smoky it seemed and the smell of stale beer on top of the smoke was giving her a headache.

Once in the bathroom Katie stripped down and climbed into the shower. The hot water felt good rinsing off the filth from the day. When she finished she grabbed a big fluffy towel and wrapped it around her wet body tucking the end into the top by her left breast.

She was so tired. Picking up her dirty clothes off the floor she bundled them up like she was carrying a football. As she reached to unlock the cellar door she found it was already open! A chill rippled through her. She froze, just stood there for a moment, listening. It was too quiet. Quickly she tossed the bundle down the stairs and locked the door. She ran up the stairs to her room, slammed the bedroom door behind her locking it, and realized she needed to breathe.

Maybe her imagination was running wild, but something definitely felt off. She started to second guess herself, thinking it was maybe just her imagination, maybe just fatigue conjuring ghosts. She sat down on her bed and all sorts of things began to run through her mind, but it was as if they dissipated into nothing. Katie fell sound asleep in no time.

Several minutes past in perfect silence; the stealthy stranger worked his way out of the attic and into Katie's closet. He had practiced earlier, knew where to step so as not to make the wooden floorboards creak. He cautiously peered around the door frame of the closet, seeing Katie lying so perfectly still on top of the covers he smiled.

"Now, I know what took the druggie so long." The stranger thought to himself.

There were only two sounds in the room; silence, and the sound of his heart beating heavily in his chest. From the closet, to the left of Katie's bed the stranger watched his prey sleep. He had all the time in the world. No one knew he was there or that he could come and go as he pleased. He watched every breath she took, savoring the rise and fall of her breasts. Hugging his little secret to himself, she never knew he slipped her a little surprise in her drink before leaving work. He wanted to touch her to smell her essence. But for now the stranger just watched her sleep. He ventured from the safety of the closet to rifle through her dresser drawers. He wanted to learn all he could about his sweet Katie. His thoughts, drifting through the mist of fantasy, were real enough to stimulate him into an uncomfortable erection. Soon Katie, I will make you happy. But time was short, it was almost sunrise, he'd have to leave.

***

In the morning Katie awoke with goose bumps. It was the strangest feeling she had yet! She just couldn't shake the belief that someone was watching her?

After a morning shower, some coffee and a slightly burned piece of toast, she started to feel half way human again. The only sour note was a dull throbbing headache.

The phone rang. "Hi, Billie, what's up? Sure, the mall, that sounds good; I don't have any plans for today. Just let me get dressed and I will be ready when you get here."

Katie climbed up those old steps to find some clothes to wear. She finally just threw on a pair of jeans and t-shirt, which was good enough for her. She had no plans on impressing anybody. "Now where did my other sneaker go?" A few pairs of shoes in her closet had been knocked over, and a shirt lay on the floor where it had dropped from its hanger. She picked up the shirt, wondering if maybe she had mice or a squirrel.

Just then Billie let herself in and bellowed "Lucy I'm home!"

Katie shook her head and hollered back, "I'll be right down!" She could already hear Billie's footsteps coming up the stairs. She hung up the shirt and finished dressing.

"You're wearing that?"

"What's wrong with it?"

"You don't even have any make up on, and it looks like you just rolled out of bed!"

"Well, I kind of did...We're only going to the mall right? I will be your ugly friend today so all the guys will only notice you. How's that?"

"Ha ha, you're real funny Katie!" Billie said sarcastically.

They spent almost an hour in the car to drive up to a mall in Milwaukee. Then spent a few hours walking around the mall, but neither one really found anything to buy. Of course, in the last store they stopped in, Billie talked Katie into buying a cute little summer dress. "I really don't know when or where I will ever wear this Billie."

"You will! Besides it looks great on you and it accentuates your cleavage!"

"It does huh?"

Katie stopped trying to figure out all of Billie's idiosyncrasies years ago. She was a lot of fun to shop with, and go dancing with; she was just one of those people that made everything a party.

They returned to Katie's house only to find Cal sitting in his cruiser on the side of the implement dealer building next door.

"Now I bet you wish that you took the extra 15-minutes to do your hair and makeup?"

"Thanks Billie!" Katie said sarcastically, while getting out of the little 4-banger with her shopping bag.

"Well, see ya!"

"Where are you going?"

"Actually I am going to Mom's for dinner, and besides it's not my turn to watch you..." She motioned toward Cal's cruiser and then she drove off beeping her horn at Cal and waving good-bye!

Katie smiled and waved at Cal as well, then walked up to her door and unlocked it. Once inside, Katie looked out the window to see if he would drive up but he hadn't moved. Taking a moment, she brushed through her hair and tied it up in a loose pony tail. Then she put some moisturizer on and a little mascara. Oh well, I can't be made up all the time, she thought!

She took two bottles of water out of the fridge and went out the door.

Cal was still in his cruiser watching Katie walk down the gravel drive toward him. Her 'girl next door' charm enticed him. *Damn! I should have called her or something. I'm such an idiot*, he thought.

Katie handed him a bottle of water through his open window.

Smiling he took it. "Thanks Kate!"

"What's going on?"

"Oh, we got a call about a couple of guys hanging out by the equipment. You didn't see or hear anything did you?."

"No, but it seems to me you can't see anything from inside your car way over here?"

"Actually, I've already checked it out. I'm sitting here because you weren't home. So I waited. Okay! I'm an idiot; I should have called you sooner."

Katie gave him a huge smile, "Well now that you are here, what did you want?"

He sensed an air of mystery surrounding Katie. She wasn't at all like any of the women from his past.

Though he didn't date much, and he had no idea what to expect from a woman like Katie, it was making him feel like a green teenager.

"I suppose I should move the cruiser."

"You do that," She said with a friendly smile.

He drove around the machinery and parked in front of Katie's. She was a bundle of nerves on the inside and, she noticed, clammy of hand on the outside. *"Oh, doesn't that just figure!"*

He shut his door and leaned up against it, casually folding his arms across his chest.

Katie mirrored his body language and leaned up against the front quarter panel next to him.

"Katie, if you're still interested, I'd like to finish our conversation from Erik's party?"

"I am. What did you have in mind?"

Cal's radio came alive with some beeping noises and static. "125, copy."

So much for that, she thought, as she stood there, taking a sip of water, and listening to the dispatcher who had interrupted their too short visit.

"Sorry Kate, I gotta run. Thanks for the water." He got back in the squad, backed out and took off over the bridge.

Such is life...Katie watched him drive away until she couldn't see him anymore and then went inside.

Chapter 8

The Brick Yard was hopping that night; the comedian Bob had hired mixed comedy with magic and was hilarious! The other good news was Katie didn't have to dump beer on anyone.

Billie wasn't working but she did come in to see the comedian. She also made herself available in case Katie needed help so she wasn't drinking and was on her best behavior. Katie knew her ulterior motive was to see Jack but she didn't overly flirt and left him alone to work.

A troop of boisterous local college boys came in and sat at the table next to Billie. They joked around with her and tried to get her to sit and have a drink with them but she politely declined. She reasoned that when you work in a bar, and then go to that same bar on your time off, you couldn't be a bitch and expect the customers to tip you later. The leader of the group called Katie over and placed their order.

She hurried back to the bar and put the order in. "Jack, I need two pitchers of PBR, 5-shots of tequila and a 7-up."

Jack looked over Katie's shoulder and saw the group of guys conversing with Billie. "The 7-UP is for Billie?"

Katie smiled, "Yep!"

Bob and Eddie emerged from the office; they had been in there a while. Eddie immediately looked away from Katie, avoiding her glance he knew she had caught him staring earlier.

While Jack was filling up the pitchers of beer Katie asked him, "What do you think of the new guy?"

Jack glanced over at Eddie but only gave a non-committal shrug and then placed the shots on her tray next to the pitchers. He stuffed a cute little plastic pick full of extra cherries and hung it on the edge of the 7-UP glass, giving Katie a wink.

With the tray of shots balanced on one hand and the two pitchers grasped in the other, Katie made her way to the "frat" table. After serving them she turned and, with a flourish, she deposited the 7-Up in front of Billie.

As soon as Billie saw the cherries she turned around to find Jack, flashing him a huge smile. He blew her a kiss which sent a shiver up her spine and a blush to her cheeks; he thought she had never looked more adorable. Of course the locals noticed as well, so much for trying to pick her up any more!

Katie looked beautiful; sparkling with laughter at Billie and flushed from the hustle and bustle of the busy night. She turned to head to her next table and, not paying attention to where she was going, ran right into Eddie. Looking up at him she realized he was much taller than she thought, and hitting him felt like walking into a lamp post.

Eddie had instinctively reached out to catch Katie before she could fall. He realized his large strong hands could more than go around her soft upper arm. He took in her glossy hair, coming undone from her pony tail, her shining eyes and her lush, kissable mouth. It took his breath away. Even through the smoke filled bar, he thought she smelled like sunshine.

"Oops! I'm sorry...I didn't spill anything on you, did I?"

It took a moment for Eddie to realize Katie had spoken to him, "Nope, not a drop. First day with a new pair of feet?" He flashed a quick smile to show he was only joking.

Katie played along, but there was just something about him that wasn't quite right. Katie sensed it when he was so close to her, she had an overwhelming desire to run away, but she still had to work with the guy so she shrugged the feeling off.

After the bar closed Billie waited for Katie. "This was fun! It felt kinda weird not working and just hanging out."

Jack came up from behind Billie and joked, "I see you found some new friends tonight? A little young for you weren't they?"

Katie had to chuckle, it was so obvious to everyone that Jack was into Billie. This little cat and mouse game was kind of cute but really, just kiss her already!

"Not really my type, Jack." She replied pertly.

Leaning into her ear he asked, "And what is your type, sweetheart?" Then loud enough for everyone to hear, "You know, so I can send them your way if I find anyone."

Billie blushed furiously and smacked his arm. Everyone standing near-by all laughed, except Tanya, of course.

When the laughter died down Billie and Katie grabbed their belongings and started up the stairs to head home. Eddie and Erik were standing near the door in deep discussion, but when the girls walked up they stopped talking.

"Good night ladies!" Erik gallantly held open the door for them.

"G'night guys!"

Once they were out of hearing range, Erik and Eddie continued their discussion.

Billie turned to Katie, "So, what do you think they're talking about?"

"I couldn't tell ya! But I am curious about you and Jack..."

Billie was grinning from ear to ear. "He just keeps flirting, and joking around. I hope he might be trying to see if we can be friends before anything else."

"That sounds logical. Cal told me he takes things slow."

"Ugh! It's a good thing I really like him because it is so hard not knowing if we are dating or what we're doing! Wait a minute – Cal? You didn't tell me you've been seeing Cal!"

"I'm not...I have barely talked to him since Erik's party but we chatted a bit then."

"Okay, so then why was he waiting for you?"

"Oh he wasn't waiting for me! He had been called to the equipment yard because someone had called in a suspicious person report. He was looking around and just sat there for a while. We talked for just a couple of minutes when he got a radio call and left. End of story."

"Right" was Billie's one word reply.

Just as they got to their parking spots Cal pulled his cruiser in front of Katie's car. Billie rolled her eyes and stuck her tongue out at Katie, then waved to both of them as she left in her little car, windows down and music blaring.

Katie saw that Eddie was watching her out of the bar's front windows. She shook off the shiver and ignored him.

She unhurriedly strolled over to the passenger side of his car. His windows were down so she leaned in resting her folded arms on the door. "Good evening officer, is there something I can do for you?" She said with a huge smile and playfully batting her eyes at him.

Cal couldn't help but smile back. He looked at her beautiful eyes sparkling in the light from the neon sign, and her megawatt smile. Cal knew without a doubt, he was hooked.

"Actually, since we didn't have a chance to talk earlier, I was hoping that we could have that date?"

"A date huh?" She said toying with him. Of course she wanted to go on a date with Cal. "I think that can be arranged."

"Great! I know you work every weekend but I do have Tuesdays and Wednesdays off, well usually."

"I don't work on Tuesdays either so I think that will work out fine. May I have your cell phone for a second?"

"Why?"

"Just hand it over..." She put out her hand and he placed his phone in her palm. She typed in her name and number for him. "There, now you don't have an excuse not to call me."

She winked and gave him back his phone. Turning back toward her car she looked over her shoulder, "Have a good night, officer!" She said in her best Jessica Rabbit voice.

As the Nova rumbled to life she noticed a stranger in her rear view mirror, standing in the shadows, smoking a cigarette. Then putting her car in gear she saw out the corner of her eye Eddie looking back at her. Talking aloud to the car, "why is everyone so interested in what I'm doing?"

Cal knew that Eddie was watching them, too; his law enforcement antennae were twitching. *"There is something about that guy I just don't like!*

***

Katie pulled into her driveway and was pleased to see the porch light still on. Letting herself into the house, she checked the basement door latch and found it, too, locked. Well she thought things are finally looking up!

Humming to herself she climbed the stairs to start her bedtime rituals. Taking a quick hot shower, some moisturizer on her face and a nice long brushing of her hair, Katie began to think of Cal.

Those thoughts of him made her joyful. Thinking about how easy it was to talk to him. How sometimes, he was just as awkward around her as she was around him. She wanted to know so much more about this charming man and just kept thinking about Tuesday night.

Snuggled deep into her bed, Katie fell fast asleep with a smile on her beautiful face.

***

The stranger waited until he heard her making the soft sleeping sounds he had grown to love. He waited patiently, silently, after lowering himself into her closet using the sound of running water for cover. He loves the way she looks while she's sleeping, so sweet and peaceful. It was not enough to just get close to Katie; he had to have her, like a man needs air or water.

Carefully placing each practiced step, he inched closer. The stranger became more daring with each visit he had made. Now he stood directly over her. He could see the tiniest movement of her eyelids, the faint pulse in her neck. He inhaled deeply of her fragrance so he could carry her with him in the recesses of his mind. The stranger touched her exposed arm with caution, only using the tips of his long fingers. He was cautious not to wake her, it wasn't time yet. The heat of her body, her scent and the softness of her bare arm gave him a tingle in his loins. A chill ran up his spine. He had found the one, the one he had searched for, the one woman who was going to be his.

A crooked smile stretched across his already wide mouth. We will be happy; you and I, and I will give you great pleasure. He was going to enjoy his time with this one.

Chapter 9

Two nights later the stranger had to wait his turn. To his horror, he almost came face to face with the little parasite that visited the attic for his pot. Annoyed, but patiently, he waited. Finally the creep left and the stranger proceeded to Katie's room via the closet. She was sleeping on her side facing away from him. This aggravated him even more. He liked to see her face. He yearned to reach out to her, to touch her and feel her warm flesh. Slowly taking calculated practiced steps, he gets even closer to her lying there before him. Heartbeats later he was at her bedside. He felt the heat radiating off of her as she slept. He watched his own hand reaching out to touch her hair. He boldly granted himself the liberty of kissing her cheek, the mere touch of butterfly wing. His face a scant inch from her, he inhaled deeply. She had her own soft scent, so clean, so fresh and he worshiped it. But his moment in time with her was all too short this night; the parasite had eaten up the time he wanted with his love. He must consider what to do about this minor complication.

***

Katie realized strange things were occurring more often at the farmhouse. In the middle of the night she would be awaken to strange sounds outside. She couldn't find things or they would be moved. Katie felt like she was losing her mind. She hadn't been sleeping well and was exhausted all the time. She'd been waking up with terrible headaches but she had to go to work regardless of how she felt.

Erik was already at the front door carding people when Katie came in looking completely drained.

"Hey darlin'!"

"Hi Erik." Katie replied sounding very melancholy.

"Everything alright, Hun?"

"Yeah, I'm just really tired and have a nagging headache tonight."

"With all the work you've been doing on that old house of yours you're probably a bit run down. Why don't you go grab some o.j. from Jack? The vitamin C will do ya some good."

Katie appreciated Erik's concern. He was a sweet guy. "Thanks, I'll do that." As she stepped back she turned right into Eddie who had been standing right behind her.

"Oh pardon me!" Katie was a little startled. She hated people sneaking up on her.

Eddie just peered down at her with his ugly mouth sneering into an unsettling grin.

Katie stepped around him and high tailed it down the stairs.

Erik said flat out, "Eddie you are an ass! That was a shitty thing to do!"

"What? I didn't do anything. She walked into me!"

Erik gave Eddie one of those looks you'd give a child who'd just disappointed you.

Minutes of silence passed until Erik told Eddie to take the door. Disgusted, Erik marched downstairs to check on Katie.

Eddie hated to be treated like a child, but sat at the door doing the job he was hired to do. A couple of young women, well actually they were still girls in women's bodies came to the door. They did their best to flirt with Eddie, and although they were minors they amused him, so he let them enter. "What the hell." He thought.

Downstairs, Erik found Katie setting up the waitressing stand at the far end of the bar. She had her glass of orange juice half empty sitting next to her.

Jack saw Erik walking over, "Erik, what's up?"

"Just getting some fresh air, it was getting stale up stairs."

Jack frowned, and then caught on. "Eddie getting under your skin again?"

Erik nodded to Katie, and walked over to her. Jack followed suit from behind the bar.

"Feeling any better?"

"I just took something for my headache. It should kick in soon enough."

Erik placed his hand on her back and gently started rubbing it in circular motions. Of course Jessica chose that moment to walk in and wasn't happy seeing "her man" rubbing Katie's back.

"I'm fine Erik. I just haven't been getting much sleep lately. Just dragging a little; thanks though."

Jack spoke up, "Well you do look like you've pulled an all-nighter."

"Thanks Jack, just what I wanted to hear! Do I look that bad?"

"Let's just say you don't seem your normal happy self."

Erik looked over and saw Jessica glaring at him, "I'll check up on you later Katie."

Erik then made a point of going over to Jessica and kissing her on the cheek before he went back upstairs.

Just Jack and Jessica were bartending tonight. Steve had called in to say he wouldn't be in, something came up. By 10 o'clock the down stairs bar had started to pick up. Katie was glad for that. There is nothing worse than being tired and having a slow night. Around midnight Eddie wandered down just to hang out; leaning against the wall near the stairs. The pretty young girls that he let in were still eyeing him. A tall lanky guy with long black hair came in slipping past Eddie. Katie served the guy a draft. He sat by himself at a small table with his back against the wall. He had a perfect view of the entire lower level.

Eddie slipped into the storage room.

Seeing this, Jack interrupted whatever Eddie had in mind.

"What are you doing in here?"

"I uh," as he grabbed a bottle of scotch, "was sent down for a bottle they needed up stairs." Eddie quickly left and went back up stairs.

Jack was a little suspicious. He knew he stocked the bar with scotch and they don't ever use that much.

Katie was puzzled by the guy with the draft, since he was still nursing the same one from an hour ago. *"Ick! That has got to be warm by now."*

"Can I get you anything else?"

His icy blue eyes, outlined by such thick black lashes, gave him an eerie appearance. She felt he was looking right through her. Then he shook his head 'no'. His reptilian demeanor gave her the chills. She couldn't walk away fast enough. Thinking to herself, "*I wonder if that is the guy Billie was talking to*".

Erik had come back down and was standing at the bar with Jack; they saw Katie's reaction to this dark haired stranger.

Katie walked over to Erik's side and asked, "Things slow up stairs?"

"Not really, but I'm taking a break. What's up with that guy?" Erik asked as he gave a nod in the stranger's direction.

Sensing that he had brought attention to himself, he gulped down the end of his warm beer, and then gave Katie one last look, before ducking out.

Katie turned back to Jack and Erik. "I think that might be the guy who's been talking to Billie."

Jack barked, "It is - and I don't like him!"

Katie agreed, "Whoever he is, he's weird!"

Erik summed it up, "If he comes back, we'll keep an eye on him."

***

Katie was utterly exhausted after her long shift at work. She knew, as soon as she pulled into her driveway, that something was wrong; the porch light was out again. She unlocked the front door, flipped on the kitchen lights and looked around. The cellar door was unlocked and slightly ajar.

"That's weird; I could have sworn I locked that door before I left."

She hung up her keys on the hook, set her purse down on the flour bin and strolled over to the cellar door. As Katie reached for the knob she heard a soft creaking sound coming from upstairs. The hairs on her arms stood up. There was a lump in her throat and she swallowed hard. Closing the door she noticed her hands begin to shake as she slid the bolt over to lock it. Gathering her courage she quietly walked through the living room to the stairs. She stood there for a moment looking up the stairway listening intently. "Maybe I'm just overtired and hearing things, I could call Cal, maybe he's in the area." As she quietly went up the stairs she heard it again, but it wasn't from her feet on those old wooden stairs. It was more up to her left side and muffled.

"This is an old house; it is probably just settling noises." She reassured herself.

At the top of the stairs she stood poised; listening for what she thought she might have heard. There were only two rooms up here; her bedroom on the left side and a spare room to the right. Silence, complete and utter silence greeted her.

She convinced herself that it was just an old house; she was overly tired and just needed some rest. Kicking off her shoes and pulling her shirt off over her head, she wandered over to the window by the side of the bed and cracked it open to let the night air in. A soft breeze gently ruffled her curtains and freshened up the stale warm air in her room. She felt almost mechanical, she was so tired. *"Why am I so groggy? Maybe I am starting to come down with something?"* Wearily she unbuttoned her jeans, stepping out of them, and then unhooking her bra and dropping that to the floor as well.

She opened up her dresser drawer to grab an old nightshirt and realized her panty drawer above it was not pushed in all the way. *"That's strange?"* She closed it, looked quizzically at it and then opened it again.

"What the hell?" She said out loud. Someone definitely had been in her room and had gone through her drawers.

Katie felt violated and sick. She threw on her old night shirt, and then she froze for a minute, her thought tangled up in a crazy mind numbing swirl. Swallowing hard, her anger motivated her to turn lights on and search the house. *"Am I crazy? I know someone was here. I know it!"*

She searched under her beds, in her closets, even behind curtains. After pronouncing the second floor empty she moved on to the first floor. It was empty as well but now her head was spinning like she was drunk *"after adrenalin rush?"* she wondered. She then looked at that ominous cellar door. It was 3:30 in the morning and she didn't have the courage to proceed to the basement. *"Nope! Door is locked."* To be on the safe side she dragged out a dining room chair and wedged it under the knob. Now feeling even more sluggish and having lead weights for feet she shuffled into the kitchen. Her head was spinning and everything was starting to get foggy. She was looking around for something, for what, she didn't know; she saw headlights coming back up the driveway from the quarry. "Cal?"

Katie tried to watch the police cruiser slowly driving around to the front up by the large farm equipment. She wasn't sure it was Cal, but if it were, wouldn't he stop if he saw her lights were still on? She winced when he shined his spotlight toward the house; she hoped he was checking for something, anything out of place.

Then remembering the very large sharp knife in the top drawer, she fumbled with thick fingers and grabbed it. Holding the knife awkwardly in her right hand she went for the door. Her legs were giving her trouble. She felt intoxicated but she hadn't drunk anything except orange juice and water. After what seemed like hours she finally reached for the door; everything seemed to be moving in slow motion.

The cruiser had stopped just in front of the house. Katie opened the front door only to fall through its opening as if she had been pushed.

Cal quickly slammed the car into park and jumped out, but he couldn't get to her fast enough to prevent her from tumbling down the few steps and sprawl out into the grass.

The grass was cool, and slightly prickly against her skin. Katie laid there looking up toward the night's sky; she saw Cal's face staring back at her. *"What is he saying? I can't hear you, you sound like you're under water. Am I dreaming this?"* She couldn't form the words that were running through her mind. Everything was closing in as she tried to move but couldn't. Her eye lids were so heavy. Darkness.

Cal was stunned. Katie fell out of the house with a knife in her hand and wearing only a night shirt. She just lay on the lawn looking up at him. "Kate? Katie, can you hear me? Katie are you alright?" With no response Cal called for rescue.

Sirens could be heard in the distance and the flashing lights were quickly coming over the bridge.

Cal held Katie's hand. "If you can hear me Kate, everything is going to be alright. Just hang in there."

From the attic vent the stranger watched everything unfold. He would just have to wait it out until he could sneak out.

Damn you, Chapman!

Cal told the EMT dispatch that he would be with her until they arrived, and then he watched as rescue took Katie to the hospital.

"Now what in the Sam hell, were you doing with that knife?"

Cal radioed in to dispatch to let them know he would be searching the house. Since it was a small force calling for back up wasn't really an option. Relying on his training, Cal entered the front door to search the little white farmhouse. Nothing really stood out of place except for the dining room chair propped up under the cellar's door knob. He removed the chair, and flicked on the lights to the cellar. With his gun drawn and hugging the wall he proceeded to check out the cellar. From what he could tell it was empty. Katie had a washer and dryer down there with a work bench for a folding table. Nothing exciting, just a few boxes on the canning shelves labeled Christmas or Halloween, and some cob webs here and there. Checking the cellar door that lead to the outside he saw the bolt was in the locked position.

The stranger took this opportunity to escape through the attic opening and shimmied down the tree.

As he did, Cal heard a slight scratching above him. Cal turned his attention to the stairs again. His gun still drawn, he cautiously headed back up the steps to the kitchen.

By the time Cal made it to the kitchen the stranger was gone, hoofing it down the tracks.

Cal searched the entire house and didn't find anyone or anything. Everything appeared to be in order except for the chair that had been propped up against the cellar door. This was confusing, and he wondered what made Katie react in such a way. So, he decided to head over to the hospital to see how she was doing.

***

Tony, the EMT driver was filling out his paperwork when Cal arrived.

"Hey, Tony."

"Hey, Chapman! That's crazy huh?"

"How's she doing?"

"I can't tell you much, she hasn't said anything coherent. The doc's running some tests now. But he thinks she was slipped a drug of some kind."

"Thanks Tony. Say, how's your Sister?"

"Oh she's ready to pop! As big as a house!" Tony answered with a chuckle.

"Tell her I wish her the best with delivery."

"Yep, will do!"

Cal found the emergency room physician that was handling Katie's case. "Doctor Greene? I'm Detective Chapman. Regarding Katherine McGuire, I'd like to know what you can tell me."

"Well, she's been trying to talk, but I can't make it out. I have her on I-V fluids, and I have run a full tox-screen, urine and blood. I should have those results soon enough."

"Can I see her?"

"Sure, she's in room 4. I will let you know as soon as the results are in."

"Thanks!"

Cal pushed the little curtain aside, then pulling it back behind him. Katie looked pale and disheveled as one would expect someone to look like who went through what she did. The machines made beeping sounds and the I-V drip seemed to make a sound as well.

She seemed frail, so still. Cal reached down for her hand, holding it and was surprised at how cold it felt. He began to talk to her softly. "Katie, sweetie...can you hear me? I'd like to know what happened...I searched your house. I couldn't find anything wrong. What happened to you Katie?"

Hearing Cal's voice she turned her head slightly to face him. Her eye lids were heavy, but she forced them half open. She was still groggy but made the effort to smile at him. Her throat was dry and she could barely swallow.

He pulled up a stainless metal stool from the corner and sat close to her. Resting his elbows on the side-rails of the bed, he just held her hand.

Katie tried to speak but nothing really came out. She was completely out of it. She dozed in and out for an hour or so. The doc came back to talk to Cal.

They stepped out of the little curtained off area to speak.

"Well, my suspicions are correct. Somebody did slip her something."

"Do you know what?"

"Looks like Rohyprol. Someone must have slipped it in something she ate or drank. She should be fine in a few hours, but she'll definitely have a hell of a headache."

"Thanks. I will stay for a while if that's alright."

"Sure. Just let me know if you have any more questions."

It was almost 7 a.m. before Katie was awake enough to really say anything.

"Cal?"

"Good morning pretty lady, how are you feeling?"

"Like someone dropped me on my head." Her voice was so hoarse she could hardly speak.

"Katie, do you remember anything that happened to you last night?"

Katie motioned for some water. As Cal poured her a cup of water, she began to tell him what she could remember, which wasn't very much. In fact Cal told her more about what happened last night than what she remembered. Katie spent that day in the hospital letting them flush whatever was given to her out of her system.

Cal called Bob at the Brick Yard to let him know about Katie. Bob was deeply concerned that anyone would drug someone at his bar and was more than willing to help Cal find out if it was one of his employees.

"Tell Katie to rest. Billie can cover for her."

Cal needed to find answers. He couldn't believe someone would drug Katie. That and the fact that the bartenders were the only ones who really had access to whatever Katie drank was even more disturbing to him.

Chapter 10

Katie was standing at her hospital room window, arms crossed, staring blankly out when Billie walked in.

"Hi Katie!" Ready to get sprung? I brought you some clothes to wear. I heard from Cal that you were in your nightshirt when they brought you in last night. We've shared clothes before so I hope it all fits!" Billie's upbeat attitude was not what Katie wanted to hear this afternoon. She still had a nagging headache and felt a bit weak, but under the headache was a profound anger. Who would dare enter her house, who would dare to slip her a "Mickey" at her own job! Yes, anger was playing a huge roll in her attitude today.

"I stopped at the nurse's station and they said the Doctor had finished up all release forms and aftercare instructions for you! They should be in any minute for you to sign." Billie continued on.

Where's Cal? Katie asked.

"I don't know the details but something came up so he called me, he said he would call you later. I hope you don't want to sit here and wait for him" Billie ventured a small smile, finally realizing that Katie was in no mood for talking.

"No." Katie sounded weary. Just then the equally cheery nurse walked in with a sheaf of paperwork. A pamphlet explaining drinking and drugs was included, really? Katie sighed and signed everything then put on the clothes Billie had brought for her.

They were quiet on the ride home. Billie thoughtfully turned off her normally loud radio in deference to Katie's headache and mood.

After they pulled into the driveway and Billie turned off the car, Katie sat silently staring at her house for a few moments. Billie's normally exuberant personality remained subdued as she gave Katie the opportunity to decide what her next steps would be.

"What should we do for dinner tonight?" Billie quietly asked.

"I don't know Billie. I have laundry to do and some bills to pay..." Katie's voice trailed off.

"Let's do Chinese."

"Whatever then, I really don't care."

"Sheesh! What's with you? I'm only trying to help!"

At that Katie finally exploded. "Why are you still here? I don't need a baby sitter! Do you think I did this to myself? Is that what everyone is thinking? I'm some sort of psycho drug user seeing ghosts to cover my overdose? Damn it, someone was in MY HOUSE! Someone I know, someone I work with, drugged me! You're damn right I'm angry and I don't need someone to watch over me to make sure I don't 'hurt myself'!" Still fuming Katie got out of the car and slammed the door shut.

Billie followed slowly behind her. She really hadn't realized how angry and hurt her friend was, she also hadn't seen the pamphlet.

Stomping up the steps, Katie suddenly stopped, looking up. She motioned Billie up behind her. "Do me a favor, Billie, see if that light bulb is loose please. Just humor me."

Billie had to stand up on tip toes to reach the light but at the merest brush of her fingers the bulb fell. KA-BANG! Both girls jumped at the loud sound and stared at the shattered remains of the bulb on the concrete porch.

Billie let out a little scream "What the heck was that?"

"Shhhh." Katie looked around knowing a light bulb doesn't sound like that. Then she saw the source of the loud sound. The guys next door at the equipment shop were moving a dumpster; they must have dropped it or something.

"How did you know the light would fall out? You scared the crap out of me!" Billie was now just as jumpy as Katie.

Taking a deep breath she turned to Billie to explain, "That light bulb was tight and working last night when I left for work, it was out when I came home. It's been unscrewed and it's not the first time! Well maybe it's nothing but I have this funny feeling sometimes that I am not alone, and I mean when you aren't here."

Billie just shook her head and sighed. "Okay...I'm ordering Chinese. Then when we pick it up we'll stop at Fox's Liquor and get some wine coolers or whatever to loosen you up."

Frankly the idea of some Mongolian Beef and a couple of cocktails sounded really good to Katie. It would be 20-minutes before their take out would be ready, so they stopped at Fox's first.

They left the house without ever going in.

***

Katie opened the glass door to the liquor store, making the little brass bell ring. Fox came out from the backroom, "Hi, Ladies! What a nice surprise!"

"Hey Fox!" They reply together in an upbeat tone.

"What are the 'partners in crime' up to tonight?"

"Katie and I are on our way to pick up some Chinese and thought we would grab something to go with it."

"That actually sounds pretty good. I only had time to pick up a lousy burger on the way in. Well if you're interested I have a special on Cancun coolers up by the register!"

"Sure, what's the special?"

"They're two 4-packs for $6."

Billie made a beeline for the display announcing, "We'll take two then!"

Fox always liked to visit with Katie and Billie when they were in the store. He never hit on them he just liked to chitchat. "What have you girls been up to lately? I think it's been a couple of weeks since I saw you last."

"Yeah, well, we've had to work every Friday and Saturday night and by Sunday I am just too tired to go out or drink."

"Brandon asked about you the other day, Katie. He said he saw you working last weekend but didn't get a chance to talk to you. He did say you girls were hopping."

Billie blithely butted in, "It has been crazy busy over there. And this Friday we have a really fun band, so the Brick Yard will be packed again!"

Fox took the money and handed Billie the paper bag, "Well don't be strangers. Have fun tonight."

"Thanks, Fox!" They chorused again.

Turning to Katie, Billie had to ask, "So who is Brandon?"

"Billie, you know who Brandon is! He works at Fox's, stocking and whatever."

"I do?"

"Yeah, the biker dude with all the tats?"

"Oh! I didn't know his name was Brandon?"

"Well, now you do."

Unlocking the doors, Billie put the wine coolers in the back seat, and then fired up her little car. As they were leaving Billie saw Jack, for a moment their eyes met, they smiled and then he pulled into the lot she was just pulling out of. Billie debated going back in but Katie cleared her throat in a 'don't you dare' way.

The Great Wall Chinese Restaurant was relatively empty, so pick-up was fast, but for the rest of the drive back all Billie could talk about was Jack. It truly was brain numbing at times and Katie had no answers for the multitude of questions being fired at her, however it did keep her mind off last night's unpleasant incident.

Parking under the big oak tree, Katie carried the Chinese food as Billie got out the brown sack from Fox's.

Putting the key in the door, Katie got that all too familiar funny feeling. She pushed open the door and flipped on the lights to the kitchen. It was a strange unsettling feeling that washed over Katie, like déjà.

Billie, who was still prattling on, shouldered her way past Katie through the door. She walked over to the fridge emptying the contents of the paper bag and placing two bottles on the counter. After her initial stillness, Katie set the food boxes down and took two plates out of the cupboard. Billie got some silverware and set the two drinks alongside the plates. Billie wasn't a guest here, she was more like family.

A wine cooler and good food brought Katie back to her usual self, getting up to do the few dishes and she finally felt normal. Billie packed up what was left and placed it in the fridge.

Katie walked over to the cellar door to toss the used damp dishtowel down the stairs when she noticed that the door she had locked last night wasn't locked anymore. She remembered not only locking the door but pulling a chair up under the door knob! Cal probably moved the chair but he wouldn't have left it unlocked surely!

"Billie? Did you open this door?"

Cracking open a second wine cooler, Billie looked up, "Huh, no, why?"

"Because I locked the door last night before that drug hit me. Billie, I searched this house top to bottom last night looking for someone or something I heard! I didn't go downstairs but I know I slammed it shut, locked it and pulled a chair under it. I know the light was off. I know someone was in here; my panty drawer was partly open, the door to the cellar was cracked open. I HEARD someone!"

"Are you sure about that Katie? That drug you were slipped was pretty strong."

"YES"

Slowly opening the door Katie saw the light was on too. With Billie close behind, the two went down into the cellar to check the outside door. That was still locked from the inside, but there was a damp footprint that did not belong to them leading away from the door toward the stairs.

Adrenaline kicked in and they sprinted back up the stairs; slamming the door behind them. Billie, hand to chest, leaned against the door trying to catch her breath and hoping she wouldn't have a heart attack.

"I'm calling Cal!" Katie, just as breathless and shaken, said as she pulled out her phone. With a single thought passing between them, they were out the door and in Billie's car with the doors locked in no time. While they sat there waiting for the police; Katie looked over at her freaked out friend and started to laugh.

Billie in turn looked at Katie like she had grown a third eye. "What do you find so funny?" Although some thought Billie was a 'flighty' blond, she wasn't really and she was truly scared right at this moment.

"We look like idiots sitting in the car waiting for the police, and oh lookie, here they come." Katie couldn't stop laughing.

Billie frowned; she wasn't sure if Katie was still high from the drug or had truly lost her mind.

It was Cal who had pulled in behind her.

Katie still couldn't keep herself from laughing. With everything she'd been going through lately this was her release or was it bordering on hysteria? She didn't know and didn't care. She was laughing so hard she couldn't catch her breath.

Cal was slightly confused at the scene.

"Don't mind her Cal. She's losing it; I think."

"What's happening?"

"We think someone might be in the house or was in the house."

"Why do you think that? I believe you but what happened or what did you see?"

Billie answered in a rush because Katie was still not able to do anything but laugh. "The front porch light was unscrewed again and Katie knew she had tightened it last night. The cellar door was unlocked again but she was sure you had locked it after you checked out the house last night. We went downstairs, oh and the light was on when it shouldn't have been, and there was a footprint by the back door that didn't belong to us. Is that enough?"

"Okay, stay here I'll go check it out."

Cal radioed dispatch and told him he was checking out the premises.

A few minutes later, Katie was finally able to control herself and stop laughing. Tears had run down her face and she looked as if she'd been crying hard.

Cal finally emerged from the house.

Billie and Katie got out of the car and met him half way.

Cal, observing an array of mixed emotions on Katie's lovely face said, "Sorry, I didn't find anything. Are you sure someone was in the house?"

"Cal, we know what we saw." Billie said flatly.

Katie finished the comment with, "There was a wet footprint by the cellar door coming in from the outside. I know I had locked the cellar door last night, if you remember; there was a chair under the doorknob! We came back to the house after Billie picked me up and that's when I asked her to see if the light bulb was loose, it was off again last night when I got home. It was not only loose, it crashed to the porch, and you can still see glass. We didn't go into the house but left to pick up dinner and after dinner I went to throw a towel downstairs and the cellar door was unlocked. I had a weird feeling about the house when we walked in, too."

"Let me check out back and see if I can find anything."

Cal walked around the perimeter of the house, specifically checking the lower door but everything looked fine.

"I don't see anything. I know you're edgy and you probably don't want to hear this, but after last night, maybe you're letting your imagination get the best of you?"

Billie spoke up, "But what about the foot print? It wasn't ours."

"I saw a damp mark; I suppose it could look like a footprint. It looked more like the washing machine could have overflowed now but I can only go by what I see. If you feel you need me to come back you have my number, or call the station and someone will come out to check."

"Okay. Well thanks for checking." Katie said feeling foolish, but what about everything else?

After Cal left, they decided to look around the house themselves to see what else was out of place. After a thorough check they felt somewhat better.

"Billie, do you mind spending the night?" Katie asked.

Billie agreed to stay but did not like the spookiness. After all Katie was her friend and she would have wanted Katie to stay if roles were reversed.

Billie made some popcorn and lemonade, and then they sat and watched the X-Files, while Katie finished folding her laundry. Not the best show to watch when you had strange feelings about the house you were in.

Katie knew there was something happening in that house. Being a rational person, the creepiness she felt within the house was not going to get the best of her. There had to be a legitimate reason for the weird stuff happening.

For instance, the clothes in her closet would sometimes be on the floor and her shoes were tipped over or askew. Katie always lined up her shoes on the floor in the closet. Her favorite nightgown had vanished, and so did the red panties she wore with her red outfit. Though they were skimpy enough for the washing machine to eat them, she didn't think that was the case. She would wake up sometimes in the middle of the night and notice a peculiar odor in the air. "There must be someone coming into my house!"

Billie listened intently to Katie as she revealed her thoughts. Her big blue eyes looked like saucers by the time Katie spilled all.

It did make Katie feel better to say it all out loud.

***

The stranger watched from a safe distance, hoping the whole time that Billie would leave. As it got later and the lights began to go dark, he realized that he wasn't going to be able to spend any time with Katie again. This frustrated him immensely.

Chapter 11

She awoke late in the morning, sitting up in bed and just surveying her room. Then realized what day it was, "Tuesday!" Two days had passed and Katie hadn't heard from Cal. She suddenly became very apprehensive. She fell backward onto her pillow and sighed, "Date night…"

Billie who had stayed with Katie for a couple of days left early, leaving Katie a note on the kitchen table.

'Katie,
I didn't want to wake you. Call you later!
I hope you have a great time with Cal tonight.
You'll have to tell me all about it!'
Hugs - BJ

The morning dragged on, and her dreaded anticipation grew. Katie finished putting her laundry away, vacuumed, dusted, and even cleaned the bathroom. Of course now she needed to shower, again.

Her phone rang, it was Billie. "Hello!"

"Hey! So do you know where you are going yet?"

"Not yet!"

"So how are you going to know what to wear?"

Katie hadn't even thought that far. She was still just trying to think about what to say to him and to try not to blow their first date. "Thanks a lot Billie! Now I have something else to worry about!"

There was a beep on the line and she told Billie she would call her later.

The caller ID showed it was Cal. "Hello!" She answered in a light friendly voice.

Cal wanted to see if he could pick her up a little earlier, and advise her to wear something comfortable.

"Comfortable? Does that mean I can wear sweatpants?" She joked.

"If you really wanted to, but I think you would be happier in jeans, oh, and comfortable shoes!"

"I think I can handle that!" Katie was quite curious about where Cal was taking her, but at least now she didn't have to figure out what to wear.

Cal pulled up to Katie's at 10-minutes to 4 p.m. She was ready but didn't want to seem overly anxious.

He knocked on her door. She let him wait a few seconds before she answered.

"Hi! Ready to go, Kate?"

She liked the way he said her name, *Kate*. It almost had poetic undertones to it; besides being kind, deep, and smoky.

Even casually dressed in jeans Cal thought she was 'doll'.

She locked the door on her way out.

Cal politely walked her to the passenger side of his car and opened the door for her. She liked this. Cal walked around the front and slid behind the wheel.

Katie gave him a big smile, "So, I finally get a ride in the big bad Roadrunner!"

Cal laughed, "I knew you'd like her."

"Like her? She's a 1969 Roadrunner! What's not to like?" Katie said with such enthusiasm that Cal had to laugh.

"So is it me or the car you want to be seen with?"

Katie had to laugh at his wry question. She loved that they had similar interests and it made her feel more connected that he was a car guy. She was going to enjoy this.

Cal idled up the gravel drive and out on to the road. Then he put his foot on it, just a little more gas and the Roadrunner screamed down the highway.

"Are you going to make me guess or are you going to tell me what's under the hood?"

"It's just a little ol' 383 Wedge." He answered with a jest of insignificance, and then gave her a sideways smirk with a wink.

She flashed him an impressive smile in return. "Where are we are going?"

Cal shot Katie a mysterious grin. "It's a surprise."

After about 20-minutes on the highway Cal turned off onto a dirt road. Driving very slowly as to not kick up a lot of dust, he just let the Roadrunner idle down the drive.

They veered around a cluster of large pine trees and then Katie saw where they were.

"A shooting range?" She wasn't expecting that. Usually guys take women to a park for a picnic or dinner and a show. She thought it was kind of funny that he was taking her shooting for their first date.

Cal chuckled "Have you ever been shooting before?"

"Once or twice out on Gram's farm."

Cal pulled the orange and black beast to a stop off the main parking area.

Katie couldn't help the smile that was plastered across her face.

Cal carefully closed his door with a solid thud, and then walked around to open the door for Kate. As she got out of the car she noticed there were only two other cars there.

"It's not very busy?"

"Well, that would be because it's Tuesday. It picks up by Thursday." He said shutting the door behind her.

He took the key and opened the trunk which was immaculate. He grabbed his black gear bag and a hard case with a handle, and then closed the trunk. Katie walked along side of him to the office to check in.

"Well, would you look what the cat dragged in!" A puffed up jolly white haired man, who could double as Santa Clause, declared with glee.

"Hank, you old son of a gun!"

The two men laughed and shook hands like they hadn't seen each other for quite a while.

"Who's this pretty young thing and why is she with you?"

"Hank, this is Katie. She is my guest today. Katie, this old codger is Hank. He runs this place."

"It's nice to meet you Hank."

"And you Miss Katie Belle."

Katie smiled at the sweet princess like sound he gave her name.

"Enjoy, oh and make sure you stop back on your way out."

"Will do Hank, thanks!" Cal said as he signed the guestbook.

The sun felt good, so warm on Kate's face. Her red hair had a glossy sheen to it that made it appear to be on fire in the sunlight. The gentle breeze softly blew a few tentacles of flame across her face and ignited the green-gold flecks in her eyes. Cal couldn't help notice how beautiful she was, how alive and bewitching. She took his breath away. This couldn't have been the same woman he sat with in the hospital.

Katie caught him studying her and gave him a warm assured smile.

Cal even loved the shaped of her lips. How he wanted to kiss those lips.

They must have walked the distance of 2-football fields before they reached their destination.

Katie took the gun case from Cal, so he could set up the table. After laying out a piece of leather, he opened the gun case and placed two weapons down on it.

"I wasn't sure if you had ever fired a gun before so I brought two different ones just for practice. This one here is light and easy, it's a Ruger .22 revolver. This one is a semi-auto Colt .45 Government model 1911."

"Ooh, pretty!" Katie said with a teasing laugh.

"Well, you're not going to shoot her until you can handle this one." He said picking up the Ruger.

"Fair enough, so show me."

Cal took a sack filled with aluminum cans from the recycle bin, Katie noticed the second can marked "pick up your trash" filled with holey cans, and walked out about 10 yards to set them up in a row on a huge wooden pole lying down. When he returned he instructed Katie how to properly hold the gun, to pull the hammer back, line up the sights and squeeze the trigger. He had her full attention as to his instructions. Then he loaded the gun.

Katie knew how to fire a gun, but she acknowledged his expertise and need for safety. After all, he was a cop.

Katie felt comfortable and relaxed with Cal. He was soft spoken with a quiet confidence that she admired. Cal was strong, sharp and possessed a dry wit that made her laugh. He had almost a regal John Wayne quality about him. Katie was attracted to his good looks and his genuinely warm wonderful smile. His intelligent steel-grey eyes coupled with his soft short looking brown hair made him seem older than he was. Cal wore a short sleeve polo shirt, a pair of Levi's and running shoes. All of which showed off the great physical condition he was in. He was definitely an attractive man.

Cal handed her a pair of shooting glasses and ear plugs.

Katie took position with the .22 in hand.

Cal stood behind her. He wasn't encroaching in on her space but she felt him subtly brush against her.

Katie pulled the trigger and missed.

"Okay, good, just remember to just squeeze the trigger, don't pull. Now try it again."

Kate took a second shot and hit the first can. Then the second, third, fourth and fifth can.

"I guess you've either done this before or its beginners luck?"

"Only a couple of times. I'd forgotten how fun it was."

A box of .22 rounds and a lot of cans knocked over later, Cal decided to show her how to shoot the semi-auto.

"Would you like to try the Colt?"

"I sure would! But just to warn you, I have never fired a semi-automatic before." She flashed a large smile.

Cal returned the smile. He instructed Katie on the mechanics of the weapon and showed her how to load the magazine and take the safety off when she was ready to fire.

This time Cal stood behind her and held on to her arms in just the correct stance. He leaned in and calmly instructed her. "Once you have lined up your target, I want you to close your eyes, breathe in, then open your eyes, and as you breathe out gently squeeze the trigger."

Katie did as she was instructed. She was surprised how much stronger the kick was from this gun, much stronger than she thought it would be. Smiling up into Cal's face she said softly, "So that's why you are standing so close; to save your Colt from flying out of my hands?"

He laughed, "You caught me, and I thought I was smoother than that."

Katie shot a few more rounds to get a feel for the .45 but she enjoyed it.

"Are you ready for dinner?"

"Dinner?"

"Yeah, dinner that meal you have about this time of the day." He joked.

"I thought *this* was the date, but if there's more, I'm in!"

Cal loved Kate's enthusiasm, and smiled wide.

Cal made sure the guns were unloaded and then wiped them off with a soft rag. He packed them back up into his case to be cleaned later. Katie picked up the cans, or what was left of them and threw them in the barrel. Then she helped Cal pick up all their brass.

Walking back to the office Cal reached his hand out for Katie's and in a fluid graceful manner she accepted it. The walk back to the office seemed a lot shorter. Hank was still sitting in his same spot behind the desk watching an old western on his little television when they came in.

"So Miss Katie Belle, did you have a good time?"

"Why yes I did, Hank."

"Don't let her fool you; she is a damn good shot. I think she was playing me."

"Well good for her. Someone has to keep you on your toes." Hank came out from behind the counter and then Kate realized he was missing both of his legs. "Cal, she's a keeper. Bring her around sometime, Martha and me would love to have you over soon. It's been too long."

"You got it Hank! Tell Martha I said soon."

"Ya bet boy. It was very nice to meet you Katie Belle."

"You too, Hank."

Cal opened the car door for Katie to get in and then closed the door for her. He put his gear in the trunk and then took a deep breath before getting in beside her. "Ready?"

"I suppose I'm at your mercy today, Cal."

"I like the sound of that." Giving her a wink, he turned the key and brought to life the orange and black beast. It purred and idled back out the dirt drive.

"So how do you know Hank and Martha?"

"Well, Hank was my dad's Marine buddy back in Vietnam, and Martha she is the love of his life. She's the reason he keeps getting up in the morning."

"Tell me about your parents?"

"Let's see, dad served 25 years in the service then he went to work for the government. He was a Provost Marshall full bird Colonel working for CID, when I moved out here with Mom and Diana. Now he's working out of the Pentagon and Mom is more than ready for him to retire. I think she's a saint for putting up with my father all these years and us boys as well. We gave her hell growing up. I have two older brothers Bill, and Mathew, and a younger sister, Diana. Bill is an electrician who lives in Michigan. Mathew is a carpenter who owns his own business in Brookfield. They're both married with children. Diana lives here and teaches second grade in town."

Cal pulled into the parking lot of a quaint little Mexican restaurant on Browns Lake.

"I love this place!"

"I know."

"How did you know?"

"Billie told me."

"She knew all along what I'd be doing tonight? I guess she can keep a secret!" Katie laughed.

They were seated by the windows facing out over the lake. The sunset had been beautiful.

Katie couldn't help but show her joy. Cal was making this evening wonderful.

They peeked over the tops of their menus at each other.

His bright eyes met hers, and they awkwardly smiled at each other.

She was still a little apprehensive but was having a great time with Cal.

"Do you like Margaritas?" Cal asked.

"Of course; strawberry?"

"Sounds good!"

Flagging down their waitress Cal ordered a pitcher of Strawberry Margaritas.

"They have the best here." Katie interjected.

While they waited for their waitress to return with the drinks, Cal placed his hand on top of Katie's and looked deeply into her beautiful eyes. "Miss McGuire I do believe it is your turn to tell me something about you."

"My turn already?   But, I still have some questions about you."

"What haven't I told you?"

"Okay, for one, if you went to school at Quantico why are you in Burlington working for a small police department?" Her eyes were bright with curiosity.

Taking a moment, thinking about how to answer, "Well like I said, dad was in the military. We moved all over the world while I was growing up. My father wanted one of his boys to follow in his footsteps. He pushed us boys in the direction of the military. My brothers did their 4 years each and went into the construction field. I was dad's last hope, so he pulled a few strings to get me into Quantico. I did fairly well but decided that wasn't what I wanted. Colonel Chapman was not too happy with my decision either.

I was so tired of all the moving, the military and the politics. Therefore when Mom and Diana moved back here, I came with them. I just wanted a quiet life."

"I guess I understand. But nothing ever happens here, I'm sure you could have gone anywhere with your qualifications."

"That's my father's dream not mine." He gave her a warm smile. "Okay - now it's your turn. I want to know all about Katherine McGuire."

"Not quite yet, I still have one more question"

"Okay, one more..." He said with a smile.

"Do you mind if it is a personal question?"

Shooting her an inquisitive look, "I suppose not..."

She was eager to know, "I've been wondering how an attractive, intelligent, fun guy like you isn't already married?"

He gave her a shy little smile. "I don't know how to answer that one."

"I hope I'm not overstepping?"

"No, no...I haven't really dated much. I've always either been absorbed in school, or the service, and now my job. There was *one* girl I was involved with back at Quantico but that didn't work out so well. I guess I've never married because I haven't found the right one yet." His smile was warm and his eyes flirtatious, "Now, is it my turn?"

Katie dreaded this moment. She wanted to be forthright. Honesty was very important to her but there were certain things in her past she didn't think she was ready to share with anyone just yet.

"Well, there isn't much to tell. I lead a pretty boring life actually. I grew up in Geneva. After high school I went to the Chicago Art Institute. I graduated summa cum laude with a degree in design and minored in history. My mother, Sarah has lots of hobbies and sits on numerous committees for various things. My father, Don is a mechanic and owns his own garage in Geneva. I have a younger brother D.J., who works with my dad building hotrods and races."

Cal commented, "Well that explains your beautiful car."

Katie smiled, "Yeah, well..."

"Let me get this straight. You graduated top of you class, studying history and design and you're slinging beers in a bar? How does that work? It sounds to me like you're over qualified to be a waitress."

"Hey, waitressing is an honest job." Katie said laughing just as the waitress delivered their drinks and putting a large pitcher down in front of them. They placed their orders and continued with their conversation.

"Then answer me this, what do you *want* to do?"

Katie took a sip, reflecting on what he asked.

"It's more of a dream actually. I've always wanted to design big beautiful homes or refurbish old historical places. I love history."

"That I get. So why are you working at the Brick Yard and not for some architect or design firm?"

"It's not so bad. Most of the people I work with are pretty great. When I moved here there wasn't any where for me to get a job in my field. I liked Burlington, so I stayed."

"Couldn't you have gotten your dream job in Geneva? There are lots of wealthy people who live there, vacation there and how about all those old beautiful homes in old town?"

Katie knew he was right, but she couldn't tell him that she couldn't go back there. It would be too painful. "I'm sure you are right, I probably could. I just wanted to get out on my own; get away from people I grew up with who never go anywhere. I guess that's why I'm here." That was the best answer she could give. She refrained from telling him too much about her past; at least for now.

Their food came. It smelled fantastic.

Cal reached out for Katie's hand. "Well, whatever brought you here, I'm glad."

She gazed up at this wonderful kind man. His eyes captured hers. "I'm glad too."

They enjoyed their meal and their lively conversation was great. There was more to it than their physical attraction to each other; they both reveled in spending time with each other and discovered there was a strong connection between them.

After returning home Katie was blissful thinking about her date with Cal. She couldn't remember the last time she'd been this happy. Lying in bed she kept playing their date over and over again in her head until drifting off to sleep.

Chapter 12

The next day Billie stopped in for dinner; this time she brought sub sandwiches, and relentlessly inquired about Katie's date with Cal, wanting every detail. When their conversation sidetracked to the strange goings on at the house, Billie talked Katie into having a séance. Billie was into the supernatural, tarot cards, crystal power, you name it and she tried it. Katie knew the strange things happening in her house had nothing to do with the supernatural and everything to do with some deviate breaking in. But she played along with her anyway.

"Katie this is the creepiest house I've ever been in! I can't believe you live here! All the freaky stuff that has happened has to weird you out living here all alone."

"Ya know Billie; I really hadn't dwelled too much on that until you just said it! So, thanks for that! Thanks, a lot!" She said in a very sarcastic tone.

Once it got dark out, they lit some candles and set up the tarot cards. Billie had a bunch of stuff with her. What it was all for, who knew? Katie let Billie run the show. The radio was on for back ground noise but it started to scramble and switch stations without any help. That really wigged Billie out. "I told you – you have ghosts!"

Sudden flashes of lightning were seen out the windows, and when it lit up the sky they could see the trees starting to sway and dance in the wind. Billie pointed out the radio's static and said, "You've got a ghost. I'm telling ya!"

"Seriously Billie? It is storming outside, you know, electrical storm, interfering with the signal, and since when do ghosts leave footprints or take underwear?" Katie said turning off the radio.

Billie ignored Kate's logical remarks and proceeded to do her thing.

Katie was already annoyed. After some stupid chanting, Billie Jo began to lay out cards. She placed them one by one face up. She drew the Tower card. Next she drew the Chariot.

Katie was watching Billie's reaction to each card as she laid them down. Katie however was unimpressed and asked, "What's the big deal"?

"This one, the Tower is a card about war. And this one here, the Chariot also implies war. It's a complex card but this means you have some obstacles."

"Billie I appreciate what you're trying to do here" Katie began to say, but, lightning flashed with a loud crack just before the thunderous boom shook the house.

***

This night, the stranger lingered outside watching them through the set of windows on the North side of the living room. He was quite agitated because Billie was there, again. She talked too much and they wouldn't go to sleep soon enough. The stranger was addicted to Katie. She had become a narcotic for him. He needed to be near her, watching her sleep. He wanted to touch her, and the nights he was able to slip the drug into whatever she was drinking were the nights he treasured.

***

Billie told her something bad was going to happen because of the placement of the other cards with the Moon card.

With that the wind picked up and a thunderstorm bellowed and boomed. They ran around closing the windows.

Katie thought, *"Oh great, that's all Billie needs is encouragement!"*

Lightning flashed, the candles flickered out all at once and the thunder sounded as if it hit the front door. They both jumped.

When the lightning flashed again Katie thought she saw someone outside the window.

"I think my heart just stopped!"

Billie's eyes were wide and she sat, frozen in place, only nodding her head in agreement.

The candles flickered back, but maybe it was just an illusion given the lightning was so bright that they only thought the candles went out.

Whatever Katie saw out there was gone now. She gave herself a mental head shake; this business with Billie was, indeed, affecting her.

Even if Billie did freak herself out; she was still quite pleased with herself. Now she brought out some books she had with her, to show Katie about haunted houses, Poltergeists and the like.

Katie was not amused. She knew it was not a supernatural problem she had in the house. Sometimes she would wake with chills, but it was as if someone were there watching her.

She asked Billie to stay the night since it was Billie's fault she was frightened.

***

Sometime shortly after she fell asleep, her restless thoughts transformed into something truly ugly.

Katie woke with a start. She was dripping with sweat and her heart was pounding a hundred miles an hour.

The despotic fiend had been watching Katie and he got a kick at how easy it was to lie in wait for her to fall asleep. He could be bolder on the nights he drugged her. But tonight was different. She was restless and whimpered in her sleep. He longed to hold her and comfort her, to love her, and this frustrated him. Especially since Billie had stayed the night. That made it even more risky for him, but he enjoyed the challenge. He wouldn't be able to spend the time with Katie he craved, although sometimes just to watch her sleep was enough.

Too restless to sleep Katie got up and slipped on her robe leaving her room, and him.

Disappointed, he dejectedly left the way he came in, through the attic vent.

***

Katie tried to be quiet descending the old wooden stairs, but Billie wasn't able to sleep too well either and heard her friend going down. She got up and followed Katie down, "Hey! Are you alright Katie?"

Whispering a response, "Yeah, sorry to wake you."

Billie giggled, "Why are we whispering? It is just us." Giggling again, "I couldn't sleep either."

"See, it's your fault!" Katie teased. "You freaked us both out with that chanting and candle bullshit!"

"Yeah, well don't forget about the radio changing channels on us! That was freaky too!" Billie reminded her.

Katie stood in the middle of the kitchen in the dark, with flashes of lightning illuminating the room every now and again. "I don't even know what I want. What are you in the mood for?"

"I don-know? Got any ice cream?"

"Yeah, I picked some up the other day. Rocky Road?"

"Sure! That will work!"

Billie went to the silverware drawer and retrieved two spoons while Katie took out the quart of ice cream from the freezer.

The two friends sat down at the table and proceeded to dig in, each taking a spoonful in turn. They were quiet for a few minutes, just looking out the windows and eating spoonful after spoonful of Rocky Road. Katie finally broke the silence. "You know, I have to tell you, I woke up in such a panic. I was drenched in sweat, and I had this overwhelming feeling that I was being watched. Call me crazy, I know that you are here and I shouldn't feel like that, but it was weird. It was so real. I thought I even 'smelled' someone in my room tonight. I just can't explain it Billie."

Billie wasn't sure what to say. She knew Katie was touchy on the subject of her rape but thought maybe now that she was seeing Cal and getting closer to him, she was having some doubt about her future because of it.

"Katie, I know you don't ever want to discuss what happened to you, but do you think your subconscious is playing games with you? Maybe deep down you're skeptical about your new relationship and you feel this sudden doom knocking at your door?"

Katie had a painful expression on her face when she shot Billie a look.

"What? I'm just sayin'!" Billie said defensively.

Sarcastically Katie said, "Well, isn't that insightful." Intuitively Katie knew that what Billie said could be true. It was just very hard to admit it.

Dropping the sarcasm and defensiveness Katie decided to get honest. "That may be, I do have a tendency not let anyone get too close. I know I'm falling for Cal, harder than I anticipated. I would love to be able to just let my inhibitions go and take me wherever they lead. But I can't Billie! I know that every man is not Derrick, and I have to let myself live again. I am trying, very hard by the way, to get over it. Easier said than done! And what I experienced is something that will never really go away. I am well aware of that, but I can't have it control my life. Now, with all these goofy things happening in my house...I don't know Billie and I really don't believe that it is a ghost!"

Billie sat attentively listening to Katie unleash her thoughts, occasionally scooping out a spoon full of ice cream.

"And another thing, we still never found out who drugged me! Why would someone do that? I can't imagine anyone we work with doing it, which leaves a customer. How were they able to get to my drink?

Someone drugged me; someone is breaking into my house and screwing with my mind! While I'm trying to get my life together and work on a new relationship...when you put it all together - of course I can't sleep. Maybe I'm overly tired, but I can't be imagining it all. Something just doesn't seem right.

Chapter 13

The following night Billie and Katie worked. It was just busy enough to keep them from being bored but slow enough for them to chat.

Katie, so wrapped up in her own problems, hadn't thought to ask Billie about her love life, "What's going on with you and Jack?"

Billie rolled her eyes, "He just doesn't seem that into me." Then changing the subject Billie mentioned that the guy with the icy blue eyes who was interested in Katie had come in and then just left.

Katie felt something was not right about that guy. "What did he want this time?"

"He wanted to know if you were seeing anyone." Billie answered.

"Well? What did you tell him?" Katie already knew the answer.

"Nothing, not a damned thing, not after you all yelled at me! I just shrugged my shoulders. I was going to tell you about him being in here, but then we had that softball team come in and they distracted me."

"Do you think that could be the guy who drugged me?"

"I don't know...maybe." Billie answered.

"Son of a...next time he's in here you have to point him out. The jocks can wait for their damn beer!"

Billie felt bad for not saying anything sooner.

After they finished cleaning up the bar, they walked out to their cars together. As Billie started up her little Escort she noticed the same man, who had inquired about Katie, in her rearview mirror. The hairs on the back of her neck stood up and she got goose bumps all over. When she went to pull out of the parking lot she checked her mirror again. He wasn't there this time. "Now Katie's got me worried for nothing? There's nothing wrong with that guy!" she told herself.

* * *

That night Katie just couldn't relax. Thinking over what Billie told her and trying to remember anything that could explain this man's interest with her, she began to wonder if he had anything to do with the stuff happening at the house.

Katie grabbed her robe from the bed and walked downstairs to the shower, turning the faucet handle to get just the right temperature. She pulled her shirt off dropping it to the floor, unfastened her denim skirt, sliding it down and then stepped out of it. She reached in testing the water. Picking up her smoky clothes off the floor, she stepped into the little hallway to drop them down the basement stairs. Locking the latch to the door she reentered the bathroom. With a heavy heart Katie stepped into the shower. She stood there for a long time just letting the hot water wash away all the cares of the day. Her head was swimming with all the things going through her mind. She lost track of time, not knowing how long she was in the shower, but noticing the water was now cooler; she shut it off and grabbed her towel. It felt good to rinse the off the day and put something comfy on. Katie brushed her teeth, slipped into her soft robe, and then slowly made her way up the stairs.

She never heard the predator enter her house.

She sat down on her bed going over the happenings of the day, trying to remember if she saw Billie talking to anyone in particular. Finally relaxed, completely exhausted and still a bit aggravated, Katie didn't bother to put on a nightshirt. She just lay back on her bed in her robe and closed her eyes, thinking until she fell into a sound sleep.

***

Once the predator knew she was sound asleep he cautiously crept forward and looked down at his prize. She looked so sweet, and smelled so good to him. Her hair was still damp from the shower.

Tonight, however, he decided to take the next step. Knowing she would not awaken but cautious anyway, he bravely, yet gingerly, untied her robe slowly exposing her supple fragrant white skin. Just the thought of her lying there before him utterly exposed gave him an erection. "I want you Katie and soon we will be together!" The words came out a mere whisper from his lips.

With the fantasy of making love to Katie in his head, he knelt on the floor beside her bed. He gently takes her hand, stroking it, kissing it, and caressing it. He studies the shape and color of her firm exposed breasts. He liked the way her nipples were so perky, even while she slept. They were a dark pink almost raspberry in color. Now accepting the challenge that lay before him; he softly glides the back of his long figures tracing the side of her full breasts, across her rib cage and on to her stomach revealing even more of her nakedness. As he explored her unconscious body he was very careful not to disturb her but he felt the need to kiss her; the feel of his lips on her silky fragrant skin. He wanted her so badly that he boldly yet slowly slid her legs apart to expose her nether region; he just couldn't resist the prospect of entering her. Although he was only able to feel the tender curve of her inner thigh before his fantasies were cut short. His erection exploded in his jeans before he could go any further.

Now that he was finally able to spend the time he wanted with Katie he was thwarted by his own elevated desires. Furious with himself and with her for being so lovely, he has to do something else. He needs a plan to take her away from here...soon.

Katie, oblivious to the stranger pawing her body, watches a vivid dream, yet feeling it as all too real.

***

She felt funny, almost like she was floating. She had closed the bar, saying good night to everyone as she walked out. The night was slightly chilly. Oddly, she noticed there were no stars out. "Now, where did I park my car?" She rounded the building to the alley; maybe she parked in the back and forgot. There was a light on but it was at the street, the one by the back door must have burned out. Fumbling for her keys in her jacket pocket, a beer bottle suddenly skids in front of her then rolls away. Not wanting to show she is uneasy she presses on. Just as she steps behind the building, a tall lanky man steps out from the shadows. He strolls right for her. Katie steps aside to let him by, not looking up at his face, just keeping an eye on her car. Not much farther she thinks. He steps in her path, making her stop to acknowledge him. It is really dark and she can't see his face. He is nothing but a shadow with a florescent glow.

"Can I help you?"

He doesn't say anything. She knows he is smiling. "Fight or Flight, right?" Katie knows he is up to no good. In that fraction of a second it took for her to move it is too late.

He grabs her right arm holding it down, and places his forearm to her throat walking her backwards. Only three steps back but very fast and her head hits the brick wall behind her. She feels the wind get knocked from her, and his forearm is crushing her throat so she can't make a sound. He holds her slightly off the ground with one arm on her neck and with the other she feels a cold metal blade slice through her T-shirt exposing her bra. He hikes up the khaki skirt she is wearing and rips off her panties. She can smell the stale beer breath in her face and that odor. What was that? She forces herself to fight, it isn't much but she would be damned if she'd just let him do this to her. She manages to get a knee up as hard and as fast as she can to hit something important. Maybe? Kicking and struggling. He just drops her. THUD! That was strange...it sounded hollow and more like a wood floor than pavement.

***

The stranger watches her rapid eye movement; he knows she is dreaming and believes she is dreaming about him. He knows she is feeling his hot love for her. She doesn't fight him but falls sweetly into his arms. Tonight he didn't bother sneaking out the vent in the attic. Tonight he would walk out the cellar door not taking any chances that a certain cop would see him leaving by the front door.

***

Katie awoke in a cold sweat and found herself lying on the floor in her bedroom. Her robe was wide open exposing her cold pale flesh. Now full of goose bumps, she was so cold, that her nipples were purple. Feeling dazed and confused she determined it was just a dream; a dream and nothing more, but it did feel so real to her. Her head was swimming, she felt completely hung over. There was a buzzing in her ears. She slowly got up off the floor. Her legs wobbled and she felt a little stiff. "Something isn't right." Katie wanted to cry. Was she losing her mind? "Wasn't it just a dream?" The thought scared her. She gingerly walked down the stairs to the shower, her body trembling. She felt dirty and had to wash off the thought, the dream...it felt so real!

***

That night at the Brick Yard it was so busy that the girls never had a chance to talk. The place was hopping, upstairs and down. The band that played that night was the Booze Brothers. They were always a lot of fun, and they brought in big tips too.

Once again, the man with icy blue eyes was watching Katie work. He never said anything to her, only stared at her with his cold eyes. This time Katie was aware that he was watching her. Was he staring at her or was it just her imagination? Was it her dream from last night that kept returning to haunt her that made her so jumpy because, really, it felt so real? She spotted him about 11 p.m. He was tall and lanky, with dirty black hair, and an unshaven face, but it was his eyes that made her feel cold the way they seared into her. His thin dark lips slightly parted into a sneer when he smiled revealing something dark within. He wore a gold chain around his neck barely visible under his black concert shirt worn with a flannel shirt over it. He had on a pair of tight black jeans and black cowboy boots. It was him, the man in her nightmare. At least she thought he had to be the one since she shivered from head to toe when she saw him. He leaned against the brick wall placed right between the two waiting areas where he had a perfect view of her. She noticed Billie had been watching him as well.

Katie had just managed to shake the feeling off and finish cleaning her tables when a minor uproar ensued.

Eddie couldn't help himself; he enjoyed sneaking up on Katie and had waited all evening for the right time to do it. When the bar had quieted down a bit between sets he knew the opportunity was right and took full advantage of the situation. Towering over her, he was just going to give her a little "BOO", when she abruptly turned into him. Her tray, filled with glasses and debris, tumbled to the floor with a shatteringly loud crash and the sound of Katie screaming.

She shivered being in such close proximity to him, she really didn't like Eddie. Her temper flared and she snapped at him. "Why do you do that to me, you jackass!" She threw the bar towel at Eddie hitting him in the chest. "Now you clean it up!" And she headed back to the bar with purpose.

Eddie was highly amused with himself for his prank but didn't expect all the attention it brought him. Katie got the applause and he got the hard time from the patrons.

Jack, who was pouring a draft, looked up at the commotion to find Eddie towering over Katie. *"What in the hell is he doing? He doesn't belong down here; he's supposed to be carding at the door up stairs."* He watched as Katie yelled at Eddie and called him a jackass. *"Well, she has that right!"*

Jack gave Katie an approving grin. "That's tellin' him!" He got a smile out of her anyway.

Eddie brought the tray full of broken glass up and dumped it in the trash behind the bar. Jack shot Eddie a disgusted look. He got the picture, "Yeah, I know, I'm going." Eddie said.

"Thanks Jack!" Katie said, "Why is he down here anyway? I thought he was supposed to work the door upstairs?"

"He is," Jack said in an irritated manor.

Just then a very attractive young girl bellied up to the bar. Jack noticed her immediately, along with everyone else at the bar. She was a long leggy brunette with incredible accouterments that she had pushed up teasingly through her blouse. The two hounds on either side of her offered to buy her a beer.

Jack knew she wasn't 21. "What can I get ya?" He politely asked.

"A draft will be fine."

"Can I see an ID?" He asked and winked at her.

Her friendly smile disappeared. "I was carded at the door."

"That may be sweetheart, but now I'm carding you. You should be flattered; I card anyone I don't think is over 30."

Jessica, the other bartender caught on that Jack's little missy wasn't old enough to be there. "Jack, I got the bar."

The young lady got up and strolled back up stairs only to be followed by Jack.

Erik saw him escorting her up the stairs and knew that Eddie let this one in.

Considering how large and intimidating Erik was, he was actually a very nice guy. "Excuse me miss, can I check your ID again?"

She knew her charade was up. She looked over to find Jack standing at the top of the stairs behind her. "I know, busted." She said. She wasn't going to put up a fuss, she had less than a year to go before she could hang out here and she wasn't going to blow it.

She pulled out her ID to show Erik.

Looking at it he smiled. "Jennifer, Sweetie, come back in 10-months and I'll buy you one."

He gave her license back; she took it, slipping it into her purse. Then as she left the bar, she turned to Erik and said, "I'll hold you to that." She said with a flirtatious smile.

He chuckled, "You do that."

Jack approached Erik, "Damn Eddie! How many 'Betties' you think he's let in here?"

"Don't know, but that one wasn't too obvious. Do you suppose that's why he wanders off the door, to get a little for letting them in."

"Oh I don't doubt it."

"We're gonna have to do something about him."

"I know it... The bastard was downstairs just before this and scared Katie. She dropped her tray and all the glasses on it crashed to the floor."

"What an ass!"

"Oh, don't worry, Katie whipped a towel at him and told him to clean up the mess, then called him a jackass as well! At least we are all on the same page when it comes to Eddie being a jackass. He's got to stop messing with Katie."

Back downstairs the stranger, who watched Katie, was amused that she went off on Eddie.

As Eddie moseyed back to the front door he knew he was going to get an ear full.

Instead Erik excused himself and went down stairs to get some sugar from his sweetie Jessica.

Katie was leaning against the wall at the bottom of the stairs quietly keeping an eye on the stranger when Erik tried to squeeze by.

"Oops! Pardon me." Erik then noticed the guy too, "I didn't see him come in, is he bothering you?"

Shaking her head, "No, I uh – it's fine."

Once again the stranger nursed his beer until it had to be warm and flat. Just before 2 a.m., closing time, he simply got up and left.

After closing, Katie and Billie went through the bar picking up all the empties left on tables and ledges, and made sure no drunks were left in the rest rooms.

"I know you saw him tonight." Billie Jo said.

"I did".

"Well? He doesn't look like a psycho!"

Katie had nothing to say; to put it simply, the guy gave her the creeps.

The girls walked into the women's room. Billie picked up the couple of empties that were left on the sinks. Katie looked under the stalls for feet as she pushed on the doors.

"That figures!" Katie said in a disgusted tone. Naturally on a night she really just wanted to get out of here, something or someone had to mess it up. She knocked on the door to the stall, "Hey, Miss? It's closing time and we need you to leave."

Katie knocked again. "Hey – are you okay?" She tried the door, locked.

Not wanting to get on her hands and knees on this floor...Katie bent over to look under and sure enough there was a passed out drunk woman sitting on the pot.

"Billie, could you go get Erik, please?"

Billie just laughed, as she turned to go out the door.

Moments later Erik knocked on the door.

Sounding like they were playing 'the Price is Right' game, Katie hollered, *"Come on down!"*

"So what do we have here?" He said with a big grin plastered on his face.

"Well, see for yourself...I have to crawl under and unlock the door."

Katie got down and reached up, unlocking the door. The door swung open.

Katie looked up to see the expression on Erik's face.

His large grin quickly disappeared, "Oh, you have got to be kidding me?"

Now Katie was the one with the big grin. "I'll get one of the guys to help. It looks like you might need all three of them!" She said laughing; it felt good to laugh.

Jack and Steve both came into the women's room to check out the situation.

"So what have you got Erik?"

"No way!" Steve blurted out.

Jack just cracked up. "How in the hell are we gonna pull her out of there?"

The woman was huge! She had dark brown hair which was lacquered and teased into a big eighties hairdo and lots of makeup which by now was looking more like Mimi from the "Drew Carey Show'. She had on some kind of skimpy top that was laced up and extremely tight jeans that they couldn't figure out how she got them on in the first place. However, those now were down around her ankles. She filled that stall, side to side. She was passed out and wedged in place.

Erik huffed, "Well you wimps won't be able to pull her out, but you can both try to pull up her pants!"

"What the HELL!" Jack and Steve both protested.

So Erik pulled her out, and the guys tried to yank up her pants. No such luck. Katie even tried to help.

"Well now they're half way up. So what do we do with her?" Billie asked.

Erik, with the help from Steve and Jack dragged her up the stairs and out through the main street entrance. They set her down on the front steps, leaning against the building bathed in the neon light.

"I better call Cal to let him know she's out here for pick up."

Erik would always call to let him know of drunks or fights or whatever might come up. He didn't want anyone to tempt fate by driving drunk, so the cops would either find them a ride home or they'd spend the night in the drunk-tank.

They made their way back in and Erik noticed what a big help Eddie had been. In a loud angry tone Erik bellowed, "Eddie! You lazy ass – where the *hell* did you go?"

Naturally no response from Eddie. He wasn't in the bar anywhere. Once again Eddie slipped out and left work early. Erik was fed up with having to deal with him.

Billie and Katie cleaned up the mess left in the bathroom.

"This sucks! How is this part of our job?"

"Billie, someone has to do it. Could you just help?"

They continued their conversation on their way back to the bar.

"Hey, can I take a shower at your place tonight? I want to go to the after bar party, and I don't want to be all nasty."

"Yeah, sure, but I don't think it is such a good idea to go to the after bar party."

"Wow...what's your problem? You sound like my mom."

"Nothing - you want to go, so go! I just think you'll regret it later."

"Why's that?"

"Billie...do you have any idea what happens at those parties?"

"It's a party...duh! You're just jealous cuz' you weren't invited?"

"I think you know me better than that! I hear some of them talking and it's just about getting a piece of ass! It isn't what you think it is, and what about Jack?"

"What about him? I want to go have fun, and dance. Jack won't commit to anything; sorry if you don't like it!"

Katie just dropped it. Billie wasn't going to listen so what was the point. She was warned.

Jack over heard their discussion and shot Billie one of his disappointing looks, turned and walked out. He might not be one for words, but she could tell he didn't like the idea of her going either.

"If he doesn't want me to go, then why doesn't he say something?" Billie thought, a little put out.

As Katie and Billie left the bar one of the squad cars pulled up. The drunken throw back from the '80s had tipped over and rolled across the sidewalk, sprawling out in the street with her head up on the curb. The officer got out, and called for rescue. He didn't look too happy either.

Billie who was still annoyed just grunted.

Katie noticed the stranger standing in the shadows, lighting up his cigarette like he always did but chose to ignore him and just went home.

Billie followed, of course she was still planning on going to that after hours bar party and wanted to freshen up. However, once she got to Katie's she had a sudden change of heart.

Katie's cell rang, it was Cal calling.

Billie waited patiently while Katie spoke to him on the phone.

"I didn't want to do this over the phone but I am going to be tied up for a while at the station. Do you have plans Tuesday evening?"

"No, not yet." Katie's voice was sweet and light.

"Would you be interested in going out with me again?"

"I would like that very much. What did you have in mind?"

"How about dinner, at my place? I'll even cook for you."

Katie was looking forward to it and impressed he was going to cook. They said their good nights, and hung up.

Billie, who never bothered to sit down for the length of their conversation, gave Katie a hug and said, "I'll just see you later. I'm not going to go to that party after all."

"Did you want to stay here?"

Normally she would have but Katie was just too happy for the mood Billie was in.

"Nah, I'm just going home." With that she left.

Chapter 14

The stranger now more determined than ever to take what he wanted; pays close attention to driving in the dark through long winding dirt roads surrounded by tall pines on both sides. He tried to recall the way. The area had changed little since the last time he was here. An occasional deer or two trekked across the road in front of him. His head lights reflected back in the eyes of some smaller critters. A raccoon and maybe a skunk also hustled across just in time. Summer was over and fall was here. The cool crispness of the autumn air brought back memories from when he was a boy coming out here to his grandfather's hunting cabin. He finally reached the over grown drive he'd been looking for. He couldn't drive through it, so he needed to hike the rest of the way on foot.

In his mind the idea of starting over with Katie was all the motivation he needed. Some of the leaves had already begun to fall. The leaves crunched under him with each step the tall dark man took. He walked only a short way when the beam of light from his flashlight struck what he was looking for.

The little cabin in the woods stood all alone as the wind whispered through the trees. Opening the door for the first time in all these years gave him new vigor. Shining the light around inside, it was just as he had remembered it. It was a disheveled dusty mess but when he was finished, it would be perfect for him and the object of his affection.

He found the generator out back and started it. Now that he could have better light, he swept the floors, shook out the old bedding and replaced it with new. The man dusted and cleaned. He turned on the water and checked the fuel in the tank outside. It was going to be a long winter for them.

He brought in a box from his car. His chest filled with pride as he unpacked the contents.

He took out a couple of framed pictures which he set up around the room right away. He even bought some feminine items and such that she would need, including makeup, which he placed in the bathroom. He knew everything about her, even what shampoo she used. He knew she'd be very happy here. As he set up the more personal items his mind drifted into fantasy. He couldn't wait to see the look on her face when he showed her their new home. He loved her more than anything and would see to it that she was happy. He'd give her everything she ever needed.

Then he got busy attaching some cuffs and leg irons to their bed. When he was finished, he placed with great care her favorite night gown on their bed. He stood in the doorway looking back around the little cabin and a dark smile crept across his face. The drive to Wautoma was only a few hours from Burlington, so he had plenty of time to get back.

Chapter 15

Tuesday came and Katie thought maybe she could finally wear that little summer dress Billie talked her into buying. She tried it on, and looked herself over in the mirror.

"Billie was right, it does accentuate my cleavage!" She chuckled to herself.

The little summer dress was lovely shades of peach with cream Hibiscus flowers throughout the fabric. The length was perfect; it hit her just above the knee. The cap sleeves and fax wrap around skirt gave her incredible curves. She was thrilled to be able to wear it and she had the perfect pair of shoes to go with it. Looking in her closet for the cream colored high heeled strappy sandals she noticed her clothes were in disarray and her neatly lined up shoes were toppled over again. "What the hell?" She didn't have time to dwell on it she had to get ready for her dinner date with Cal. But this really bothered her. She just couldn't figure out how her things could be in disarray when no one else lived here, she didn't even have any pets.

She grabbed up her shoes and bounded down the stairs. Sitting on the couch she slipped her foot into one of the shoes and fastened the little buckle and then the second one. She was so excited and happy to see Cal again. She had already brushed her teeth, but she brushed them again anyway. Reapplying her Cabernet Cashmere lipstick, and then fluffing her hair with her fingers. She took a deep breath, "time to go."

Cal had given Katie the address. It was easy enough to find on the corner of W. Chandler and Kane Street. There was his house number. She double checked. Sure enough this has to be it. She pulled her Nova onto the brick paved drive down to the side of the house. Getting out of the car she gawked at the three-story Victorian with a huge wraparound porch. It was enormous, and gorgeous! Walking up the steps she noticed all the spindle work had be redone and freshly painted. The white wicker furniture on the front porch looked very inviting. His yard was neatly manicured and beautiful.

She thought to herself. "When did he ever find time to do all this work?"

Cal opened the front door, which was painted a deep plum and had very pretty art glass.

She couldn't keep the smile off her face.

Cal's heart skipped a beat. Katherine was absolutely breath taking. He motioned for her to come inside. He gave her a hug and kissed her on her cheek. "You look beautiful Kate."

Blushing a little she said, "Thank you." Then catching a whiff of the heavenly scent emerging from his kitchen she said, "Mmm, something smells good?"

"Well thank you, I like to cook. I hope you're going to like it."

They walked into the large open kitchen, which was full of wonderful smells.

"Wine?" Cal offered.

"Yes, please."

He uncorked a bottle of Merlot and poured a glass for both of them.

Cal was a very attractive man, and he was tall, over 6'; even in heels she dwarfed next to him. He handed her a glass and bent down to kiss her soft lips tenderly. It was a very nice welcome. He looked into her beautiful bright eyes and said, "Dinner should be ready soon; would you like to see the house while we wait?"

"I'd love that."

Taking their wine glasses with them he led Katie on a tour of his beautiful home. The kitchen was open and gorgeous. All the cabinets and wood floors were walnut and he had granite counter tops including the island. A large window let in a good amount of natural light. The dining room was just as beautiful, and the crown moldings were deep and really put the finishing touch on this room. He set a lovely table with old china and even flowers among the candle sticks. Cal had soft jazz music playing in the back ground. As they walked through each room he explained to her what he'd done, or what he wanted to do. The formal living room was quite large as well. All the case work in this room was also walnut. The crown moldings were very prominent in here. He had decorated with more modern furniture in this room, over sized heavy leather couches and chair with solid mission tables. The front parlor was where Katie had come in. Under the stair case Cal had put in a powder room. There wasn't anything else in this room other than a grand stair case, made of walnut and the spindles had just been refinished. A new runner ran up the stairs. Cal continued to lead Katie up to the second floor. There was a long hallway that stretched across 6-doors which concealed four bedrooms, a bathroom and another stairway to the third floor which was basically a walk up attic.

Katie admired the accrue-colored wallpaper. It looked old but it was new. Cal showed her the empty rooms and told her of his ideas for each of them. One was the room he was using for now, but at the end of the hall were a pair of double wooden doors. They opened up into a large room under construction, with one wall torn down to open up into another room.

"This will be the master bedroom, with a walk-in closet and its own bathroom."

"I can't believe you've done all this work. It's wonderful. The house will be absolutely gorgeous when you are finished with it."

She could tell the pride he had in showing her his home. They walked back down to the dining room. Cal pulled out a chair for Katie and asked, "More wine?"

"Yes, thank you." She listened to the soft jazz. The vocals of the woman singing intrigued her. "Who is this?" She asked.

"Viola Cummings." He answered as he refilled both their glasses. "It was one of my grandmother's favorites."

"I like it." Kate smiled.

Cal lit the candles and then excused himself to the kitchen.

"Would you like some help?"

"No, thank you, tonight I get to wait on you."

Katie looked around the dining room attentively admiring the beautiful wood work while she waited. She started to day dream about how amazing he was. He was almost perfect. However, Katie wasn't sure if she couldn't trust her feelings and this started to make her even more nervous.

Cal reentered carrying a large chilled bowl with salad and all the fixings. He set it on the table retreated into the kitchen only to return with a tureen filled with a thick potato leek soup. He placed it on the table and sat down across from Katie.

She could tell he was also bit nervous and found it comforting. She smiled at him. "Is that vichyssoise?"

He returned the smile, "It is."

Katie silently was in awe at the extent of which Cal superseded her expectations. He was so proper, and seemed to be a jack of all trades, including cooking. They had light friendly conversation warming up to each other. The vichyssoise was incredible. Katie loved it and told Cal so. She admired his many talents.

When they finished the first course Cal retrieved the main course.

He waltzed in with a lovely platter containing London broil garnished just like at a fancy restaurant.

"That looks wonderful!"

Cal smiled, he was really enjoying this. He slipped back into the kitchen to retrieve the rest of the meal. Freshly made bread, asparagus spears drizzled with a little olive oil, baked potatoes with real butter and sour cream.

He placed another bottle of Merlot on the buffet table next to them.

They clearly enjoyed each other's company and made each other laugh. Dinner was fantastic. Katie felt full; she wasn't going to eat another bite until Cal cleared the table and brought out dessert.

"Ooo...I love cheese cake!"

"Okay I have to confess, I didn't make the dessert. Annie's in town did. All I did was put it on a pretty plate. You just can't beat her cheese cakes."

Katie laughed; she loved Cal's humor and honesty.

He was right, Annie's cheese cake was the best.

Their date was progressing nicely so they relocated to the living room with their wine.

Settling themselves on one of the over sized sofas they seemed to talk for hours. Cal loved the ease in which he could be with Katie. Her smile was genuine, and she was warm, smart and funny. Cal was falling head over heels for her. And although Katie was usually pretty straight forward, Cal began to suspect that there was more to Katie than she was willing to share with him. Cal thought maybe in time she would open up to him. For now he wanted to enjoy the moment.

The soft jazz played on and seemed to become a part of the aura. Cal set his glass down on the coffee table, and then leaned in to kiss Katie full on the lips. Katie returned the kiss. She too set her glass down. At first their kisses were exploratory and friendly. But then the intensity of their kissing got heated as their passion grew. Cal enveloped Kate's curvy petite body in his long strong arms. His hands had a mind of their own slowly caressing her body as to hold to memory every inch of her. The heat radiating from Kate stimulated Cal with her essence and made Cal eager to know more about her. Cal's touch awakened her flesh and with every stroke of his touch she felt electricity, even in their kisses. All her senses were heightened beyond anything she had ever felt before.

His fingers ran through her soft silky hair while their hungry kisses elevated them to the next course. She felt high, she was euphoric with desire for this man. She'd never had this connection with anyone prior to Cal. Then in the heat of their passion Cal made a move, albeit a slow non threatening move to change her position, she suddenly froze. Cal noticed how frigid she instantly became. He stopped. He wasn't sure what just happened to this passionate woman in his arms.

Scary memories of her rape poked holes through her happy moment. Katie was abruptly over whelmed and began to feel ill, her head was spinning, and she broke out into cold sweats.

"Is everything alright?" Cal asked sounding confused about what just happened.

"I – I ah, better go." She said as she jumped up.

Cal couldn't believe the painful expression on Katie's face. Cal stood with her.

"Oh – alright, let me walk you to your car."

She hurriedly walked out the door and down the front steps to her car with Cal trying to keep up with her.

Cal opened her door for her. "Kate, is everything okay?"

A veil of confusion covered his face. It was a very awkward moment for him. Their evening was going great up until then, and he didn't understand what went wrong.

"It's fine, really. Thank you for dinner. It was lovely." Katie wanted to crawl under a rock and die. She couldn't believe she acted like that and spoiled such a perfect evening.

Cal was gracious and the perfect gentlemen. He took her hand in his and kissed it. "Thank you, Kate, for a wonderful evening." His velvety voice was steady and melted her heart. "Please drive safely."

Her heart raced and the water works were coming, she had to quickly leave.

The sound of genuine concern for her in his voice made her feel even worse.

"I will. Thank you again for the lovely evening."

With that she left with him watching her go. He was completely dumbfounded.

She couldn't look up at him. All the way home she felt horrible. "What is wrong with me? Cal was great, more than great, he's wonderful". The water works just flowed. She knew that if this was going to work he had to know the truth about her past. She couldn't always control what triggered her fears. She was angry with herself for spoiling the best night of her life. She asked herself, "How could he possibly want me after I tell him? I'm damaged goods. Why would anyone, especially Cal want anything to do with me?"

Katie cried herself to sleep that night.

Chapter 16

For weeks the stranger would watch her work but not say anything, and made her feel very uncomfortable just the same. Then after hours she would notice him smoking in the parking lot as he watched her leave.

Erik noticed him also. He would make a point of walking the girls to their cars. Katie appreciated the effort.

Katie was much more careful as to what she drank. She never left anything open making it more difficult for whoever was trying to drug her.

And in that time, Cal had called her a few times to make other dates but she always had an excuse. Cal had given Katie some space, but it had bothered him too much to let things go any longer before finding out what happened. That Friday night after Katie got off of work Cal was parked alongside of her car, waiting to talk to her about it.

She knew she couldn't avoid him any longer.

"I'll catch ya later Billie."

Billie got the hint and left.

As Katie approached Cal's metallic grey Crown Vic he got out to greet her.

She gave him a smile but it wasn't her natural happy smile. Cal tried to read her but she was too guarded.

"Hi Cal, what's up?" Her tone even sounded distant to him.

"I was hoping we could talk about what happened."

This time Katie didn't have an excuse and she wasn't ready to share her secret with him. She had strong feelings for Cal but couldn't lead him on only to have it end badly. She stepped up into Cal's arms and held him tight not wanting to let him go.

Cal felt something was off. He couldn't figure out what this was all about. Even through her embrace he could feel how much she wanted to be with him. "Is everything okay Kate?"

As soon as Cal asked he felt her body language change.

"It's fine." She said. Then she made the mistake of looking up into his soulful steely grey eyes. They looked back at her with deep concern, searching for answers.

"I am sorry I haven't returned your calls…"

Cal remembered this feeling. He knew where she was going with this conversation. It wasn't going to be easy to hear this.

"Cal, I really like you and want to spend time with you, but I don't think I can be with you right now. I need some time."

Cal had never felt about a woman the way he felt about Kate, and now she was ripping his heart out. He still didn't understand why. "So you're telling me you need space? Kate, did I do something wrong?"

"No." She said looking into his beautiful yet sad eyes.

Cal thought "Oh here it comes."

"It's nothing you did...it's me. I'd like to be friends...I just don't know if there can be anything else right now." Katie held back the tears. She hated it when women would pull that line on men, and now she was doing it.

Cal who was a mess on the inside was cool and collected on the outside but his eyes gave him away. He was deeply hurt. "I guess there isn't anything else to say." He got back in his car and left.

She never wanted to hurt Cal. She was in love with him. Katie hated herself for what she just did. She never would have said that to anyone she cared about. Her thoughts were now all on Cal. The relationship she wanted to have, and the reality that she was "damaged goods," or at least in her own mind.

***

Katie had never felt really lonely before even when she was. Lately not only did Katie feel lonely, but she didn't feel things were right. She would go to bed and could hear a car without its motor running just rolling down the gravel drive outside but would never see it. She would hear strange noises in the basement and sometimes the roof would creak as if someone were walking on it. Her imagination ran wild and drove her mad. Katie took up sleeping with one eye open, always alert to any sound and her hand on the very large knife under her pillow. Was it just her imagination working overtime? Or was this stranger bothering her more than she thought? She couldn't take much more of this. She was bound and determined to find out more about this guy that took so much interest in her.

But first, she had to call Pete. He was her rock. They had been friends since fifth grade. She could tell him anything. Dialing his number she remembered the last time she had called him in the middle of the night. Katie's insides were all in knots. Her life had not been the same since then, and she didn't want to think about it now? She shook the thoughts of her past from her head as Pete answered in a very groggy tone.

"Pete? It's Katie."

"Tiredly he answered, "Is everything alright? It's 3:30 in the morning…"

"I don't mean to wake you; I have to talk to you."

"Sure Hun, what's up? Are you okay?" Pete knew something was up.

Katie started with the typical small talk; I'm fine, things are good, got Billie Jo a job working with me at the Brick Yard…then plunged forward telling him about BJ and the stranger, and the weird things she would hear or see, Pete told her he would come down and spend the week with her. They talked on the phone for almost an hour. She was so relieved Pete would stay with her; she finally got some long overdue sleep that morning.

Chapter 17

Monday afternoon Pete pulled into the drive. Katie was planting some flowers in the yard and could hear his pickup rolling down the gravel drive. Billie of course was laying out getting some sun. Billie Jo had one of those "look at me" personalities and she loved any attention she could get. She was about 5'7" had long shapely legs, a bit flat-chested but had one of those "ballerina bubble butts" the guys like to check out. Along with her long wavy dishwater blonde hair, big blue eyes and a bright smile she could easily get dates, however her insecurities stifled her opportunities. Today, she enjoyed getting attention from the guys at the implement dealer watching her sip her ice tea while they ate their lunches. She wore over sized sunglasses that took up most of her face, with a royal blue and silver barely there bikini so shiny, it sparkled like a fishing lure in the water on a bright sunny day.

Pete observed her combing through her long wavy locks with her fingers and teasing the men with her straw. Pete just shook his head. He just couldn't get over how she never seemed to grow up.

Parking his big Dodge pick-up truck on the side of the drive where Katie was digging in the dirt, he laid on the horn. Katie knew Pete was there but he loved to be loud and obnoxious whenever he could. Now Pete was not a tall man, but resembling a badger, his 5' 10" 210 pound build kept many thinking twice before messing with him. Katie however knew he was a teddy bear. She noticed he cut his sandy blonde hair really short, almost a buzz cut, and he grew a beard and mustache.

"Wow! You look great! You sure are a sight for sore eyes…" she jested with a big grin.

Pete gave Katie a big ol' bear hug, and cracked her back as he did so, "So do you Sis!" Pete wiped at the smudge of dirt she had on her check. They hadn't seen each other for about a year. It was long overdue, and Katie was so happy to see her friend.

BJ feeling left out had to get up and run over to hug Pete too.

"Let's go inside, I think maybe Billie's had a little too much sun" Pete smiled as he lifted her sunglasses to reveal the white raccoon eyes against the hot pink face.

"Billie could you get him something to drink while I wash up?"

"Sure thing!" Billie opened the fridge door to reveal Pete's favorite beer and grabbed one for him.

"Thanks! So what's - umph!" Pete could not finish his statement as BJ hopped in Pete's lap, giggling.

Pete twisted off the top to his beer and tossed back a swig while Billie wiggled in his lap.

Billie was laying it on thick, "So tell me, have you been working out? Are you still with Barb? Tell me what's new?"

Pete went along with her little game, and mimicked everything she had said to him, in a girly voice.

"Stop teasing Pete…seriously!"

Smiling, Pete gently placed his cold beer against her bare back and enjoyed the reaction he got in return.

"Ooooh!" She shot out of Pete's lap and squealed. "Hey! That isn't fair! You haven't changed a bit!"

Laughing his big hearty laugh, "Sorry Billie...No, I have not! I just couldn't help myself." Then he laughed a little longer.

"Hey, before Katie gets out of the shower, I want you to tell me what you two have been up to."

"Huh?"

"Katie told me she thinks there is someone stalking her. That there are strange things happening here at the house."

"Her ghost?"

"Ghost? What ghost? Is there a ghost that hangs out at the bar watching her too?"

"Pete, Katie is just skittish or paranoid or something...that guy at the bar seems okay to me, maybe a little weird." Then whispering, "But she does have a ghost in the house...I've seen things!"

Pete knew that Katie wasn't one to believe that a spirit was responsible. He also knew BJ was all too willing to blame it on the spirit world or supernatural or whatever you wanted to call it. Billie was a trusting soul, a little naive but had a good heart.

***

They all caught up on each other's lives and had a great Chinese takeout dinner. Katie was starting to get tired of Chinese all the time, but the food was always really good. Billie decided to go home about 10p.m. Not soon enough for Pete and Katie, because they wanted to catch up without any interference.

"I know she means well, but I don't have a ghost."

"I've heard her interpretation of what's going on, but I'd like to get your spin on it."

She told Pete all the things that have happened, minus the stay at the hospital. He would have been upset she didn't call him at that time.

"I just have this feeling that someone is not only watching me but getting into the house. I can't figure out how they're doing it. Maybe I am losing my mind, and the stress from starting a new relationship after all this time is putting doubt in my head. But I can't be imagining it all. Even Billie has been here when some really weird stuff has happened. That almost makes me think my house is haunted! Hell, I don't know Pete! Maybe I am nuts, right?"

He laughed. "You're funny. Heck yeah, you're nuts, but a good kind of nuts. You know the smoked kind that goes good with a beer!" Then he laughed even harder.

Katie punched him in the shoulder. "Ha. Ha, smart ass!"

Pete gave her a big hug. "You know I love you. I have to pick on you. I've missed you, and I have so much time to make up for."

"Well, I've missed you too."

"From what you and Billie have said about this, you're right, it's not supernatural. Some of it you probably are imagining though. Or at least blowing out of proportion, what's really happening. This guy that you've been seeing, is it serious?"

"I'm not sure any more; I think whatever it was I blew it." She said while averting her gaze.

"You shouldn't let life just pass you by because you are afraid of getting hurt."

Pete struck a chord, and her green eyes started to well up, but Pete took her hand in his beefy rough mitt. "You know I am right."

Pete was more than just a best friend, he was family. He was like her big brother, always looking out for her. Even in school, he was always there. They did everything together. She trusted Pete with her life. Hearing what he had to say rang true. Katie knew he was right, she had been playing it safe.

"Pete...I don't know if I could ever let someone get that close to me again. How do I trust again? I was in love with Derrick! And...what he took from me...I don't think I can do this again." She said, as her voice started to crack, "It's not fair to the man that I have been seeing."

They sat there without speaking for a few moments.

"Katie, you are a strong woman, a smart woman. You can sum up a person in the first 5-minutes you meet them. Give yourself a little credit where credit is due. Sometimes, sometimes Kate, people we love lie to us. Fool us into false truths. Derrick led me to believe he was the one for you. He fooled me too Kate. I feel like what happened to you was my fault!"

Katie tried to interrupt "Pete..."

"No, the door is finally open, now let me finish! For the last two years you have been blaming yourself, but I have been blaming me!"

"Stop it Pete! You're right...it isn't my fault, but it isn't yours either!"

With that, all the guilt Pete had been carrying around for the past two years let loose. Katie had never seen Pete falter. His eyes welled up and he took Katie in his arms. "I'm sorry Kate. I am so sorry I wasn't there and that you had to go through that."

Katie knew he had to say it out loud. She still never blamed him for any of it. Derrick was a friend of Pete's. One that Pete had trusted with his "little sister". But in the end he wasn't the person either one of them thought he was. Derrick had a secret cruel dark side. One that he didn't let anyone see until it was too late.

***

Earlier Pete had parked his truck alongside the implement dealer building, so it still looked like Katie was alone. If anyone tried to break in tonight they'd have a hell of a surprise waiting for them. Pete stayed in the bedroom next to Katie's upstairs. That night was the safest Katie had felt in weeks.

At around 3 a.m., Pete heard a car rolling on the gravel past the house. He got up and looked out the window. He didn't see anything, so he walked into Katie's room to check on her. Then he noticed a shadow bouncing off the implement building next door. As he walked over to look out her bedroom window the floor creaked with his weight and Katie jumped up with a start. "Who's there?" She demanded holding out her knife.

Pete swiftly yet quietly said, "Whoa! It's just me."

"You scared the shit out of me? What's wrong?" She whispered back.

He pointed to the window, and they both looked outside. Scanning the premises, they couldn't see or hear anything more. Pete said to Katie, "Why don't you try to go back to sleep, I'm watching."

Pete lay in bed just listening to all the noises of the night. Trying to determine what sound belonged to what. It wasn't long when he heard a metal creaking sound just below his window.

"What the hell is that?" He thought to himself.

Getting up slowly to look outside his window. There was definitely someone down there. He couldn't make it out but he knew who ever it was didn't belong at his friend's house at that time of the morning.

He yelled out the window at the shadow, "Who's out there?"

SLAM! The cellar door came down hard. The shadowy figure took off running through the cow pasture to the west of the house.

Katie jumped up with his loud bark. Simultaneously, Pete yelled for her to call the police as he took off running down the stairs and out to the pasture to see if he could catch the intruder.

By the time the police arrived, Pete was on his way back huffing and puffing from chasing whoever it was down the train tracks. The cops found the screwdriver the guy had used to pull the pins from the cellar door to get in.

One of the officers was Cal Chapman.

Katie proceeded to tell the police about the stranger at the bar. Sgt. Nelsen took notes and made a list of persons to contact.

She told Pete. "Thank God, you were here. I knew something wasn't right. Pete, I told you there is someone stalking me! I could just feel someone watching me while I slept."

Cal over heard her comment. Though Cal was cool on the outside, he was a mess on the inside. He wanted to be there for Kate and he didn't like this other man holding her.

While Nelsen was taking Katie's statement, Pete rubbed her back in support, as she told what she knew; he could feel how tense she was. He couldn't bare it if anything bad happened to her again. He felt he needed to protect her this time. He wasn't going to let there be a next time.

Pete noticed Cal attentively paying attention. So Pete stepped away, while she was talking to Sgt. Nelsen and approached Cal. "Officer Chapman, can I speak with you?"

They moved just out of earshot from Katie. "Officer Chapman," Pete began.

"Cal is fine, just Cal." Any other given time Cal was very good at locking up his feelings and be a professional, however this time it was more difficult. All he wanted was to hold Kate tight and keep her safe.

"Cal, Katie thinks this guy has been in her house before. She's like a Sister to me. When she called to tell me about all the unexplainable things happening and that she couldn't take it anymore, I came to help. I'm going to be staying with her until this bastard gets caught."

Cal was relieved to hear what Pete's relationship was with Kate, yet he was hurt and couldn't understand why she didn't call him.

A Stranger in the Night

Pete continued to say, "Katie thinks it's this weirdo that hangs out at the Brick Yard. If this is true, I think this guy has followed her home. And I'm sure he's been in her house already."

"Why would you say that?"

"First of all, this is a pretty easy house to get into if someone wanted to. She says at times during the night she can smell a peculiar odor. She hasn't been able to sleep too well. Locked doors are mysteriously unlocked. Lights turned off are turned on, and someone keeps taking the outside light bulbs. There are strange sounds at night, even on the roof. Things in her drawers and closet are moved around. Some things have turned up missing and she is the only one living here."

Cal listened intently, wondering if Pete knew about her ending up in the hospital. It wasn't his place to tell. Cal knew Katie had thought someone was in the house and felt awful for not looking harder. He even had a couple calls of some guys hanging out late at night by the Implement Dealer, but never found any evidence of that either.

"I don't want her freaked out any more than she already is...but could I get you to have a squad drive through periodically just in case?"

"I can do that." Cal had already thought of that and he would most likely be the one doing it.

Cal walked over to Katie, "I don't know if we can get a print off the screw driver, but I will have someone drive through here to the quarry every now and again. We will find him Kate."

He sounded very reassuring. And by the expression on his face, she knew he wanted to say more.

Katie was so exhausted from lack of sleep that her body shook. Cal put his arm around her and walked her to the house. Pete took notice. "Nah, it couldn't be. I wonder if that's the guy she was seeing?"

Cal sat Katie down on the couch and took the throw off the chair to cover her up.

In a soft sad voice Katie said "Thank you, Cal."

He could see she wanted to say something more but Pete interrupted. "Thanks, I've got it."

Cal gave her one last lingering glance before he parted.

Katie felt terrible. She realized what a mistake it was for her to push Cal away. She should have confided in Cal what was happening.

After the police left, Pete made some hot tea, and brought it to her. She was lounging on the couch, trying to keep her eyes open.

"Pete, thanks, I needed something to calm my nerves."

Pete asked. "Why don't you try taking a nap? I can take care of things, and I will make sure Billie doesn't bother you today either. Okey dokey?"

Pete looked down at her. "Hey, on the bright side you aren't nuts!"

Katie replied sarcastically, "Thanks, Pete! Leave it to you to put a bright side on this." Taking a sip of tea, she then placed it on the coffee table.

Pete left the room thinking to himself, *"I better check out that cellar door."*

Stepping outside he felt the sun's rays warm his face. He strolled over to the cellar door, inspecting the latch and hinges he realized this fuck had been in her house many times.

He walked all the way around the old farmhouse. He didn't see anything else out of the ordinary. Frustrated, Pete leaned against the oak tree in front of the house, resting his head back to look up at its sprawling branches. Reaching in his shirt pocket he pulled out a cigarette, then placing it between his lips he searched for his lighter in his front pants pocket. Finding it, he lit the cigarette and inhaled deeply. One of the oak's branches reached out towards the roof of the little house. Something about the vent caught Pete's eye. Trying to climb the large oak with a cancer stick hanging from his lips was not an easy task. He reached the branch which hung over the roof, he slowly swung down. He was careful not to make much noise as to alarm Katie. The attic vent was ajar. Pete removed the vent so easily. It was only set in place and held with one screw. Pete took out his mini Mag-light that he always carried on his keychain. Turning it on, he entered the attic. It was very hot and arid, and lined with marijuana? Every rafter was lined with the shit hung upside down to dry out. "Well, that explains Katie's headaches." She gets terrible migraines from pot. There was obviously a connection to whoever owned it, and the creep watching Katie. Continuing his search of the dark attic he found a panel that led into Katie's closet.

"Son of a bitch!" Pete couldn't believe it. Katie was in real trouble. Whoever this was had been coming in through her closet. Pete went back the way he came in. Replacing the vent and then climbing back down the tree. The sweat was just dripping off of him. Between smoking, being a bit out of shape and trying a trapeze act from the tree to the attic, he was surprised he didn't have a heart attack!

He went into the house to check on Katie. She was sound asleep curled up on the couch with a blanket.

"She needs the rest, maybe I will keep this to myself for now."

He needed another cigarette, not really, but it went good with a jolt of caffeine. Grabbing a cold Mountain Dew out of the fridge, he stepped outside for another smoke. Pete had a lot to contemplate. Taking a long drag from the cigarette he lost himself in memories of Katie's horrible ordeal with Derrick. He couldn't get the image of finding Katie out of his head. Even shaking his head trying to dislodge it didn't work. He was glad he was the one who found her, but what he witnessed was etched into his soul forever.

Katie was so badly beaten she spent almost a month in the hospital. Pete knew that is reason she moved away, to start a new life where no one would know her secret. Derrick got what he deserved. Pete just wished he were the one who did it. If only he had gotten there sooner then maybe he could have prevented her from getting hurt. "Don't worry Kate I won't let anything happen to you this time." Pete said to himself. Then he left a note on the kitchen table for Katie in case she woke up before he got back.

He started the truck, put it in gear and pealed out onto the highway leaving only dust and some gravel bouncing down the drive. Pete wasn't quite sure what he was going to do, but he decided he needed to talk to the officer from last night.

Pete pulled into the station just over the bridge from Katie's.

Cal, who was getting in his car to leave, saw Pete pull in.

Both men shut their doors and walked toward each other.

Shaking hands, "What can I do for you Pete?"

"Is there somewhere we talk? I have to fill you in on something."

"Sure, do you want to go into the station or something less formal like the picnic table over there?"

"If you don't mind, over there is fine. I'd like to smoke."

They sat opposite of each other; Pete pulled out another cancer stick and lit it, taking a long drag. "Cal I found something. But first I need you to understand something, and I don't want what I am about to tell you go any further than you and me?"

Cal gave Pete a strange look. "I'd like to tell you it won't but if..."

Pete immediately jumped in, "Whoa, stop right there. Nothing I am about to tell you is criminal...not really. It's personal very personal and it relates to Kate."

"All right, go ahead!" Cal was puzzled but hoped some of his questions about Kate might be answered.

Pete drew in another long drag and let it out. It was difficult for Pete to talk about, but if the police were going to get a better understanding about the situation, especially Katie's reaction to certain things, they had to know all of it. "About two years ago Katie was seeing this guy..." He took another deep drag from his cigarette, as he slowly let it out he said, "he brutally raped her, and beat her to a bloody pulp so there was almost nothing left of her!"

Cal could see how angry and upset Pete was.

Pete's leg was now nervously bouncing, as he continued. "I had walked in just when he was through with her. He saw me and took off. Walking in on that..." Pete closed his eyes, and shook his hung head. "I was shocked." Pete looked back to Cal, "I chased him out the back door only to have him get hit and killed in the street. It took a long time for Katie to come back from that. Too many people knew Derrick and Katie. And after everything that had happened, she had to leave to start over. Get a fresh start, ya know? It's very difficult for her to trust again."

Cal sat quietly listening, nodding every now and again. Hearing what Kate went through, pain and anger grew in the pit of his stomach. "This explains so much."

He understood why it was so hard to for Pete to tell him.

Pete took the last drag on his cigarette and put it out on the bottom of his shoe.

"Cal, this was Katie's fresh start. Moving to Burlington, the only ones that knew about her past besides her folks were Billie and I. She cut everyone else off. What this guy is doing to her..."

Pete's hand started to tremble. "What this guy is trying to do..."

"Pete, I get it."

"No, there is more." Pete told Cal about what he found after everybody left. The vent, the pot, the access panel in her closet, everything. "I really want to help you catch this guy. I know Katie has nothing to do with the pot. That isn't her, I think this guy came back for the dope and found access to her!"

Cal was furious. He couldn't believe he missed that when he searched her house. "Pete, I am getting the picture, and I think you are correct about the guy from the bar." Cal was making a mental connection to her being drugged and all that Pete just revealed to him.

"What did you find on the screw driver?"

"Nothing, it was a stretch; I wasn't so sure we would find anything."

Chapter 18

By the time Katie awoke it was time for dinner. Pete was in the kitchen unpacking the groceries he picked up on his way back from speaking with Cal.

"You're alive!" He teased. "I am going to make you dinner."

Although she wasn't really hungry, she said, "All right, just as long as it is something simple".

Katie went up stairs to get some clothes so she could take a shower. She was glad to have her dearest friend here with her.

"I will be right out," Katie said closing the bathroom door behind her. Then she yelled through the door, "What are you going to make me?"

"You said simple, so I guess something simple!"

And with that, Billie comes through the front door; making Pete jump a little.

"Don't you ever knock?" Pete asked with deep resentment in his voice.

"Why? Katie doesn't care." Billie of course not smart enough to acknowledge anyone's annoyance with her.

"What do you want, Billie?" Pete asked with a frown.

"I haven't heard from you guys, what's up? I figured we would be hanging out, maybe party like the old days."

"No Billie, I am just here to visit with Katie."

"Sheesh! What's your problem?" BJ asked with attitude.

"For one thing, we had the police here last night! There is no poltergeist bothering her, there has been a man breaking into the house!"

"Oh my God! Is she all right? Did the police catch him?"

"No and Katie is exhausted. She is taking a shower now. She is going to take a few days off from work. We are going to break up her routine, just in case it is the guy from the bar. So, you don't need to be bothering her right now!"

Billie who was now insulted and totally pissed off with Pete stated, "She is my friend, too! You think you are the only one who cares? Screw you, Pete!" Then BJ stormed out to her car. She slammed her door, and the little engine raced. She looked up at Pete through her windshield, glaring. Not sure if she wanted to say something else to him or not.

Pete half amused with himself thought, "Well that is one way to get her out of here."

Noticing that she hadn't taken off yet, he sighed and walked over to her car knocking on the window.

Debating whether or not she wanted to hear what else he had to say, she reluctantly rolled down her window. "Now what?" She asked.

"I'm sorry for being rude, Billie."

"I don't want to argue with you, I really do just want to help. I can't help feeling like this might be my fault somehow."

"Not that I don't doubt you probably did do something, I just don't think this time it is your fault. But, what do you think you did?"

Billie began to tell Pete about this guy at the Brick Yard.

"We already told the police about him. What else?"

"Pete? Has anyone contacted her landlord?"

Pete was speechless - maybe she wasn't so dumb after all. "It never even occurred to him to ask the landlord who the previous renters were! Do you know who the landlord is?"

"Sure, it's the old man in the brown house on the other side of the implement dealer. Mr. Warren."

Pete was now on a mission and turned to walk away, "Tell Katie I will be right back."

Before Billie could answer, he was already halfway across the lot.

***

Katie stepped out of the shower, calling to Pete; "I think a juicy burger with grilled onions sounds real good about now. What do you think?"

"Katie?" Billie spoke through the bathroom door. "Pete said he would be right back."

The voice she heard was not Pete's. "Oh great!" She sighed.

Pete rapped on the door to the landlord's house.

Slowly the old man answered, "Yes?"

"Mr. Warren? My name is Pete. I am a friend of Katie's. I was wondering if I could ask you a few questions about..."

Quickly replying, "I don't want any problems young man. I know that the police were there last night. I can't have troublemakers in my house."

Pete instantly interrupted, "Mr. Warren, someone tried to break into the house last night. That is why the police were there!"

Changing his tone, "Oh, is Katie okay?"

"Thank you for asking, yes, she is. What I was wondering is if you could tell me about the people who rented the house before?"

"Pete, is it?"

Pete nodded.

"I cannot give you information like that."

"I just want to know if you had any problems with them or complaints against them."

"No, I had my hired hands for the farm across the street living there with my nephew. If you work for me you get a roof over your head. I had to downsize the cattle, and let them go. So, then I decided to rent out the house you see."

"Your nephew didn't want to rent it from you?"

"My nephew? Scott is a no good son-of-a-bitch! Please let me know if she has any more problems. I will be over first thing in the morning to change the locks for her, okay?"

"Thank you, Mr. Warren."

Pete walked away slowly, and paused long enough on the edge of the gravel drive to light up another cigarette. He knew changing the locks wouldn't stop anyone from breaking in, that's not how they're getting in, but it was a nice gesture. "I wonder if it could be the nephew's pot." Pete pondered this on the way back to Katie's.

Before Pete got to Katie's doorstep he had taken the last drag on his smoke and flicked it into the gravel. By the time he was back in the door, Katie was dressed.

"Where were you?" Katie asked.

"Just checking something out." He answered.

Katie gave him one of her looks to let him know she knew there was more to it.

Katie asked Billie, "Pete's cooking, do you want to join us?"

"Not tonight, I just stopped in to say hi!"

Pete and Katie were dumbfounded.

"I will stop back tomorrow before work. Well, take it easy." With that, BJ turned on her heels and left, flipping her long hair behind her.

Katie asked Pete, "What just happened?"

He chuckled, "Your guess is as good as mine!"

Pete was cooking hamburger patties on the grill and Katie sliced the onions. They joked back and forth, laughing; picking on each other like they did when they were kids. It felt good.

Cracking open a can of cold Mountain Dew, Pete got serious. "How much do you know about your landlord?" Pete took a swig with his left hand and flipped a burger with his right.

"My landlord?"

"Just work with me..."

Katie answered with an inquisitive frown, curious about the question. "He is my landlord. I answered an ad in the paper for the house. The guy owns the dairy farm across the street, a couple of rentals, and about 600-acers. He rents out another chunk of land for the quarry behind the house. He's widowed, has a girlfriend and two sons. The sons have been trying to get him to retire from farming. What else do you want to know?"

"Do you know anything about his nephew?"

Katie gave Pete another puzzling look. She thought for a moment and then remembered, "When I was moving in, there was a bunch of his things still in the house. I told Mr. Warren about them, and he told me to just throw it away or put it in the garage, and he would let his nephew know about it. One morning I woke up and it was gone."

Pete asked, "Are you sure you never saw this guy?"

"I am pretty sure. Do you think the nephew is the guy trying to break into the house?"

"I don't know. Anything is possible! All I know is Mr. Warren's nephew lived in the house before you, and that Mr. Warren is not fond of his nephew."

Pete took the foil full of sliced onions with butter and seasoning, off the grill.

"Pete, do you think this guy will come back tonight?"

"I am not sure, Hun, but I kinda doubt it!"

Katie ate but wasn't very hungry, so she just toyed with her burger. It tasted good, but somehow nothing seemed to satisfy.

After dinner Katie just wanted to go back to bed. She was still exhausted. Sitting up against her over sized pillow, cross-legged on her bed, Katie went over in her head every strange thing that had happened since moving into the house. "What am I missing?"

Pete got her a glass of water and some Advil. "You okay, Sis?"

"No – not really." She took the Advil and swallowed them down with some water. "Why is this happening to me?"

Pete sat next to her on the bed trying his best to comfort her. "I don't know, I wish I..."

"I can't do this. I can't go through this again Pete, I can't!" With that Katie just lost it, and started to cry. She had to let it out and with Pete she could do that.

The woman he saw before him wasn't the same woman he knew only a few short years before. The woman he knew would take names and kick ass, this woman had that one locked inside screaming to get out. Pete hated to see her like this. He put his arms around her and just let her cry it out.

Neither one said another word.

By morning she woke up with Pete lying by her side, still holding her.

"What would I do without you Pete? I couldn't ask for a better friend."

Katie moved to slip out from under Pete's arms, "Huh? Umm...morning."

Pete let her up, as he yawned, and stretched.

"I'll make some coffee." Katie said as she threw on her robe and tied the belt.

"Sounds good." Pete said as he yawned and stretched again.

Katie headed down the stairs and heard Pete cough that smoker's cough. *"I wish he would quit."*

Pete trudged his way down, listening to every creak the stairs made.

Pete paid attention and he backed up and counted which stairs made the most noise. Just in case - for later reference.

While the coffee brewed Katie freshened up and Pete stepped out for his morning smoke.

Katie poured two cups of coffee and brought one out to Pete, who was sitting on the front stoop, "Thanks, this is great."

As Katie copped a squat next to her friend she said, "Thank you for last night."

Pete took his free arm and put it around her, pulling Katie close so she could rest her head on his shoulder.

"Pete? Remember when I told you I was seeing someone?"

"Yeees..." Pete dragged the answer out.

"I was sort of seeing Detective Cal Chapman."

"The cop that was here the other night?"

"Yeah...but I think I blew it. I really had something good with him and I screwed up."

"You did, or did he?"

"No, I did. Cal has been great. You're right, I can't let anyone in. I am just too afraid to let anyone get that close again. Things were going great and I pushed him away. What the hell is wrong with me?"

Pete kissed the top of her head. "Sweetie, you should probably go talk to him. I had a sneaky suspicion that night that he seemed a little too concerned about you to just be doing his job."

"I don't know Pete. If I tell him the real reason I've been avoiding him he's going to run. And I can hardly blame him, why would he want to be with someone who's damaged?"

"Katie, you don't know that and where did this self pity come from? I still think he should know if you care for him at all, give him a chance."

She sipped her coffee deep in thought.

Katie quickly changed the subject asking, "What are we doing today? I better call in to work and let them know I can't work for a couple of days."

"Is your boss there early?"

"Well, yeah, he gets deliveries today."

"Maybe instead of calling him, we should go see him?"

"Oh, okay?"

"Honey, you can't go to work until we find this guy and besides Billie agreed to cover for you at work tonight."

"Billie? Shit...I have to let her know what's going on."

Pete interjected, "She already knows. I've already talked to her."

***

By 2 o'clock in the afternoon Pete drove Katie to The Brick Yard.

Erik opened the door a little surprised to see Katie so early in the day.

"Hey, Katie! Paychecks won't be ready 'til later."

"Oh I know I just stopped in to talk to Bob. Is he here yet?"

"Yeah, sure he's in the office."

Erik eyeing up Pete asked, "So are you going to introduce us?"

"I'm sorry Erik; this is Pete, my very best friend in the whole world. Pete this is Erik, the guy who keeps me out of trouble." She said with a big smile.

Pete joked, "That must be a full time job." Pete shook Erik's hand, and exchanged friendly greetings. Pete was no small man, but Erik made Pete look small.

"Do you think Bob would mind if I go on back?"

"Nah, his door is usually open."

Pete followed Katie down the hall to the back of the bar where Bob's office was. Standing outside the office door, Katie over heard Bob on the phone. He sounded concerned. "Yeah, we'll keep an eye out. No, I haven't had any complaints. I don't need that. You got

159

it. Yep, will do. No... I'll make sure Erik calls you. Thanks." The phone hung up.

Katie lightly rapped on his door. "I hate to bother you, Bob."

"No, come in, come in."

"Bob, this is Pete, Pete this is Bob."

The men shook hands and Bob gestured for them to sit. Katie took a seat, however Pete remained standing behind her.

Bob was already behind his desk, and sat back down. His chair was oversized and ugly. The casters were worn out and the seat had duct tape holding the naugahyde together. His desk was cluttered with papers. And there were pictures of his kids up everywhere. He loved his kids, but didn't see them much. His wife divorced him because she couldn't stand the bar scene. Katie found that strangely amusing because that is how they met in the first place. She sure loved to spend his money. She just didn't want him anymore.

"Bob, I don't know how to ask this..."

Bob seemed to already know what this was all about and jumped in. "I just got off the phone with Chapman. He told me what happened. Are you all right?"

She was getting tired of everyone asking her that, but answered anyway. "I am, thank you, but I need to ask for some time off." Katie averted her eyes as if she were a little girl getting into trouble for something as she said it. Pete sensed she didn't like asking for the time off, and placed both of his large callused hands on her shoulders.

Bob took notice of this, puzzled about who Pete was to her.

"Katie, I understand that you believe the guy that tried to break in is a customer here?"

"Well, I have a pretty good idea that it is."

"I wonder if this is the same one who drugged you at the bar. Can you describe him to me so I can have Erik keep an eye out for him?"

Pete was taken aback by this revelation. Katie felt his grip on her shoulders tense. He couldn't believe she would keep that from him. He stood there listening to every word, so he could question her about it later when they left.

Katie cringed, knowing full well Pete would read her the riot act for not telling him.

"Actually, Erik noticed him watching me before. Erik has already seen the guy that I think it is."

"Well, shit, Erik just left...I will have to talk to him when he gets back."

"So why didn't Erik bounce him if he has been bothering you?"

"I can't have everyone that stares at me or tries to hit on me bounced out!"

"Yes you can...if a guy gives you the creeps it is usually for a good reason. Kate I don't want you or anyone else that works here to have something like this happen to them or worse."

Katie nodded in agreement, "Okay...but Billie was the first one he approached. He asked her about me and he has been hanging out here for months just watching me work. He creeps me out, but ..."

"But nothing! We are like a family here. At least I'd like to think so. We spend a lot of time together and we need to trust each other and count on each other. I want my family to be safe. You have no idea how much it bothered me that you ended up in the hospital. I couldn't imagine anyone here doing that. And now we can be pretty sure it's a customer. I wish you would have said something to me before the jerk tried to break in to your house."

Pete spoke up, "I know this puts you in a bit of a bind, but I talked to Cal, and he said to break up her routine. So if she doesn't come in tonight that may throw him off a bit. BJ knows who he is so she and Erik can watch for him to show up."

"Pete, Cal didn't say if he thought the guy was dangerous. So what do you think?"

"I really couldn't tell you. Though he tried to break in, which makes me think he isn't a bad ass, just a thief or perv."

"Well, Katie don't you worry, come back when you can. Billie better pick it up a notch though. We'll let you know if anything happens here tonight. Okay?"

"Thanks Bob. I am sorry about this."

"Nah, go home and try not to worry."

Pete got up and shook Bob's hand again. "Thanks man."

Bob just gave Pete a weary smile.

On their way out of the bar Katie noticed Jack and Steve watching her closely as they stocked the bar.

"Hi guys. I want you to meet a very good friend of mine, Pete."

They stepped out from behind the bar.

"Pete this is Jack, and Steve."

Shaking their hands in turn, "It's good meeting you."

Jack gave some distance but Steve had to give Katie a hug.

"Gee, thanks Steve. What was that for?"

"I am just glad you're okay! My brother was on duty that night you called them."

"Oh...I'm good. He didn't get in. It's scary though."

Jack had a low gruff voice, "Is that what you came to see Bob about?"

"Yeah, sorry to leave you shorthanded but I won't be in for a few days."

Jack sized Pete up, and looked back to Katie. "We've got you covered kiddo. No worries! Nice to meet you, Pete." Jack started back to stocking the bar then turned to ask, "You don't suppose this is the guy who drugged you?"

Now that was the second time Pete heard about her being drugged. Katie knew she had some explaining to do. She could feel Pete's mood intensify.

"Yeah, Kate!" Steve said with some enthusiasm. "I bet it's the same guy."

Katie tried not to waiver in her strength but what they were asking made perfect sense.

"I suppose it is a good possibility. But Billie doesn't seem to think so."

Jack had a troubled look in his eyes. "I saw Billie talking to the guy we're talking about. I never saw him near the bar Katie. But that doesn't mean anything. I will work down stairs from now on and keep an eye out for him too."

The drive home may have been short, but the silence was long. By the time Pete and Katie pulled into the drive, Billie was already waiting in her car.

Pete pulled in front of the house like usual. He would have to hold it in a little longer.

Billie got out greeting Katie. "Hey, lady!"

"Billie thanks for working tonight. I want you and Erik to look for that guy, just don't be so obvious about it! Oh, and Jack will be watching too."

That put a quick smile on Billie's face. "I am sorry for even talking to him. I know...never talk to strangers. But it is a little hard not to! We do work in a bar for goodness sakes! I am just sorry for everything."

Katie gave BJ a hug, "I know you are, but you don't have anything to do with him following me home."

"Do you want me to stop back after work?"

"Well, I kind of want to know what happens tonight. Do you mind?"

"Yeah, I'll swing by."

"Be careful Billie, and remember Erik and Jack will be watching too."

BJ turned to walk back to her car, commenting over her shoulder. "They'll get him, Kate!"

Katie wasn't sure what to do with herself. She felt bad for bailing out on work. Once again too many people knew her business, and it made her uneasy.

Pete opened up the fridge and took out a beer. "Do ya want anything?"

"Maybe just some ice water. Thanks!" She knew what was coming next.

Katie didn't watch much television so the first thing she did was turn on the radio. Some background noise was good. She plopped down on the couch and put her feet up on the coffee table.

Pete entered with her water, worried about the expression on Katie's face. One could usually read Katie pretty well. Not that she tried to hide her thoughts, but you just knew without having to ask. Only now, Pete had to ask.

"Thanks, Pete." taking the water glass from him.

"Now..." He paused calculating his tone, "When in hell were you going to tell me that you were drugged and ended up in the hospital?"

She knew she should have told him. They used to tell each other everything.

"Pete, I really don't know why I never told you."

"Well you've had plenty of opportunity to bring it up. Especially since someone tried to break in! Why haven't you ..." Pete stopped there, he realized Cal already knew. "Cal was here...you had him to lean on." He wasn't hurt. He was glad she had found someone to trust.

"Pete, Cal is the one who found me. He called the ambulance and stayed with me at the hospital."

"Okay, but didn't you think any of this could be related?"

"I suppose I did. I should have told you."

"Yes, you should have. You shouldn't have let things get this far before calling your big brother. But at least you were in good hands." He teased.

"Are you still mad at me?" She asked.

"Yeah, but I'll get over it!" He paused momentarily then asked, "Earlier you seem like you were somewhere else. Where did you go? Is everything okay, Hun?"

"I really wish everyone would quit asking me that!"

"Too bad, Kate! That's just the way it is. When we care enough to ask we're going to ask. So get over it! Now tell me what's really on your mind."

"I feel like there's more to it. I'm missing something, like I should have been more aware somehow."

"Sweetie, I don't know how you could have? This isn't someone you know. This isn't Derrick..."

Pete had to swallow hard when he spoke his name. It hurt to even mention him to Katie. But he had a feeling that she was thinking it.

Katie took Pete's hand in hers and squeezed, with some assurance.

"Pete, I know this isn't the same, but somehow, it sort of feels that way. It's scary and not knowing is the worst. Before I called you I had a nightmare about what happened, but it was different. It was happening now, and it was this guy - and when I woke up, there is this odor. I can't quite place it. I think I have smelled it before I'm not quite sure where. It makes me sick. Literally! I get migraines that won't quit! Almost like this house doesn't want me here."

Pete knew now was the time to tell Katie what he found in the attic. He put his beer down and turned to her. "Katie, now it's your turn to be mad. I found something in your attic while you were passed out on the couch."

"What? I have an attic?"

"I didn't want to say anything just yet, but I think I know what you smell."

Pete stood up and gently pulled Katie by the hand to get her to follow him. He led her up the stairs and into her room. He slid some of her clothes down the rod to the front of her closet and showed her the outline of square panel way in the back, barely visible. Pete took out his pocketknife and inserted it in the seam and pried with little effort. Katie saw the little door swing open. The aroma hit her like a ton of bricks.

"What the hell! How did you find that? What's in there?"

There was no way Pete would fit through the door but Katie could. Pete moved away so Katie could take a better look. As she got down on her knees she tried to take shallow breaths. The smell was pungent.

Pete started to explain to her how he found it, "I saw that the tree out front isn't that hard to climb, and one of its branches reaches across to the vent in the peak of the roof. It looked like it was opened so I climbed up to see if my suspicions were true."

"Hey, there is a cord here, and buckets?" Katie felt a thin chain dangling down on top of her head. She reached for it and lightly pulled. The attic softly buzzed but barely came to life. There were black lights hanging with cords running down and over to some power source. The buckets were full of dirt and dead plants. There were rows and rows of marijuana tied and hung upside down from the rafters. Katie was stunned; she just sat there halfway in between the attic and her closet in disbelief.

"Pete, we need to call the police. Don't you think this is why that guy is trying to break in?"

"Kate, I already told Cal about it. But I don't think he's trying to break in. I have a feeling he has been in."

Slowly Katie backed up out of the opening, then exited the closet. She sat on the edge of her bed.

"Kate?"

"So that is what you meant by 'don't be mad'?"

"Kate, I just wasn't sure how to tell you. I know this is freaking you out, and I didn't think telling you that he has been in your house would help any."

"Pete!" She hesitated; horrors rushing forth she started to tremble. "Do you think...?"

"No I don't...You would have been aware."

"Really? What about me being drugged! Why would he drug me if it wasn't so I couldn't fight back? You know I'm right! And if he only wanted to get his stash then why hasn't he taken that stuff out already? Why does he play games with me?"

"I don't know, Hun."

"Pete, he has been in my house! My room! While I sleep! How am I supposed to...?"

"I am so sorry..."

She felt so deeply violated and angry her hands were shaking. Her hazel green eyes almost had a deep emerald glow to them. A rage was building from deep down inside of her.

Pete tried to console her but she pushed him away and flew out of the room, stormed down the stairs and forced her way out the screen door to get outside. Pete followed as quickly as he could not sure what to do. Katie stood there in the front yard taking deep breaths. Trying to fill her lungs with fresh air and replacing that stale weedy hot air from the attic. Now the screen door slammed behind Pete. He stood there in front of her studying her expressions carefully, trying to determine what was about to happen next.

Katie was stronger than some gave her credit for. Now, that she could fill in the blanks a little better than before, everything imploded. She was so mentally over whelmed and was breaking down into an emotional puddle of goo. She mumbled to herself recounting all of her terrifying thoughts.

Pete couldn't help her. He just let her go through everything she had bottled up. It didn't take too long before she very softly and slowly addressed Pete. "Pete, if you are waiting for me to hit you or scream at you...I hope you aren't too disappointed. I know you have my best interest at heart and I love you for that. But I can't help feeling we still don't know the whole story here." She then raised her voice with some anger behind it. "Big deal, Scott has pot in the attic. Granted it's a lot of pot! But if he was coming into the house he could have just taken it. Thrown it out the vent while I slept and been done with this house."

Pete had thought the same thing. "Hun, I don't have the answers for you yet, but we will. And you won't have to worry about this guy again."

Smiling wearily, "I know that Pete. I know this dumb ass will screw up, and we will nail him. But I feel so violated and dirty. He must be taking my things."

Pete didn't know what to say, he just shook his head shrugging his shoulders.

Katie was tired of the mind games and tired of feeling helpless. She never wanted to be an emotional wreck. That wasn't who she was. Katie felt she had taken all she could take, and she wasn't going to let this guy win.

***

In a small town police department you have limited man power. Cal pulled two guys to help him with a stake-out at the farmhouse. They knew there was pot in the attic. They knew someone kept trying to break in. Now they needed to catch him in the act.

An officer was set up on top of the implement dealer building. A second officer sat hidden in the cab of a tractor. Cal set up waiting behind the over grown brush of the southern tree line. The night rolled in and the waiting began. Luckily Cal brought some bug spray because the mosquitoes were out in full force.

Time dragged on. Katie paced from room to room, tidying up here and there. Rearranging magazines, and putzing in the kitchen. Pete sat with his feet up on the coffee table in front of the TV flipping through channels, looking for anything that could pass the time.

"Can you please sit down you are wearing me out. Do you want to talk or play cards?"

"Since when do you play cards?" she said with a little laugh.

"I can play Rummy!"

"You really want to play Rummy?"

"No, but we need to do something, the suspense is killing both of us."

"I think I'm going to get ready for bed, but then we need to talk..."

Pete knew what she meant. They never really "talked" about Derrick, and maybe that's what she needed right now so she could move on. "If that's what you want? I'll step outside for a quick smoke while you change."

Slowly climbing the stairs Katie heard the screen door close behind Pete. He sat down on the little concrete porch and lit his cigarette. He knew Cal was out there somewhere in the dark. Pete just happened to look up, and with the glow of head lights coming down the road back lighting the building before him he could see a man crouched down on the roof. He knew it was an officer.

Katie was glad Pete was here but having him there brought back some raw feelings she never dealt with. She always figured if she didn't talk about what happened on that fateful day, it would eventually go away. Out of sight out of mind, but that wasn't the case. That weight was heavily hanging on her heart and she needed to let it go.

Her thoughts soon drifted to Cal. She felt horrible about how she left things. He was the one good thing in all of this that made her feel everything was going to be okay.

She needed to fix things between them. *"I'm such a fool! What am I so scared of?"*

Chapter 19

Billie was having trouble keeping up with the crowd. The music was pumping and loud and actually giving her a pounding headache.

Erik sat on his stool, carding the little "chickie babes" with their fake ID's, then sending them away; all the while watching for Scott Warren. Erik asked Jack to take his place so he can have a break.

Jack asks, "Where's Eddie?"

"Who knows? He's always just wandering off!"

Jack gave a nod to the back and of the room.

"What's up?" Erik took notice. "Scott. How the hell did he get by me?"

Billie was bringing a tray of drinks over to a back table. She didn't even notice the tall dark man with the eerie icy blue eyes standing not three feet from her. She put her drinks on the table and took their cash. As Billie turned to leave the table a large hand reached out to grab her arm.

"AUGH!" Billie gasped, but it was Erik that grabbed her arm.

"A bit jumpy, aren't you?" he said with a smile.

"You startled me!" She said completely flustered.

"Sorry about that, I wanted to see if you could send some drinks over to Jack and I at the door?"

Looking up and over to the front door, Billie noticed Jack. He smiled at her, and she gave a shy smile back. "Sure, I'll get right on that", she said a little puzzled as to why Jack was at the door.

Billie walked away oblivious to the man who stood right next to her, but Erik did not. Erik passed by Scott not giving him another glance and stepped into the storage room like he was going about his business. Once inside he pulled out his cell phone, still keeping a watchful eye on Scott. "Cal, he's here. Yep. You got it."

Cal radioed Sgt. Jim Nelsen, an eighteen year veteran, to get over to the Brick Yard.

Scott watched Billie go to the bar. Then he moved even closer to the restrooms, leaning on the center brick wall. He had his back to Erik.

"Not the brightest bulb in the box!" Erik thought keeping his distance, but made sure he was close enough to grab him if need be.

Billie waltzed the sodas up to Jack. "Thanks, Billie!"

"You are welcome!" She said sounding all bubbly. She could have been floating on cloud-9, if she wasn't so flustered with all the people in the bar. As Billie turned away, Jack reached out to her, catching her by the wrist. Billie stopped, and then spun back around. Her heart was pounding; she had such a crush on Jack. He scared her a little but that was part of the attraction. Her big baby blues met his wanting eyes. Gently he pulled her in closer to him. She cocked her head like a puppy dog questioning, but she allowed him to bring her towards him. With the other hand he brushed her long waves from her face to behind her ear. Her heart skipped a beat. He drew her in even closer, now she stood between his legs as he sat on the stool. He moved his hand from her wrist to her shoulder - gesturing for her to lend him her ear. She responded in kind, bending down ever so slightly, he whispered, "He's here, but don't look around for him. He is standing behind you - back by the restrooms."

Billie had to remember to breathe. She nodded as if she were in a daze.

Jack gently kissed her cheek and gave her a wink, then sent her on her way patting her behind.

Billie didn't know if she should be happy or cry. She was so uneasy about what was about to happen. She was a bundle of nerves, but in a way Jack made her feel calm. Billie went back to the tables and worked the floor. Not really looking for Scott, but aware of him at all times.

After about 15-minutes or so, Scott approached her. "Say girlie! Where is your friend tonight? Isn't she working?"

Billie was feeling very uncomfortable; even though she knew that Jack and Erik were watching closely, and that the cops were on their way. "Oh, she wasn't feeling well tonight, sorry. Do you have a message for her?"

Scott just shook his head, "That's alright I will catch up with her later."

That statement put a knot in the pit of her stomach. She tried to act casually and turned away to get back to work.

Scott had no clue what was waiting for him outside.

Sgt. Nelsen pulled his squad up front and parked waiting until his cell rang. He answered, "Nelsen."

"Nelsen its Erik. He doesn't have a clue that we are onto him. But he looks like he's leaving."

"Thanks, we're out front. We're ready for him."

As Erik hung up a loud commotion started up by the restrooms. "Shit! Now what?"

Finding a brunette who was wearing way too much make up and another girl, somewhat chubby but very pretty were yelling at each other; Erik walked over to break it up when out of nowhere 'POW'! He walked right into the brunette's right hook intended for the other woman. She hit his broad chest. It didn't hurt, but it surprised him nonetheless.

"Ladies – I think maybe you should take this outside?"

"That cow is messing with my boyfriend!"

"Cow? He's not your boyfriend! You stupid bitch..." this time the prettier one threw a punch.

Erik stood between these two brawling Betty's and was looking for his backup. Eddie came from out of nowhere and quickly took the brunette under control, and he led her up the steps to the front of the bar; followed by Erik walking the other girl out. The whole time they were screaming at each other.

Scott, of course was now out of sight. In the few minutes it took to bring control to the situation, Scott slipped out the back delivery door. Even Billie didn't see him leave. She was too busy watching the show like everyone else.

Nelsen met Erik at the front door. "What's this?"

Erik just shrugged to Jim, and Jack knew they blew it.

Leaving the front door, Jack gave Eddie a glaring look. Jack was more than irritated and walked away to seek out Billie. From the top of the stairs Jack scanned the room. Billie was at the lower bar waiting on drinks. *"Now where's Scott? Okay you sneaky son of a bitch, where did you go?"* Jack asked himself.

He then realized that Scott must have slipped out through the back delivery door. As he turned around to get Jim's attention; he was standing right beside him.

Jack pointed and said, "Fuck! The delivery door!"

Nelsen clicked on the mike attached to his left shoulder, letting the guys outside know to go around to the back delivery door. Turning on his heels, he left to join the other officers.

Erik was not a happy guy at this point, physically removing the Betty's from the bar. He turned the unruly one over to an officer standing outside, happily getting rid of her. Not his problem anymore!

"Jack?"

"Back delivery door!"

"That little bastard!" Erik exclaimed as he dialed Katie's cell. "Shit! It went right to voice mail."

"So call the house?"

"She doesn't have a house phone."

"Cal better catch up to him before I do!"

"Hey, Cal knows what he's doing, he'll get him. There is no way he'd let anything happen to Katie."

177

Jack pulled the keys from his leather jacket pocket.

Erik started to ask, "Where do you think you're going?" Even though he already knew the answer to his own question. He wished he could just take off to join the party as well.

Erik sat down on the stool by the front door in a huff.

From the back lot Eddie saw Jack straddle his Harley.

Jack revved it and without a care took off.

Eddie knew instantly where he was going.

Erik scanned the bar searching for Eddie but he was nowhere to be found. "Now where did he go? That son of a bitch! Everybody's taking off and just leaving me sit here!" He mumbled to himself.

***

Pete was now leaning against that big oak tree in the front yard trying to enjoy his cigarette. Katie's window was lit up and caught his attention. Her curtains were pulled but he watched her shadow dance around the room. He really wasn't ready to talk about what they had been avoiding for so long. Thoughts of Barb came forth. Pete really loved Barb. She was so much fun and interesting, never a dull moment. Unfortunately for them, when Barb found out she had a brain aneurysm. She told Pete she wanted to live life to its fullest and travel, see everything she could before her time ran out. Of course it wasn't Pete she wanted to share those experiences with. Barb broke his heart.

He remembers now how Barb was so very jealous of all the attention he gave Katie while she was recovering. And only then did Barb feel the need to drop the bomb on him about leaving. He just didn't know how to deal with both situations together. Who would?

The thunderous roar of Jack's motorcycle crested the top of the bridge; distracting Pete from his thoughts.

Jack then idled down to make the turn into Katie's gravel drive. Pete watched as Jack rode up.

Cal and the other two officers watched this all unravel from the seclusion of their posts.

Pete flicked his cigarette out into the gravel and approached Jack as he got off his bike.

"Jack!"

"Where is Katie?" Jack sharply asked.

Pete motioned with the nod of his head over his shoulder to the window with its light on. "Upstairs, why?"

Cal who had just received word from Nelsen strolled over, not comfortable with the situation unfolding. "Jack?" Cal inquired with some urgency.

Jack gave Cal a glare, "Yeah! We missed him."

The situation was making Pete uneasy.

Cal glanced up past the tree line to what he thought were running lights. "Pete, go inside with Katie, Jack you come with me."

Pete met Katie at the door and made her step back through the doorway. He quickly locked it behind them, "Katie, they think he is out back. They missed him at the bar and think he's come here."

"Was that Jack and Cal?"

"Yes, now let's turn off all these lights. Even though you have most of the curtains closed you can tell what room we're in by our shadows."

Katie felt strangely calm, "It's the nephew isn't it?" She asked while walking through shutting off lights. The only light coming in was from the implement building next door.

"Jack and Cal are checking something out by the quarry. Cal thought he saw something." Katie followed Pete up to his room, and she sat down on the bed. There was no access into this room except through the door. They sat quietly listening for something, anything that could give them an idea of what was happening outside.

Jack followed Cal but then he raised his hand to signal Jack to halt. He had heard footsteps lightly treading on the gravel, and then there was movement to the west of them. Cal had his weapon un-holstered and the safety off. Cal then motioned to Jack to move back and to the west to cut him off from the house and Cal was to come around behind him, the sound coming up from the quarry was an old Volkswagen bus full of "Deadheads". They gradually rolled up and out from down below as their head lights from the van paned across the drive to reveal both the men.

Jack and Cal were both annoyed now. "What the hell! Stupid dumb-ass hippies!"

***

With that Scott watched as their van highlighted the cop and Jack! He took advantage of their distraction and high tailed it through the cow pasture and down towards the railroad tracks. Scott knew they would find his car, well, it wasn't really his; but he still wasn't happy about it.

The stranger watched the scene unfold from a safe distance. The headlights exposed both, Cal and Jack. He chuckled to himself. This was all very amusing to him. "Well, well what do we have here?" He said to himself as the dark hooded figure headed in his direction then past him by without a clue he was there.

Now this stranger directed his interest to this individual.

Scott ran toward the tunnel under the bridge. Once he knew he was far enough away he stopped. Scott thought to himself as he doubled over trying to catch his breath. *"Boy smoking sure makes you winded."*

Scott heard a faint sound behind him, but it was too late.

***

Cal stepped forward holding out his badge and gun, forcing the hippies to stop. He could instantly tell they were all high as kites. The aroma of reefer was so strong on them, but at the moment he only wanted some answers to what they might have seen.

Jack stood patiently waiting for Cal, while keeping an eye on the house. Cal called for some back up to move the search for Scott here.

At first the hippies weren't going to divulge any information, even if they did know something. Then when they heard sirens coming over the bridge, one of the passengers in the van finally offer that there was another car that came through, but she didn't see where it went.

Cal decided to just let them go, he knew the "Dead" were in town, and they would be easy enough to find if he needed to. It's hard to miss a 1965 Volkswagen bus with peace signs painted all over it.

Jack was a bit surprised by Cal letting them go, but didn't say anything.

Once the squad cars came close enough Jack headed for the house. For now the two other officers stayed where they were watching until Cal told them otherwise.

Pete and Katie heard most of the commotion, and then they heard Jack's rapping on the door. They came down turning on the lights as they walked through the living room and into the kitchen to let Jack in.

The police were now searching for the car that was possibly out there.

Jack sat down at the kitchen table to fill them in on the situation. Katie was nervous and tense, and knew it was going to be a long night subsequently she made a pot of coffee.

After about an hour Cal came in. Katie greeted him in hopes this could all be over with. Cal shook his head with disappointment. He was very concerned and visibly upset.

Katie stepped up for a hug and Cal embraced her. He couldn't believe any of this was happening to her.

It felt so good to be in Cal's arms that she was reluctant to let go.

Pete and Jack, who were sitting at the kitchen table drinking coffee, exchanged a quiet, *It's about time* look between them.

Cal looked down at her and said, "Kate, I thought we had him."

She finally relaxed in Cal's embrace, but she still held on. "I knew it - I just knew it! I'm not paranoid."

"No, you're not! Kate how long have these strange things been going on?"

"Pretty much since I moved in; just little stuff that I over looked at first but more so these past couple of months.

Billie came in. "What did I miss? What happened?" She saw all the police outside and was worried.

Katie and Billie hugged. "He was at the bar but vanished." Billie blurted out.

"We know, he was here but they missed him too."

Jack gave Billie a smile and reached out a hand for her to come to him.

Sgt. Nelsen arrived and knocked on the door.

Cal stepped out with him.

Pete watched through the window for all of 10-seconds before he burst out the door to find out exactly what the hell was happening.

Cal didn't appreciate the intrusion but understood it.

Cal allowed Pete to be involved with the conversation, so Nelsen continued to give Cal what information he had. "We couldn't find him at the bar; he must have slipped through the back delivery doors. Then I saw Jack Carter leave right away taking off on his Harley." Motioning to the black Harley parked in front of them.

***

It was 4 a.m. when everyone left. Pete was outside finishing his smoke before going to bed. Something was bothering him. He just couldn't put a finger on it, but that nagging feeling that something bad was about to happen was there.

Pete's footsteps made the stairs creak every few steps so Katie heard him coming.

"Good night, Pete!"

"Night, Kate."

Pete laid his head down on his pillow going over all that had happened since he came here. He felt some comfort in the fact that he sealed up the access panel in Katie's closet. No one could get in there now. Not quietly anyway. He remembered Katie wanted to talk, but they had been interrupted. He was not sure if he was relieved that their conversation was postponed or not.

Morning came way too early. Neither Pete nor Katie had any reason to get out of bed until much later. However the sun was brightly shining through Katie's windows. She decided to get up but not to disturb Pete, so she quietly snuck down the stairs, even missing a couple of the squeaky steps. Katie grabbed the throw and curled up on the couch. Then she fell back to sleep.

Chapter 20

The day had been hot and sticky. Cal didn't come on duty until late in the afternoon. The blast from the air conditioning felt good as he entered the station. "Detective Chapman? These people would like to speak with you", said one of the officers acting as desk clerk.

Pete was pacing the floor as Kate quietly sat in one of the chairs off the desk area.

Chapman showed Pete and Katie into a small conference room and closed the door.

"We're hoping that you've found the owner of the car from last night?" Pete began.

"We don't have much to go on; the plates on the vehicle do not match. The plates and the vehicle are both stolen. We have a few leads, but nothing yet." Well, actually they had plenty of evidence that he was in Katie's home, but Cal didn't want to say anything yet.

Katie piped in, "Is one of those leads Mr. Warren's nephew and perhaps a pair of my underwear?" She was obviously testy.

Cal tried to keep his feelings in check and stay professional. "Why do you know something?"

"Well, no...I just thought it was too much of a coincidence that Scott used to live in my house, there's pot in the attic and all the weird stuff that's been going on over there."

"Kate, I don't believe in coincidences and I can't tell you that it is Scott Warren for sure that has been doing these things. We are looking to question him, but that is all we can do for now. I wish I had more to tell you. We'll keep an extra eye on your place and hopefully this is who we are looking for, and we will catch him in the act." Cal wanted to tell her everything's going to be alright.

"Thanks, Cal. I feel better knowing you will be watching." Katie smiled, knowing what she had just said, was pretty cheesy.

Once Pete and Katie got in the truck Pete lost it. He laughed so hard he could have wet his pants. Mimicking Katie like a pesky sibling would, "I feel so much better knowing you'll be watching!"

She punched Pete in the arm, "Stop it!" she said laughing at herself.

Pete spent the day checking around the house for ways to break in. If he saw something he didn't like he'd change or repair what he could. Pete even made sure that no one could open the root cellar door from the outside. Mr. Warren made good on changing all the locks to the house.

They sat up talking; drinking coffee and periodically Pete needed to step outside for a smoke. Pete finally told Katie all about Barb and how much it hurt when she left him. Then he said, "Katie, it is so obvious how much you and Cal like each other. Why are you shutting him out? Don't push him away. Give the guy a chance."

Katie didn't have an answer, at least not one Pete would accept.

Pete once again butted in. "Cal is doing the best he can, and I think you pushing him away right now, is wrong. You are doing to Cal what Barb did to me. Just sayin'."

Katie couldn't believe Pete would say such a thing.

"I am not abandoning him!"

"Oh really? What would you call it then? He needs to know why you are behaving like you are."

Frustrated, Katie stormed outside. Pete didn't bother going after her. He knew Katie well enough to know that she needed a few moments to herself. Picking up the remote Pete flipped through the channels surfing for anything to watch.

On the way out of the house Katie had grabbed her cell phone off the table. She walked out and around the back of the house, debating with herself over whether or not to call Cal. Then gabbing hold of some courage and taking a deep breath she decided to dial Cal's number.

She heard Cal's smoky voice answer.

"Cal? It's Katie."

"Is everything alright?"

"Yeah, I mean nothing is going on..." She gave a long pause, "Can we talk?"

Cal was reserved in his response. "Yes, of course."

"Not on the phone."

"Well I'm working all night until noon tomorrow. When did you want to talk?"

"I know you are off on Tuesday, can we meet at the Lake, at the pier?"

"We can, but I've got plans Tuesday. Can we make it later in the evening?"

"I'd like that. I just want to explain ...why ...I'll see you Tuesday."

"Katie? Are you sure everything is all right?"

"Yeah, have a good night, Cal."

"You too," he said quite puzzled about her phone call, but was pleased she called.

Katie entered the house in a different mood than when she left. Pete watched her head up the stairs to get ready for bed.

Pete didn't really find much on, even the late night movie was ho-hum. He heard Katie coming back down the stairs. He looked over to see her leaning against the doorway to the living room.

"Pete, I know you're right, but you and I both know it's going to be an ugly truth. I do like Cal, a lot. I just don't know if I could handle the rejection."

Pete reached out for Katie's hand. She walked over to him and then he pulled her in to sit with him. "Honey, I know you are scared but put yourself in Cal's shoes. I'm sure he thinks he did something wrong. You two were getting along great until you went cold on him. Now with all that's going on here, his job is to protect you. He is forced to see the person who he cares for, and she won't let him in. You need to fix it. Don't leave him wondering. Besides I have confidence that he is a guy you can trust, so trust in him. And if I'm wrong...you at least know you tried."

"I know Pete. I have to tell him, he deserves that much."

Katie went back up the stairs to bed while Pete slipped outside for one last smoke. He sat down in the cool grass and relaxed with his back up against the trunk of that oak tree in front of the house. He pulled out a cigarette placing it between his lips. As he went to light it he noticed Kate's shadow dancing around in her room. He sat there looking up at her window just holding on to the lighter. The stranger of course was watching Pete.

Pete took the cancer stick from his mouth and broke it into little pieces and dropped them to the ground. He sat there for a long time even after Katie turned off her light. With his head resting back on the tree and he closed his eyes. Thoughts of the days when he and Katie were kids, growing up, getting into trouble of one kind or another, put a gentle smile on his face. He could hardly remember a time when Katie wasn't in his life. Now when she needed him the most he was feeling helpless. He hated that all he could do was wait for something else to happen. Pete wouldn't be able to sleep with this apprehension.

He picked himself up off the ground and slipped his lighter back into his pocket. He decided to take a walk in the somewhat cool night air. Opening the door to the house he reached in for the key and then locked the door behind him. First he walked around the little house, then around the dilapidated garage. He wasn't really looking for anything in particular, just checking everything out. The garage amused Pete, *what good did it do to have a garage with no door?* It really needed to be knocked down before it fell down. There was no way Katie would ever use it. Not to park the Nova in anyway. Just before he reached the tree line, from which the stranger was watching him, something else caught his attention. He stopped, turned and walked towards the backyard where the cow pasture met the fence.

However, this gave the stranger a great opportunity to move his position. Since Katie's garage was always open he was able to slip in unnoticed. He at once found a tire iron just leaning against the inside wall. Picking it up and gripping the metal tool feeling the weight of it in his hand. The stranger determined this was the right time to eliminate Katie's overly protective friend. As Pete checked out the barbed wire fencing he found a scrap of fabric stuck to a barb. He found it odd. It was too big of a piece to have just been ripped off and for the cops not to have seen it. While Pete fished for his cell phone the stranger cracked Pete right upside the head knocking him off balance. The second blow knocked him cold. There was a substantial amount of bleeding coming from his head wound. The stranger was not his usual cool and collected self. He didn't think this through. He had to act quickly, he was sure a cop would be making his rounds to check up on Katie. So, he tossed the tire iron out as far as he could into the cow pasture. Contemplating what he was to do about Pete's body. He grabbed a hold of Pete's feet and dragged him over to his own truck; which was backed up in front of the garage door opening. The doors to the truck were not locked. Pete's limp body was no light load to lift up. With some effort the stranger hoisted Pete into the cab of the Dodge, just in time, too.

A squad slowly turned in, taking his time to shine a spot light across the yard and tractors parked on the side of the little white farmhouse. No movement. As the squad rolled past the front of the house and then the garage Officer Young shined the spot light into the garage. Nothing seemed out of place and still no movement. He flashed the spotlight onto the tree line from where the stranger was previously watching. Nothing, everything was still. When Young drove off to continue checking out the quarry, the stranger picked Pete's pockets and found not only the keys to the truck, but now he had Katie's house key too. This made the entire evening worth it to the stranger.

After about 15-20 minutes Officer Young came back on through and repeated his search with his spot light going back over everything. Little did he know that this whole time the stranger lay on top of Pete's still body in the cab of the Dodge. Once Young pulled out and drove back up over the bridge, the stranger put the key in the ignition and shifted it into gear. Since the truck had been backed in it was easy to get the truck to roll a little bit down an incline. Then he was able to start the engine without it being too loud for Katie to hear. He slowly drove the Dodge with Pete in it down into the quarry and up over to the opposite side where there was a steep drop off. When he got the truck into position, he pulled Pete into the driver's seat. Standing in the bed of the truck he slipped a long piece of pipe he'd taken through the back window so he could push down hard on the gas pedal to get it to take off over the rocky cliff. Although he knew this would be very dangerous he had to be able to jump off taking the pipe with him before going over.

It worked but as he jumped, he hurt his thigh as he exited the bed of the pickup and landed hard on his shoulder. Pete and his truck careened over the edge and landed with a heavy thud!

Of course he had to look over to admire his handy work. Sore and bruised he peered down at the smashed and bent wreckage of the truck containing Pete's body.

The stranger was pleased that he only had one more to take care of before he could have Katie all to himself. Time was of the essence and he needed to get back to his own vehicle before it was found.

Chapter 21

Morning light filled Katie's room. It was a beautiful morning. She stretched and rubbed the sleep from her eyes. Katie had slept so soundly that she didn't remember Pete coming back in. She sat up in bed swinging her legs over the side placing both feet on the floor, and stretched again. Standing up she grabbed the little silky robe from the foot of her bed. She padded lightly across the floor to peek in at Pete, but he wasn't there. *Huh? Maybe he is already up?* Katie thought as she descend the stairs. She didn't find Pete down stairs. Coffee wasn't even made. She peered out the kitchen window and saw his truck was gone. Maybe he went to pick up donuts and coffee or something. It was only 7 o'clock and she was sure he'd be back soon. She went into the bathroom to wash up and brush her teeth. While she was flossing she heard a high pitch loud siren sounding off from the quarry.

She knew it wasn't Tuesday. Maybe someone already got hurt this morning? Katie sure hoped not.

Shortly after a rinse and spit, the rescue, fire and police sirens made their way over the bridge. Katie walked out the door to take a better look at what was going on. They didn't pull into her drive; instead they passed her house and turned down the service road. Whatever it is must have happened way back.

It was now going on 8 o'clock and Katie finally decided to find out where Pete was. His cell rang, and rang, and rang again. It was just about to go to voice mail when she heard a familiar voice. "Hello?" Cal asked.

"Cal? What are you doing answering Pete's phone? Are you two having breakfast or something without me?" She said with a smile.

"No Kate, something has happened."

Katie's heart stopped for a second, then thumped back into somewhat of a normal rhythm; only beating a little faster. "Has Pete been hurt? Is he alright?"

"Kate I'll stop up in a little bit. Rescue just put him on the stretcher now."

"Stretcher?" There was a moment of silence on the line. "Are you in the quarry?"

"We are and Pete is being taken to the hospital."

"Cal? Is he going to be alright?"

"We don't know anything yet. Kate, give me a little time to get things wrapped up here, and I will stop up to talk to you."

Cal snapped Pete's phone shut. The officers took pictures of the accident. Cal and Jim Nelsen walked up to the top where the truck drove off. They saw how the tall grasses were laying down. It didn't really look like deer had been laying there but they were definitely matted down. They took pictures up there as well. While observing the tire tracks Cal spotted a boot print in the soft dry dirt. Cal knew this wasn't an accident, and since Scott hasn't been found he could very well have something to do with this.

Cal finally wrapped everything up that they needed. Pete's truck was being brought up on a flat bed to be towed to the municipal building for further investigation. Now he needed to speak to Katie.

She had made a pot of coffee and was sitting on the front stoop sipping a mug of fresh hot java when Cal pulled in.

Katie watched Cal as he got out of the grey Crown Vic shutting his door behind him and walk towards her. "Hi, Kate," he greeted her somberly.

Katie had a very worried look on her face. "Can I get you some coffee?"

"That would be nice, thanks."

Cal followed Katie into the kitchen. She poured him a mug of coffee and then handed it to him. They seated themselves at the kitchen table. Cal knew Katie was tense and worried.

She calmly said, "I need to know what happened to Pete."

Cal laid it out for her. "I don't know anything. I'll tell you what I can, but right now all I can gather is sometime last night Pete and his truck took a nose dive off a rocky drop-off in the back of the quarry."

Katie was stunned. She couldn't believe it. Her face showed deep concern for her friend.

"I know he didn't do this on his own. He had help. That's what I need to ask you. Can you tell me anything that happened last night, anything at all? Possibly something happened after I spoke with you on the phone?"

She so desperately wanted to go to the hospital to be with Pete. She just held her mug between both hands running her thumbs across the top. "Cal, I don't know what to tell you. We sat up for a little while just talking. I went to bed, while Pete stepped outside for one last smoke. I must have fallen asleep pretty quickly because I don't ever remember him coming back in. I never heard the truck start up either. When I woke up he wasn't in his room so I went down stairs and his truck was gone. That was around 7a.m. Then I heard the Siren from the quarry go off, you guys coming over the bridge and then when I finally called to find out where the heck Pete was – you answered. That's all I know." After a long pause she asked, "I'd like to go see Pete."

Cal knew how much Pete meant to Katie. That's what worried him. If someone was moving Pete out of the way to get to Katie there has got to be more to it than the pot in the attic. Something in his gut told him he was right. He just couldn't figure out how Katie was tied into all this.

Cal took a sip of his coffee and said, "We will have to wait until they put him in a room. No sense sitting in the waiting room. We are less than 10-minutes away. We might as well wait here."

"Cal?" Katie started to say something but hesitated. She had Cal's attention, but instead of taking this opportunity to tell him why she ran out on him the way she did, she couldn't do it. She only looked deeper into her coffee mug letting the silence fill the empty void.

In that moment of silence Cal got a call on his radio.

"I'm sorry Kate, I need to take this. I will be back and I will take you to see Pete. Okay?"

"Thanks, Cal. If you hear anything, please call."

"You know I will."

***

Doctor Benjamin Philips was working in the Emergency Room when the ambulance brought Pete in. With the blunt force trauma to Pete's head he ordered a CT-scan right away. Then after many hours of being poked and prodded, stitched and bandaged, Pete finally landed himself in a private room. Cal came in shortly after he woke up.

"Hey, Pete! How are you feeling?"

Pete's brow furrowed. He strained to see Cal. In a very gravelly voice Pete asked, "What happened?"

"Well, that's what we would like to know."

"Is Katie okay?"

"Pete, Katie is fine. She's anxious to see you. But I'd like to ask you some questions first."

"How did I get here?"

"Pete how about if I ask the questions?"

Pete nodded. He tried to sit up but his whole body was bruised, and his head was throbbing.

"Would you like some water?"

"Yes, please." He cleared his throat, and coughed.

Cal poured a little Styrofoam cup of water for Pete with the little plastic pitcher they left on a tray in the room.

"Here ya go." Cal was patient. He liked Pete; he didn't like to see him like this.

"Are you up to answering some questions now?"

Pete gave a nod.

"Do you remember going outside to smoke last night?"

Pete thought for a moment and forced a "yes".

"Do you remember taking your truck?"

Pete had a splitting headache, that throbbed terribly but some foggy thoughts about last night were starting to come forward. He just didn't remember taking the truck. "No."

"Can you tell me what you do remember about last night? Do you remember seeing anybody?"

Pete tried to think, but he was all fuzzy on the events. "Cal, I just can't remember. I wish I could give you some answers. I just can't right now." Pete's voice sounded strained.

"Pete, I will let you rest for now but you know Kate is very persistent. She is going to want to come see you this evening. If you can think of anything, can you write it down?"

Pete forced a gravelly "Yeah, I can do that. Hey, Cal, it's bad isn't it?"

Cal smiled, "Buddy, you have seen better days."

Pete forced a smirk.

Cal left Pete's room to head home for a little sleep before picking up Kate.

Pete laid in bed taking inventory on all of his injuries and trying to figure out how he got them.

Doctors and nurses would come and go. Pete rested, dozing in and out. *These are some good drugs.* Pete thought to himself before he fell asleep again.

Pete woke with a start. He remembered something. The pain in his head was proof it wasn't a dream. He buzzed the nurse to get him something to write with. He needed to jot this down before he forgot it.

A cute feisty nurse came in. Her smile was fresh and full. "Whatchya need Hun?"

"Ma-am, I was just wondering if I could get a note pad and a pen."

"Ma-am?" She gave a little chuckle. "That's a new one. Sweetheart, I'm not old enough to be called Ma-am. You can call me Debbie."

Pete thought she was cute and felt a little embarrassed from calling her Ma-am. "Alright, Debbie, would you mind?"

"Sure thing, I'll be right back."

Pete got a huge grin on his face, "I'm not going anywhere!" Even in pain he joked, he just couldn't help himself.

As she reentered his room with the pen and paper he realized just how pretty she was. Her sable colored hair was put up in a twist and held with a clip. Her soft bangs were swept over to one side, framing her oval face. She had a gorgeous olive complexion and high cheek bones. Her eyes were large and a golden-brown with long black lashes. She wore very little make-up and the lip gloss accentuated her full lips. Pete thought she had almost an exotic look about her. He must have been admiring her longer than he had intended because she had to tease him about it.

"Yes, I am single. No, I don't have any children. I have been a nurse for 3-years and yes, I would love to."

Pete was surprised. He just sat there speechless.

"You let me know when," she said, as she handed him the pen and paper. Debbie then turned on her heels and out the door she went.

Pete couldn't believe how bold she was. He liked it. He was so stunned he didn't have a good comeback for her and that kind of threw him off. He almost forgot what he wanted to write down.

***

Katie was very impatient. It was 5 o'clock in the evening, and she couldn't wait any longer. She grabbed her purse and swiped her keys. When she did, she noticed her spare key wasn't on the hook. Maybe Pete has it, she thought. Katie locked the door behind her and took off for Cal's. Not wanting to miss him she dialed his number.

It took several rings before he answered. "Hello?" Sounding like he just woke up.

"I'm sorry Cal; I didn't mean to wake you. I just wanted to let you know I left, and I'm on my over so we can go see Pete; that is if you still want to go with me?"

"No, I'm glad you called. Ah, just let yourself in when you get here. I'll leave the door unlocked for you."

Katie was pulling onto the brick drive when her thoughts of the last time she was here put an even darker veil over her mood. She didn't want to think of that just now. She had been waiting all day to see her friend.

Before Katie entered, she knocked on the plum-colored door. Standing in the entrance hall she happened to look up just in time to see Cal coming down the upstairs hallway slipping a shirt over his head. Katie couldn't help but to stare at his awesome physique.

"Hi, Kate! Thanks for waking me." He said as he bounded down the stairs. "Let me just get my shoes on and we can go."

"Cal, do you mind if we walk?"

He sat down on a wooden bench to tie his shoes, "Sure, it's only a couple blocks."

Katie observed how Cal's biceps flexed, and the veins in his arms pulsed. His unshaven face gave him a ruggedly handsome look.

For a moment she lost herself in thought, once again to the last time she was here, how wonderful his kisses and sweet caress felt.

She snapped out of it when he brushed his body against hers as he reached for his keys on the counsel behind her.

She felt a pang of desire for him. Katie was hoping that he wouldn't run after she told him her secret. But she had one more day before they would have that conversation.

Cal held open the front door for Katie and they left together.

There was a warm gentle breeze rustling the leaves in the trees along the way. A faint scent of some lovely flowers filled the air. Cal didn't offer Katie his hand but they strolled side by side. Neither one of them saying much of anything until Katie couldn't stand the silence any longer.

"Was Pete able to tell you anything?"

"No, but I hope you understand I really can't talk about it either."

Katie was a little hurt by his response, but she knew she couldn't put him in a difficult position. He still needed to investigate to get answers, and she kept adding to his plate. "I know you can't, I'm just concerned. Can I ask you one more question?"

Cal glanced down at her with a raised eyebrow and a grin.

"Well, it really isn't a question...I have some thoughts about whoever did this to Pete, and I think there could be more than one guy, and that they want something in my house. There has to be a connection to something we don't know about, right? Or am I reading more into this?"

"You make a good point, and I have thought about that too. But until Pete remembers something I have nothing to go on." Cal was impressed at Katie's intuition. They walked the rest of the way in silence.

At the hospital Katie poked her head into Pete's room. He was resting with his eyes closed. She was taken aback by the sight of Pete's bruised and swollen face. His arm was in a cast, and his head was bandaged. Tears started to well up in Katie's eyes.

Sensing her presence, Pete slowly turned to look in her direction and asked in his gravelly voice, "Is it that bad, Sis?"

She stepped all the way into the room; then stood over him looking down at her injured friend. She said, "What the hell did you do now, Pete?" with what little smile she could muster.

Pete tried to smile back but everything hurt too much. "I'm not sure, but I feel like I got hit by a truck."

Laughing, Katie answered, "Well you kinda did!"

Pete looked over her shoulder, "Where's Cal, isn't he with you?"

"Yeah, he's out in the hall."

"I remembered something that I have to tell him."

Katie turned to go out the door when Cal stepped in. "Oh, I was just coming to get you. He thinks he remembered something."

Pete reached for his little note pad on the stand. "I wrote it down just in case I forgot again, but I have been remembering bits and pieces of what happened."

"That's great!" Katie said.

"What can you remember?" Cal asked.

"I remembered finding a piece of fabric on the barbed wire fence. It seemed odd to me that it was so blatantly hanging there, yet you guys didn't see it."

"You're right. We didn't find anything out back. You say it was on the fence?"

"Cal, it couldn't have been there when you guys were searching around the house. You would have seen it. I remember thinking I should call you about it, and then lights out. By the hurt in my head and all the stitches they gave me, he cracked me a good one."

Cal stepped back out to use the phone. The nurses' station was right outside Pete's door. He called Sgt. Nelsen to go take another look around Katie's backyard, and told him what he needed to look for. He came back in. "Thanks, Pete; we needed something to go on. That's all you can remember?"

"Yeah, I uh...only remember stepping outside for a smoke. Then walked around the house just checking on things, the piece of fabric on the fence caught my eye and now I'm here."

Pete was really banged up and very lucky to be here. He had more than a throbbing headache. He had a concussion, a dislocated shoulder, a broken wrist, a couple of cracked ribs, minor cuts and lots of bruising. Even Cal couldn't believe how lucky Pete had been. Surely who ever dropped Pete and his truck off the edge in the quarry meant to kill him.

8 o'clock came and the nurse shoed both Cal and Katie out of Pete's room. She was very serious about her job. "Visiting hours are over. Pete needs to rest now," she said.

Katie bent down to kiss Pete. "I'll come back tomorrow."

His dose of drugs had kicked in and Pete gave her the best smile he could muster, slurring "K!" And gave her a thumbs up.

Katie had to smile. Even all busted up Pete managed to make her feel better.

The walk back to Cal's was somewhat quiet too. Katie could tell that Cal's wheels were turning. He was so deep in thought he hadn't realized they were back at his place.

"Cal thanks for going with me."

"I'm sorry I'm not much of a conversationalist tonight."

"It's okay; I know you have a lot on your mind...About tomorrow night?"

Cal interrupted before she could finish. "I am looking forward to seeing you," he said with a gentle easy smile and making sure he looked directly into her beautiful eyes. "I'll be there by 10 p.m. if that isn't too late?"

"No, 10 o'clock is good."

They had an awkward moment, both not sure what should happen next; a hug, a kiss or what? She decided to just walk away, hopped in her car and then backed out his driveway, leaving him to stand there watching her go.

Cal's cell rang, it was Jim, "Cal, you were right. There was a piece of a flannel shirt hung up on the fence and there's lots of blood."

Cal jumped in his car and headed for the station.

Chapter 22

Tuesday came and Katie was a nervous wreck. She kept herself busy futzing around the house, started reading a new book she picked up, only to keep reading the same paragraph over and over. Then took a nap until she decided to go see Pete at the hospital. When she saw him, he was looking a little better or maybe it was just Katie's wishful thinking.

"Hey, you! Feel like company?"

"If I said no would you go away?" He said teasingly with a pained smile on his face.

"Even when you're in the hospital you have to give me grief. What's with that?" She laughed.

"Oh you wouldn't want it any other way, Sis!"

"I know." She sat in a chair next to his bed.

"What's up Doll?"

"I am going to tell Cal tonight," She said with an apprehensive look in her eyes.

"Oooh..."

The tone in the room just became very somber.

"You told me I should, right?"

"Honey, if you really want to have something with Cal, he deserves to know. Usually you're an open book, but these days you are a hard one to figure out, and sometimes you knowingly or unknowingly push people out of your life."

"Then why are you still here?"

"I tend to ignore you!" He smiled at her.

"I am just so nervous about telling him. It's more than that...I think I'm afraid of his reaction, Pete. I need you for some moral support."

Pete had already told Cal about Kate, but that was before he knew that Cal was more than just a cop. There was no way he was going to tell Katie that Cal already knew. He knew that if she found out he betrayed her trust, it would certainly put a kink in their relationship. "You've always got my support." Pete was hoping that someday the old Katie would come back; the one who was so full of confidence and lust for life. He was hopeful that his intuition on how Katie felt about Cal would bring her back.

"Pete, I'm a wreck! How do you bring something like that up?"

"Do you consider him a friend?"

"I'd like to think so. We enjoy each other's company, and we were taking it slow. He's a complete gentleman. Ya, know...we really clicked."

"Sounds like things were going great. You never really told me what happened?"

"He invited me over for dinner. He cooked. It was fantastic. We had some wine and just talked. After dessert we sat on his couch and things progressed. He's very good by the way."

"All right, I really didn't need to hear that!"

Katie chuckled a little. Pete liked to see her lighten up.

"Well anyway, I don't know what happened. He was gentle and sweet. But when things got heated, I just froze, I panicked. My great evening got interrupted by my nightmare."

"I'm so sorry. What did, Cal do?"

"Nothing, he asked what was wrong and I couldn't leave fast enough. He even called me the next day, but I didn't answer him. Then he tried to set up other dates, and I came up with all sorts of excuses not to. I'm horrible!"

"Well that wasn't very nice of you!" Pete teased in a brotherly way. "I'm surprised he even talks to you."

"Thanks a lot Pete; I'm trying to be serious."

"I know you are. I don't have any answers for you. All I can tell you is to be honest with him and don't beat around the bush. Just say it the way it is. I think Cal will respect that."

Katie just nodded in agreement, thinking about what Pete said.

"What time are you going to meet up with him?"

"10 o'clock."

"So what are you planning on doing when you get booted out of here?"

"Well when Nurse 'Ratchet' kicks me out I'll find something to do." She laughed.

"Hey now, she's actually pretty sweet. And her name is Debbie by the way."

"Look at you! You can't be doing too badly if you're checking out your nurse."

"Ha Ha!"

Pete and Katie joked with each other lightening the mood, and watched a little TV until a few minutes after 8 o'clock. Sure enough Nurse Daniels came in to check on Pete and boot Katie out.

Katie winked at Pete and gave him the thumbs up behind Debbie's back. Pete just shook his head. Before she left, she bent down to kiss his cheek, "Thanks, Pete...I'll let you know how it goes."

"'Night Katie, good luck!"

* * *

Katie had almost two hours before meeting Cal. She didn't want to go home and wait around the house in case she lost her nerve. She decided to just head out to the lake and wait for Cal. She parked the red Nova and walked out to the pier. There was a bench bolted down at the end. That is where she took up residence looking out over the quiet lake. It was a perfect summer night. A warm breeze picked up off the lake, embracing her. She was never clearer on what she wanted in her life. The thoughts of what she might say flooded her mind. She rehashed old memories of her and Derrick; how happy they had once been. How what she thought was love was so wrong. Why couldn't she see the writing on the wall? There were signs...quite a few signs. She felt so foolish. Katie knew what happened to her was in no way her fault. But she was angry with herself for being blinded to who he really was. If she ever wanted to be truly happy again she needed to move on with her life and put the past as far behind her as she could. Katie was optimistic that she could have something with Cal. She felt safe with him, and he awakened feelings in her that she hadn't felt in a long time.

Soon she heard a car pulling up. Its tires rolling over the gravel parking lot, as its lights panned across the pier and found her silhouette sitting on the bench before it came to a stop. Katie didn't have to turn around to see who it was; she felt the vibration from his Mopar. She heard a door shut. Then she heard Cal approaching. She recognized his very distinctive gate. Or maybe she was the only one who noticed such things.

As he stepped up beside her she heard his velvet voice say her name, "Kate?"

Something about just the sound of his voice sent a thrilling charge through her body. She was so nervous but determined at the same time. As she turned to look up at him, she flashed him a soft smile and motioned for him to sit next to her. There was obvious tension, and yet a spark of desire hung in the air.

Cal wasn't sure what to do or what to say. It was Kate who wanted this meeting. They both sat there looking out over the lake with anticipation. She had finally worked up enough courage to break the ice.

"Cal, I have to apologize to you. You deserve an explanation for that night at your house when I left in such a hurry. I haven't been totally honest with you."

"About what?"

"Cal, I just need for you to hear me out first... Otherwise I'm not quite sure I'll be able to get through this. Then, after I tell you, if you decide you don't want to see me anymore, I will understand. You deserve better."

"Kate I'm not sure what this is about, but if I didn't want to be with you I wouldn't be here right now. Whatever you're worried about telling me, I'm listening." Cal held out his hand to her for encouragement.

Then she looked deeply into Cal's soulfully beautiful eyes and graciously accepted his hand. Her fingers were cold and her palms were clammy.

"I didn't mean to push you away; or to be so rude as to run out on you like I did. We were having such a wonderful evening. I truly want to be with you, but I won't blame you if you don't want to be with someone with so much baggage.

Cal instantly put two and two together and figured it out. She was finally going to open up to him about her rape. Cal squeezed her hand a little tighter, giving her extra support, knowing how difficult this was going to be for her, and it was going to be hard for him to hear it.

Katie averted her eyes from him to peer out over the lake. She wouldn't be able to get through this if she had to look him in the eyes when she told him. Taking a deep breath she proceeded to tell the man she was falling in love with about the most horrific moment in her life.

"About two years ago someone very close to me hurt me like no one should ever be hurt. I found out the man I was seeing was not the man I thought he was. By accident I saw him with another woman, one who later turned up raped and murdered. I told Pete I was going to confront him about it. But Pete told me to wait until he could go with me. Of course I was so angry and upset I didn't wait. I confronted Derrick on my own and he snapped." Tears started to well up in her eyes.

Cal was silent, intently listening to her tale. He couldn't imagine what she went through and was feeling the heat of anger brew inside him as she continued describing what Derrick did to her.

"He held me down...he beat me, and then he strangled me while he... raped me. He... forced himself on me. He...violated every part of me. He stripped me of everything, and took from me, what I don't know if I can ever get back." She paused, still looking out over the water which was now reflecting the twinkling stars. "I don't remember all of it, which is probably a good thing. Pete walked in on it and scared him off. Pete saved my life. I woke up in the hospital with severe injuries." She gave pause again. The tears rolled down her cheeks.

Cal was still holding her hand, but took his free hand to gently wipe the tears.

"I don't know if I can ever truly get over that, but I refuse to let what happened define me. I refuse to stay a victim." She turned to him and searched his face for any reaction. "Now you know, now you know why I moved here. I needed a fresh start. Then you came along and stirred feelings in me I didn't know I could feel again. I didn't mean to run out on you like I did. I guess I feared what might happen next. I panicked. I wanted to be with you, but you are the first man I have been with since then. I just couldn't; at least not until...now...you deserved to know the reason why I've been avoiding you. I'm sorry for pushing you away." Katie tried to read Cal's reaction, searching the depths of his soul through his eyes as her tears gently rolled down her face.

Cal held Kate's hand tightly, quietly reflecting all that she had divulged. He spoke softly and tenderly. "Why would you think I wouldn't want to be with you? Do you honestly think that I am going to run away from this, from you?"

Katie sat silently not sure how to answer. Even Cal's eyes began to well up. He put his arm around her, bringing her closer to him, resting his cheek against the top of her head.

"Kate, you are an incredible woman. You are very special to me. What that animal did to you was despicable! I can't imagine all that you went through. I only wish I could take the pain away." Cal started to choke up. "Thank you for confiding in me, Kate. I'm glad you did. I know how difficult that was to tell me." He then turned to face her, and tenderly lifted her chin with his finger ,so he could look directly into her gorgeous eyes and said, "I don't want you to have any doubts; I am not going anywhere. And if you're willing, I would like for us to pick back up where we left off? I'd like to see where our journey leads us."

She was still crying softly, but relieved to hear those words. She leaned into Cal, letting all her worries fade away.

Cal was happy having her in his arms again. He wanted to protect her.

"Kate, do you have any idea how hard it has been working on this case? I have to tell you, I'm a little jealous of Pete. He gets to be there for you and protect you from this guy and I didn't know if I'd be crossing some line if I did anything more than just my job. That has been the most difficult part."

Cal had very mixed feelings. Anger; knotted up in the pit of his stomach that someone could hurt her like that. Joy; he was happy to have Katie back in his arms. Determination; he was going to get the little bastard who was stalking her.

Cal spoke matter-of-factly, "Kate, I'm going to get this guy. No one is going to hurt you like that again. I promise you, I *will* find him."

Cal held Katie for a long time. The heat of the day gave way to a refreshingly cool summer night. The lake was peaceful aside from the subtle splash of the waves rolling into the dock or the crickets playing a song and maybe an occasional frog butting in. The stars seemed to be endless. It was quite peaceful and they were content to enjoy the moment.

Chapter 23

The sky was clear. A subtle breeze blew through the trees rustling their leaves. Dexter trotted down the dirt path happily sniffing every twig, bush and tree along the way. His owner Lynn Ketterhagen was enjoying their stroll through the park as well. She brought his ball along and threw it for him. Dex would run after it, tail wagging eagerly retrieving it. His beautiful black and brown coat just shined in the sun's rays. His face had a black mask that gave him his distinctive German Shepard markings. His intelligent bright eyes gleamed with excitement and his ears perked alert waiting for Lynn to toss his ball again. Towards the back of Bushnell Park they rested and Lynn gave Dexter some water from her water bottle.

"Come on Dex, let's head back." Dex stood wagging his happy tail.

"Oh, alright; you want your ball boy?" She threw his ball one more time.

He raced to retrieve it. The breeze shifted slightly. Dexter stood poised, his nostrils flared actively. He caught scent of something and took off to find it.

Lynn yelled. "Dex! Here boy! Dex - come!"

He took off heading east running intently searching for something.

Lynn started off after him still shouting commands. "Dex heel! Dex come!"

His ears turned back momentarily to hear Lynn's commands, but his interest lay ahead. He only slowed a little then bounded down the train tracks.

Lynn ran after him hurdling over clumps of tall grass and weeds. She carefully crawled between the barbed wire fencing. Looking up she saw Dex running into the tunnel. Once Lynn got to the train tracks she followed him to the tunnel. He was barking at something. Something that smelled really dead.

"What is it boy?" Lynn came closer. At first she thought it was a deer. Maybe it had been hit by the train or a car and fell off the bridge only to die in here. But it was not a deer. "Dex, come!" This time he obeyed her.

"Good boy." She put his leash back on him and walked out of the tunnel. She felt sick. She then dialed 911, "Hello – yes you need to send someone over to Bushnell Park. I found a body under the bridge."

Since the secondary station was practically across the street from the park 2-squad cars along with the coroner, were there in no time. Lynn and Dexter met them and walked them back to where Dex found the body.

Cal was one of the officers on scene. He made sure the crime scene was protected. Since not much usually happened here this was a big deal. Cal took lead and directed an officer to take Lynn's statement. The others started with photos of the scene and collecting evidence. Cal started with the body.

The body was located on its side. His legs were sprawled like he'd been grabbed and thrown down. A puddle of blood was found approximately 3-feet long and 24 inches in diameter and trailed to where the body finally rested. It looked like a single stab wound to the lower back, but post mortem would determine for sure. Cal crouched down to bag the corpse's hands as not to destroy any trace evidence they might hold. Using his pen, Cal carefully moved aside the tails of the victim's flannel shirt to reveal his back pants pocket. He then carefully took the wallet out to get an ID. The license read Scott Warren. There was a total of $43 dollars, a condom and miscellaneous scraps of paper folded up in the wallet.

This was not a robbery. Stabbings are personal. Cal looked back down at the body. The flannel looked familiar. He remembered the fabric they found on Katie's fence.

"Chapman, over here!" An officer yelled.

Cal turned his attentions to the officer. He had found a boot impression along the side of the tracks. It was subtle and just a dusty outline, but Cal recognized it to be similar to the tread left in the quarry. The victim was wearing cowboy boots; this was not the victim's foot print. Placing a measuring tape down and taking a photo for evidence.

Cal turned back to the body.

Because of the elements it was going to be hard to determine exactly how long the victim had been there. The body had already gone into putrefaction and along with insect infestation; his flesh had been chewed on by critters. Cal took a sample of the dried blood from the point of origin where he had been stabbed and then turned the body over to the coroner, Mitch Carter, who also happened to be Jack's father.

"I'll get this done as soon as I can, Cal."

Cal patted Mitch on the shoulder, "Thanks."

Lynn was sitting hunched over on the bumper of a squad car. She was light headed and fighting the urge to vomit.

Cal strolled over to the officer with her inquiring as to what he found out. As far as they knew Dexter was the first one to find the body. Lynn is the only witness thus far.

After they wrapped everything up Cal was the last to leave, pondering questions he had.

Was the murderer the same guy that sent Pete over the drop off?

Were Scott and this guy partners?

Which one or was it both of them getting into Kate's?

Who belongs to the boot print?

Cal also acknowledged the close proximity the body was found in relation to Kate's house. He was worried for her safety.

Cal had to let her know, "Kate, we found Scott Warren."

"That's great!"

"Kate..." He gave pause then just told her, "He's dead."

She tried to process what that meant. "So it's over? I can go back to work and have my life back?"

"It looks that way." Although Cal wasn't so sure it was over. "I just want to give you a heads up, that I'm sending a few officers over to remove the contents of your attic."

"That's good. I'll empty my closet so they can get in. Thanks, Cal - I am so relieved!"

He was not; and now he had a murder investigation to do.

Cal's next step was to call Bob at the Brick Yard and have all the employee's questioned, for the second time. The first time he questioned them it was to inquire about Kate being drugged.

It was pay day and everyone would be coming in for their checks, consequently Cal took over Bob's office. One by one they came in and were interviewed by Cal. Normally Cal would have had them come into the station for the interviews but since it was more of a fishing expedition; an informal inquiry would be best for now.

Erik was relieved that Katie wasn't going to have to worry about this guy anymore and finally come back to work. He identified Scott's photo from a prior he had as the same one who would hang out watching Katie work.

Tanya and Jessica were of no help.

Eddie came in moving like he was a little sore. He too identified Scott as the guy hanging out at the bar.

Cal asked, "I noticed you're favoring your left leg. What did you do?"

Eddie was quick to answer. "Nothing, Sir. I started working out again, I guess I over did it."

He noted that Eddie was wearing running shoes today, but could have sworn he preferred boots.

Jack identified Scott as well. "Sure, that's him. He would order a draft and sip it for hours. The creep would talk to Billie and stare at Katie. I never liked the guy."

Steve was the last one to come in. Cal noticed right away his subtle limp, and he favored his right hand. Cal coolly asked, "What happened to you?"

Laughing Steve answered, "Oh, I guess I'll never grow up. A couple of days ago I got together with some buddies of mine and played street hockey. Roller blades and no gear. Good thing we were drinking or this really would have hurt." He laughed even harder like he got his own joke.

Cal asked if he knew the man in the picture. Steve thinks he'd seen him around, but he sees lots of people. He was sure he'd been in but couldn't say much else. However, when Steve got up to leave, Cal noticed he was wearing boots that had a thick tread. Keeping in mind the two boot prints they found. He would have to check out Steve's story.

As Cal was leaving the Brick Yard, Steve was shooting the bull with Erik and Bob at the bar. Cal casually asked, "Hey Steve, I've been meaning to ask you; does Brandon Holtz still play hockey with you guys?"

Steve chuckled, "He sure does. Who do you think ran my ass over?"

Cal knew the Holtz's and they'd collaborate Steve's story about getting hurt.

Cal wanted to interview one more today; Scott's uncle.

Cal called Mr. Warren to come down to the station. He followed Cal into the conference room, and then was told of Scott's demise.

Mr. Warren was visibly upset. Even though he didn't care much for his nephew, Scott was still his sister's kid.

Cal extensively questioned Mr. Warren; "Who were Scott's acquaintances, friends, and other family members? Who was his employer, and co-workers? Did he know if Scott had any enemies or had been in any recent fights? Did he know where Scott hung out?"

Mr. Warren was over whelmed. He wasn't that much help, he didn't know anything except he saw him at a 7-ll working on its roof in the last month.

"Do you know who he was working for?"

"No. There were a few guys there with a white work van. I don't remember there being any company name on it."

"Then do you remember which 7-11 it was?"

Mr. Warren was trying to recall, "Ah...I think it's the one in Dover. Let's see...I think I was across the street at the Pioneer's Inn. Yes, I believe it was. Yep, that's the one, the 7-11 out in Dover." Mr. Warren said reaffirming his recollection.

This was the break Cal had been looking for. "Thank you, Mr. Warren you've been a great help." He reached out to shake Mr. Warren's hand. "I am sorry for your loss."

"I hope you catch whoever did this."

"We will, Mr. Warren."

Chapter 24

Katie had emptied her closet so the police could crawl in through the access panel to the attic. The smallest officer was elected to be the one to empty the contents. A heavy odor filtered through the room as he opened the panel. He slipped in and was handed lights to illuminate the space, and a camera along with garbage bags for the all the marijuana. After he took pictures of the space, he took down the black lights and pulled down the all plants lining the rafters that had been hung upside down to dry. They had very large buds with reddish hairs which was quite impressive for a small time operator. These were special plants certainly not ditch weed. When he finished, seven bags were hoisted out of the access. Then out came the buckets with dead plants in them.

"Hey hold up! You're never gonna guess what else I found!"

Sgt. Nelsen stuck his head into the hole in the wall. The officer in the attic handed him not just one but three brown paper Piggly Wiggly bags filled with wads of cash.

"Holy Shit! This just keeps getting better!"

It took them awhile to empty all the contents of Katie's attic. She was sitting down stairs on the couch trying to read a book and sipping ice tea when they started coming down the stairs with the loot.

Nelsen informed Katie that they had removed everything that was up there; she could seal up the panel again and put her stuff away.

"Thank you. I feel so much better now that it's gone."

"I'm sure." He gave her a subtle smile. "Well, that's it. I'm sure if we need anything else, Detective Chapman will let you know."

With that they were gone.

Katie was happy to be rid of the drugs and Scott. She didn't necessarily want him dead, but that solved her problems, or so she thought.

***

Cal was busy at the station compiling what little information he had and making numerous phone calls. All that the manager for the 7-11 store could give Cal was a name and number. It looked like a shady operation from Bohner's Lake. Dialing the phone Cal waited for Mark Connelly to answer. Finally! "Hello, this is Detective Cal Chapman with the Burlington Police Department. I am looking for a Mark Connelly."

"This is." Sounding like he wished he hadn't answered the phone.

"Mr. Connelly, I understand you have a roofing business, is that correct?"

"Yeah..."

"Could you tell me if you have an employee by the name of Scott Warren?"

"Yeah...but he ain't here. The looser is almost always late and he hasn't come to work in over a week. What did he do?"

"Sir, we found his body."

"You're kiddin' me? No shit?" Mark seemed amused by this. "Did he do it himself or did someone do to him?"

"Sir, I was hoping you could tell me anything that could help me find out what happened to Scott. Has he been in any conflicts with anyone at work?"

"Well sure he has. In fact the last time he worked, him and two of my other guys, ah... Cory and one of the Reid brothers were arguing about something. It got pretty heated and they started shoving each other."

"Do you remember what that argument was about?"

"I have no clue, but they stopped when the other Reid brother stepped in. That was the last day I saw Scott."

"I'm going to need to speak with the Reid brothers and Cory. What are the Reid's first names and does Cory have a last name?"

Mark suddenly didn't want to be so cooperative, and vaguely gave Chapman any information. He finally gave Cal their names and their cell numbers, but he didn't know anything else.

"Sir, they work for you, you have to have addresses."

"Nope, just their cell numbers, cuz' I pay my guys cash."

Cal knew Mark was leaving something out, but for now he'd work with what he had.

"If I have any more questions for you, would this be the number to reach you or is there a better one?"

"This one is good." Mark said with a bit of disdain in his voice.

Through cell records Cal was able to get addresses. Cory was actually a Walker, so he knew where to look for him. His family was well known in the area; his Great grandfather started the little grade school; which is now a coffee shop/diner.

Tomorrow he'd get a fresh start on the investigation.

Chapter 25

By 8 a.m. Cal met the medical examiner, Mitch Carter for the autopsy results.

"Cal," Mitch greeted Chapman in an easy friendly manor offering him his hand.

Shaking Mitch's hand, "Thanks for getting this done so fast."

"Like I had much else to do? It isn't every day we get a murder."

"So give me a summation of what you found, what was the cause of death?"

"There were no drugs and barely any alcohol in the tox screen. No sign of a struggle. Because of the deterioration of the corpse, I had to get outside help from a forensic entomologist. According to her findings based on bugs and larva and the amount and rate of putrefaction; he died approximately 10-days to 2 – weeks ago. The body was in very poor condition but the point of entry was protected.

I'd have to say he never saw it coming; death was instantaneous. The cause of death was massive trauma to the back wall, lower right side of the lumbar area into the thoracic area. Based on the length and breadth and angle of the entry wound and the organ damage; oh and the nicked spine due to the carved marks inside of the floating rib in which the bone suffered a ragged cut from the knife with a serrated edge. This leads me to believe the weapon used was a military or martial arts knife.

They are used to kill quickly and instantaneously. Whoever killed this guy knew how to use this type of knife. That's my assessment anyway."

Cal needed to recruit some help on the case; Sgt. Nelsen and two other officers; along with consulting with the Felony Assistant State's Attorney Major Crimes Unit within the County's State's Attorney's Office. Cal even called the Department of Corrections in Wisconsin and Illinois looking for anyone recently paroled who had this M.O. Then he placed a bulletin out to all Police Agencies in Wisconsin and Illinois to look for those with this type of technique and who used this type of weapon who were recently released.

While contacting the FBI, Cal received help from a forensic psychologist who profiled the personality type of the killer. In gathering as much help as he could he'd also enlist the help of the State Police for some leg work.

It was a long day for Cal. He put off calling the Reid brothers in for questioning until tomorrow morning. It had been a brutally long day and he was mentally exhausted but feeling pretty good about getting things moving on the murder case. He looked at the time and called Kate.

She was taking a nap on her couch when her cell rang. It startled her and she quickly reached for her phone to answer, "Hello?"

"Kate? I'm sorry, did I wake you?"

"Huh? Ah, that's alright."

"Have you eaten yet?"

"No, what time is it?"

"Actually it's 7:00."

"Wow, I must have been tired. What did you have in mind?"

"Do you feel like pizza? We could go to Doug's."

"Pizza actually sounds really good. How long until you're off work?"

"I am just wrapping up; 15 – 20 minutes maybe."

"Good that gives me a couple minutes to wake up. Do you want to meet there or shall I pick up you up?" She tried to fight back a yawn but couldn't.

"Are you sure you aren't too tired tonight?"

"No, I'm good." She managed to say through another yawn.

"Okay, I'm not proud, I'll take a lift." Cal lightly jested.

Katie picked Cal up and they headed over to Doug's.

She smiled and reached out for Cal's hand. "So how was your day?"

He snickered, "Oh, it was pretty exhausting. I was on the phone most of the day. Let's not talk about work. I just want to enjoy a beautiful woman's company and share some pie."

She gave Cal a sideways glance, and her green eyes said it all. Kate had a brilliant smile that could melt away the worries of Cal's day. Cal thought it was cute that Kate didn't realize how attractive she really was. He could hardly keep his eyes off of her.

Doug's wasn't very busy, and they were able to get a back corner booth right away. A pitcher of Pepsi and a large thin crust extra cheese, sausage, green pepper and onion pizza were ordered.

Cal reached across the small wooden table for Kate's hand. He loved to gaze into those gorgeous eyes of hers and take in her captivatingly smile.

Katie was flattered by Cal's intense gazing. He always made her feel special, like she was the only woman in the room.

Their effervescent conversation carried on throughout their meal. Katie was actually quite humorous and made Cal laugh; forgetting all about the murder investigation he'd been working on. Cal had dated all different types of women, but Kate was easy to be with. She was the most down to earth, engaging, realistic, intelligent, charming woman he had ever met and she kept Cal wanting more.

Time flew, and before they knew it was 10 o'clock when Cal asked for the check.

"I suppose I should take you back to your car?" Katie questioned. She really wasn't ready to call it an evening; but she could tell Cal was very tired and knew he had to be back to work first thing in the morning, so she wasn't going to push for more time with him.

"I'm afraid so. I'm glad we did this." Cal said.

Katie excused herself while Cal took the bill up to pay at the bar.

He took cash out of his wallet and handed it to the tired looking gentleman working the bar. Looking past the booze bottles on their shelves Cal saw Eddie's reflection in the mirror sitting as if a cat in waylay with an intense stare towards the hallway to which Kate was emerging. Cal didn't let on that he was watching Eddie.

Katie smiled, "Are you ready?"

"Sure thing," he said, as he placed his hand on the small of her back and casually walked out of Doug's. Now Cal's enlightened mood quickly gave way to trepidation.

Even though Kate drove, Cal still opened her car door for her. He was the constant gentleman. While he himself was getting in the car, he took a quick glance over the roof of her Nova to the window in which Eddie was watching them. Cal had a bad feeling about Eddie, and the more he observed him - the less he liked him.

Katie noticed how quiet Cal had been on the way back to the station. As they were pulling in, Cal turned to Katie and asked, "I know it is getting late, but I could go for some coffee. Care to join me?"

Happy to hear they were extending their time together, she quickly replied, "How about I make some coffee at the house?"

"That sounds better yet." Cal said, as he shut his door. Then he started up his cruiser and followed Katie home over the bridge.

Katie had the pot all ready to go so all she had to do was turn on the switch. They sat together on the couch listening to the radio while they waited for the coffee to brew.

"It's not that I'm not glad to have you here for coffee Cal, but are you sure you aren't too tired? I know you've been working crazy hours."

Putting his arm around Kate to bring her in closer to him, they sunk back into the couch. "I guess I'm just not ready to go yet," Cal said.

In no time the coffee was ready. The rich aroma permeated through to the living room. Katie poured two large mugs of hot coffee and brought them into where Cal was still sitting on the couch. She handed a mug to him and then leaning against the arm of the sofa she curled her legs up under herself. Katie sensed that there was something that happened between her leaving for the restroom, and him paying the bill. She wanted to just ask him but wasn't sure if she should; so she figured if he wanted to tell her he would. She'd play it by ear and feel him out.

Cal tried to not show concern about Eddie's venomous demeanor towards Kate. He wanted to know more about this lovely redhead who kept him on his toes; like what she wanted to do in the future. He kept the conversation light and optimistic. "So if you could do anything you wanted, what would it be?"

The question took Katie by surprise. "I'm really not sure how to answer that."

"Well, what was your dream when you were little? Has it changed?"

"Oh gosh. When I was little I wanted to be a vet, then I think I wanted to race cars. I really don't remember if I had one set thing I wanted to do." She thought for a moment. "You know, now that I think about it, I wanted to travel around Europe visiting castles. I guess I've always taken an interest in architecture."

"Didn't you get your degree in architecture?"

"Actually it's in interior design, and minored in history. But that was only after I started taking Criminal Justice courses so I could get a science degree and work my way into forensic science."

"You're kidding? What changed?"

Taking a long drink of coffee before she answered, "I'm not really sure. I guess after taking all the psych classes and getting more involved with what I was actually going to have to do, it depressed me. I always wanted to have a family - eventually! And knowing what some sicko had done to a kid...I don't think I'd be able to separate work from home, and be able to hold my child and not see the horrors of what someone could do to them. I feared that. I know that might not make any sense."

"Actually that makes perfect sense. I sometimes wonder myself if I followed the right path. I know my job, and I do it well. But sometimes it's hard to see the good through all the bad. Luckily, I've chosen a community where there are a lot of good people."

"What would you be doing if you weren't a cop?"

He laughed. "I don't think I can be anything else. It's who I am. Don't get me wrong...I have hobbies. Like the money pit I call home. But I don't think I'd want to be anything else."

He watched Katie take another long drink of coffee. Then decided to continue his thought, "I eventually want to settle down and have a family. Then my life will revolve around them. I don't want to be like my father, gone all the time, dragging his family all over God's creation, having the kids bounce from school to school. That isn't any kind of life I want for my family. I want them to have a stable enjoyable life." His eyes were fixed on her. He could see having a life with Kate. The more time Cal spent with Kate the more she surprised him, revealing more of the intriguing, gregarious woman she was. Cal was seeing her in a new light.

She caught his wondrous gaze. She smiled and put her mug down on the table, as did he and they kiss each other tenderly.

This time all her thoughts were on the man sitting next to her; the man who gave her the motivation she needed to transform her life.

He didn't want Kate to do something she wasn't ready for, so he tried to read her lips and her body and let her take the lead.

Katie loved the way Cal kissed her. Firm - yet tender, and very loving. She didn't want to push him away again. The complete and utter respect he showed her allowed her to give a little more of herself to him every time they were together. She felt safe sharing pieces of herself with him.

She faced him, taking his face in her hands, and then bringing his lips to hers. Their kisses became more passionate. His hands wandered and began caressing her, feeling her toned curves, and the small indentation in the small of her back. The way she moved, he could sense she was getting into making-out with him. He drew her nearer and ran his fingers through her silky long hair. Her curls cascaded over her shoulders. He wanted her, but restrained from letting things get too far. He never wanted anyone as much as he wanted Kate. But he couldn't rush things with her; she had to be the one to take it to the next level.

Katie lost herself in the moment and straddled Cal's lap, surprising him. Face to face he held her firmly by her hair but it was gentle, not rough. His lip service was incredible. She couldn't help herself, she was happy and wanted to play, so she gently nipped at his bottom lip.

That startled Cal for a second, and he hesitated. The passion paused, as they tried to read each other searching for what was about to happen next.

Cal quickly decided to let her play. He could control himself, and she needed to feel safe with him. He kissed her and she bit his lip again. He joked, "So that's how you want to play is it?" Then playfully turned the tables; he laid her back on the sofa and slid her under him but he hovered above her holding up his weight, stiff armed.

Katie laughed, big and playful.

Cal loved to see her like this.

She grabbed the front of his shirt and pulled him down to her.

He gave her an impish grin and quickly went for the side of her neck. He teasingly nibbled and kissed her playfully.

She giggled – which she almost never did, but his lips and hot breath on her neck tickled her so. Katie took hold of his head taking a fist full of what little hair she could grab.

He felt a chill as she ran her delicate fingers through his hair and then turned on his neck. She nibbled back, just keeping it playful.

Closing his eyes he let her kiss him enjoying her sweet caresses.

Veering her lips from his neck to his chin and up his strong jaw line, she kissed him slowly imprinting every inch of his wonderful face with her lips.

Cal opened his eyes and tenderly traced her lovely face with his finger tips, then kissed her on the tip of her nose.

They intimately talked a little while longer until they both fell asleep in each other's arms. Once again Cal had opened a little more of Kate's guarded heart.

It was the middle of the night, and everything seemed to be fine. The house was quiet and so was the property surrounding it. That is except for the stranger who had been watching everything through the windows. He was enraged at their display of affection. He felt wounded; like someone had disemboweled him. *"That bitch! That whore! How could she?"* He thought to himself. Now he needed to take things up a notch.

Like a hyena sulking away - he would return.

Chapter 26

When Katie awoke Cal was gone. She thought for a moment that she had been dreaming the whole thing. That is until she smelled sausage cooking and eggs and toast. Now she was ravenous. She sat up noticing how stale her coffee breath was from last night. She slipped into the door way of the kitchen to sneak passed to the bathroom for a quick tooth brushing.

Cal had his back to her humming quietly to himself while turning the sausages.

Looking in the mirror Katie saw how disheveled she looked. She washed her face and combed through her hair. *"I guess this is as good as I'm gonna get this morning."* She stepped out and padded across the kitchen floor. She saw Cal had set the table and made a fresh pot of coffee. Katie stepped up behind Cal, and placing a gentle hand on his back to let him know she was there, before she hugged him from behind, resting her cheek on his muscular back, remembering last night.

"Good morning, Sunshine!" Cal said happily.

Katie found it funny that Pete called her that too. "You stayed the night, and made breakfast?"

"Of course – hope you don't mind – I just helped myself to what was in your refrigerator?"

"Not at all - this is nice."

Standing on her tip toes, she reached up to give him a kiss on the cheek, and then stepped over to the coffee pot. "Coffee?"

"Absolutely, not like we didn't have enough last night!" He gave her a wink.

The toast popped up and Katie began to butter them. Searching the cupboards, Cal took out a platter and placed the eggs and sausage side by side on it. They sat down at her little table, the sun's rays beamed through the airy curtained windows.

Cal thought Kate looked beautiful this morning. He reached out for her hand and she gladly gave it to him to hold. "Thank you for last night; it was wonderful spending time with you like that." He lifted her hand to his lips and kissed it.

Katie had been drawn to Cal. He was genuine and romantic and tender and sweet and the list could go on, regarding all the things she loved about him. But he also made her feel safe.

They ate and had light cheery conversation. She flashed him one of her charming smiles, and Cal knew he was falling in love with her.

Cal didn't have the time to finish his coffee, so Katie poured a travel mug for him. "I have to go, thanks, Kate! I'm sorry to leave you with the dishes."

"It's fine! Thanks for making breakfast."

He kissed her lovingly on the mouth, and out the door he went.

After cleaning up the kitchen, Katie jumped into the shower, all the while day-dreaming about Cal. Pete was getting out of the hospital today, and she planned to pick him up.

Cal arrived at the station happier than he had been in a long time. Of course, the first one to notice his jubilation was Sgt. Nelsen, who just happened to see that

Cal pulled in from the east not the west like he does every other day.

Jim greeted Cal with a Cheshire cat grin, "Good morning, Chapman!"

Cal knew instantly that Jim knew where he spent the night. "Why yes it is Jim."

Cal wasn't going to share; he liked to keep his private life private. He walked straight through to his office. Cal picked up the phone and continued with what he was doing last night. He got in touch with the Reid brothers and had both coming in today. Next, Cal called the CID for assistance in looking at military personnel. He was interested in anyone who had less than honorable discharge or was excused based on psychiatric evaluations. He already knew that it was going to take a while for them to get back to him. He wasn't going to hold his breath, but this was his best chance of finding out who did this. He already knew before the Reid's came in that they had nothing to do with Scott's murder but they could shed some light on whom or what got him killed.

***

Katie knocked on Pete's hospital door.

He knew it had to be her. "Com'in!"

"Are ya ready to get out of here?"

"You know it! But they say I have to wait 'til noon before they release me."

"That isn't so long to wait. Where do you want to go for lunch?"

"Oh – I'll have to think about that. Everything sounds good! Although the hospital food wasn't too bad."

His nurse came in, "Are you ready to go home, Pete?"

"I sure am!"

"Wow - that was enthusiastic! Don't you like my company?" She said teasingly.

Katie could tell there was something happening between Pete and his nurse, Debbie, so she excused herself and stepped out into the hall. While she was out there, she overheard idle chatter at the nurse's station; which only verified what she already suspected. Not long after, the nurse left Pete's room with a giddy expression on her face.

When Katie reentered Pete's room he had the biggest grin on his face to match the nurse's.

"You got her number didn't you?" Katie teased.

Toying back with an even bigger smile, "What makes you say that?"

"Pete! You have the goofiest grin painted on your mug right now! That's what!"

"What can I say?" He said as he motioned for Katie to sit by him. "You look happy yourself. I take it things are good between you and Cal?"

"You can say that."

"Now, who has a goofy look on their face?"

"That would be me!" She laughed. "I am just so happy. You're getting out today; I get to go back to work, and I don't have to worry about anyone stalking me. It's great! I feel great! That and the fact that I think I found the most wonderful man alive!"

"Hey now!"

"Well, besides you...you don't count."

"Why don't I?" He teased.

She shot him a look.

"I know what you're saying. I'm happy for you, Sis. He makes you happy, and I haven't seen you this happy in...forever. As soon as I get out of here you're going to have to tell me all about it."

"Sure −", she laughed.

Dr. Philips entered the room, "Well Pete, it looks like you finally get to go home. How are you feeling?"

"Great, aside from the cast on my arm and the stitches in my head!"

"Any problems, concerns, questions?"

"Nope! Just want to get out of here."

"Okay, Pete. Debbie checked everything off so I guess I can release you. I know you aren't from town so in 10-days have your doctor check the stitches, and by then they should be ready to take out. As for your cast, I'd say you have about 4 more weeks."

"Thanks, Doc!"

***

Pete was happy to be out of the hospital. He didn't like to be cooped up. "Sis, I know what I want for lunch!"

"Is that so?"

"Yep! I want a big juicy bacon cheeseburger, some fries and a big chocolate shake!"

"Somewhere in particular?"

"Don't care...anywhere! Just drive!" Pete laughed.

Kate took Pete to Doug's. He had the best burgers in town. They walked in and Doug automatically greeted Katie.

"Katie, back so soon? Where's Chapman?"

"Working, it's Just us today. Doug this is my friend Pete. Pete this is Doug, the owner."

They shook left hands being Pete's right was covered in a plaster cast.

"How ya doing?"

"Good to meet ya, Pete."

"You, too!"

"Do you want your usual seat?"

"Sure, that's fine."

They were seated, and Katie refused the luncheon menus. "Doug, we know what we want. Two bacon cheeseburgers-medium, with grilled onions and pickles, fries and 2- chocolate shakes."

"You got it!"

Pete piped up, "I take it you're a regular?"

"Lately, anyway!" She said with a smile.

Doug soon brought their shakes over.

"Thanks!"

"Your burgers will be right up."

Katie started to daydream.

Pete noticed the vivid smile that had crept across her face. "Okay, Katie, spill!"

A huge smile took over her face, "Well, I told you that I confessed to Cal about what happened, when we met out at the lake."

"Yeah?"

"He took it a lot better than I expected. He was very supportive, and he understood why I acted the way I did. But then he said 'he wasn't going anywhere and that he wanted to start back up where we left off'. And so...we have."

"Okay? But there's something else going on; I can tell...what gives?"

"We had a great night last night, and he even spent the night, and then he made breakfast this morning!"

"Wait a minute - what? You're kidding me, right?"

"Nope!"

"You mean you..."

"Oh! No...it wasn't like that. We came here for pizza last night then went back to my place for coffee, and we just talked. We fell asleep on the couch, and when I woke up, he was cooking breakfast!"

"Wow - you seem to be head-over-heels for this guy. You mean to tell me he hasn't tried anything?"

"Not that it is any of your business... but no...he has been a perfect gentleman. We just talked, about anything and everything. He reads me so well, we just kissed and cuddled. It was nice."

"Whoa, you don't have to tell me everything, Hun. I am just glad he makes you happy and things are going well." Then he shot her an all knowing "big brotherly" kind of look that seemed to say "Don't kid yourself, he's still a man."

Katie studied Pete for a long moment. Before she could answer, Doug brought over their burgers and fries.

"Thanks, Doug! Looks great!" Katie said.

"Enjoy!" Doug replied as he walked away.

Pete picked up his large 1/3 pound burger and took a giant bite out of it.

Katie just stared at this caveman-like display. "You aren't hungry are you?" She laughed.

Then she cut her burger in half. Pete continued to scarf it down, mixing a few fries in here and there, then washing it all down with his shake. "Continue..."

Katie didn't know where to begin. There was so much she wanted to tell Pete. But even though he was her very best friend and big brother...there was only so much information he really wanted to know. So, carefully choosing her words she continued.

"I know you think things are moving a little fast for me, but this is different. It feels right; I can't explain it any better than that."

Mumbling because his mouth was full, "Uum uf."

She laughed at him. "You're eating like you haven't had food in a month!"

Pete washed some down with his shake. "Well, hell, they don't give you much and what they do give you isn't this tasty."

"I know you have to get back home. You were supposed to be back a while ago, but will you at least stay for another day or two?"

"I was planning on it...that is if you don't mind me cramping your style?"

Chapter 27

Joe Reid was the first to arrive at the station. Cal escorted him into the main conference room. Shortly thereafter Jim Reid waltzed in. Sgt. Nelsen took him to the small conference room for his interview.

Cal offered Joe a pop. Of course he took one. "Coke -thanks!"

Joe was a big burly 19 year old kid in bib overhauls and messy shoulder length hair. Not the sharpest tool in the shed. Cal knew of the family. The kids had no chance of succeeding in life; least not without better guidance. Their dad was a drunk who had prior domestic battery charges; their mom abandoned them early on because of the father. Both boys had been in and out of trouble since grade school. Minor stuff; nothing like the person they were looking for, but Cal still had to proceed in the direction the case was leading him.

"Joe, I just have a few questions for you. I won't keep you long."

"Sure." Joe popped open the can of Coke and took a swig. "Whatchya need to know?"

"I hear you had a confrontation with Scott Warren?"

"Yeah, what of it?"

"What was the argument about?"

"Don't remember..."

"You don't remember?"

"Nope! He's a jack off. Everyone has issues with the guy."

"Do you know why anyone would want to kill him?"

Joe took another swig of pop, "Nope!"

"What *do* you know Joe?"

Joe stared back at Cal. He didn't like cops, and he especially didn't like to be in the station being questioned by them either. For some reason he started to sweat and the vein on the side of his neck began to pulsate.

"Joe? I'm waiting. What do you know?"

"Nothin' - I know nothin'. Look the guy was a jerk, who knows? All I did was punch him."

"Now, why would you punch Scott?"

"Like I said the guy was a jerk!"

"Is there anyone, and I mean anyone you can think of that might want to do more than just punch Scott?"

"Nope!" Joe said with finality.

That was pretty much the extent of Cal's interview with Joe. Cal knew Joe didn't kill him and kicked him loose.

Nelsen pretty much had the same response from Jim. Jim however was so nervous he couldn't pay attention. Nelsen thought he came in high anyway. He was a smaller version of his brother, but neither one is disciplined enough to murder the way the killer they were looking for was.

It was a dead end.

Some calls started to filter in from different corrections offices in Wisconsin as well as in Illinois. None of them had a convict with the profile to match who they were looking for.

***

Pete woke Katie up from her long nap on the couch. She needed to get ready for work.

She stretched and yawned, "Thanks, Pete...What time is it?"

"It's 7:30."

"Oh...well it felt good to get a long nap in." She sat up and stretched again. "I guess I finally get to go back to work," she joked.

Pete had been eating peanuts in the shell and threw one at her. "Whatever - you slacker!"

Katie chuckled. She didn't have to punch-in until 9 o'clock but came in a little early so she could socialize with everyone she missed. Billie had brought Katie to work and she was the only one of the group that had constant contact with her through everything.

Erik was the first one to welcome her back. He hugged her, picked her up and spun her around. "Katie! I've missed you, Hun!"

"Ah, thanks Erik, but you're squishing me!"

"Ooh! Sorry!" He set her down.

Eddie slinked in and watched the warm welcomes from afar. He wasn't one to get too involved.

Jack surprised Kate when he took hold of her by the shoulders and gave her a big kiss on the cheek. "Glad you're back Red! We missed ya!"

Katie shot Billie a puzzling look.

Bob stepped out of his office with Steve and they both were very happy that Katie was back. "Welcome back, we missed ya, Sweetie!" Bob said as he hugged her.

After Bob, Steve gave her a warm hug. "Man you're a site for sore eyes. The place was drab without ya, Doll!"

"Well, thanks guys! Glad to be back!"

She had to walk past Eddie to go downstairs. Eddie held his arm up so she couldn't pass. "Katie...glad you're back." This time when he talked to her it was more than odd. It seemed sincere enough, but was really creepy at the same time.

"Thanks, Eddie." She said with caution as she glanced down at his arm blocking her way.

He moved it so that she and Billie could pass.

Erik observed the incident and was slightly bothered by it. It was innocent enough but he didn't like Eddie. He knew Eddie was hung up on Katie whether he admitted it or not. Eddie also liked to scare Katie on purpose. And that wasn't cool!

By 10 o'clock the place was really hopping. "Are we giving away free beers tonight or what's the deal?" Katie asked BJ.

Billie laughed and bee-bopped her way to the side of the bar where Jack was working to flirt with him.

Katie liked that Billie was finally happy. It looked like there might be hope for them yet. Jack was good for Billie. He seemed to ground her, and that was a good thing.

By midnight Katie was slowing down. Only two more hours to go, she sighed.

Closing time came, and the last call bell was rung. Billie and Katie picked up in no time, even cleaned out the bathrooms.

They counted their tips. "It was a better night than I thought!" BJ announced.

"Yeah, it sure was." Katie agreed.

Jack was finishing up on the bar glasses and winked at BJ.

Katie had to ask, "So - what's the deal with you two?"

Billie Jo was all bubbly, and her goofy look resembled Pete's from earlier in the day.

"Okay, you can tell me later."

As they walked out, Erik held the door open, "G'night ladies!"

"Good night, Erik!" Then the girls walked out to Billie's little car.

Katie waited for Billie to open the car door and happened to glance over her shoulder back towards the alley out of habit. She wasn't expecting to see anybody. After all, Scott was dead. But she had this lingering suspicion someone was watching. She glanced up to check, and there, leaning against the building, lighting up a cigarette, was a tall dark shadowy figure. Katie's heart stopped for a second, and a lump stuck in her throat.

She heard the door unlock, but she stood frozen in place. It wasn't until Billie called to her did she breath again.

"Hey! You comin'?"

"Do you see him?" Katie said as she leaned into the car to motion for Billie to look behind them.

Billie looked out the back window. The shadowy figure Kate saw was now gone. "Who? I don't see anybody."

Katie looked back to where the guy was standing. She felt a wave of de`javu as she stood there contemplating what she just saw. She was sure someone was there.

"Kate?"

She hopped into Billie's car, "No, I'm good, just go."

Billie's little 4-banger raced as they drove away.

"Who did you see?"

Katie just looked down at her lap shaking her head in disbelief.

"If you think you saw someone we should stop in to see Cal."

"No take me home...Pete's waiting."

"Are you sure?"

Billie thought Katie looked green around the gills.

When they pulled in less than 3-minutes later, Pete was waiting sitting on the front stoop.

Katie shut the car door behind her and walked towards Pete.

He said, "Hi Sweetie, how was..."

But she just past Pete by and walked right into the house, closing the door before he could finish.

Pete instantly knew something wasn't right. Billie was waving Pete over to the car.

"Billie? What just happened?"

"Pete, it was so weird. We had a great night then just as we were getting into the car she froze like she had seen a ghost. I asked if she wanted to stop and see Cal, except she insisted on me bringing her home. I don't know what she saw. I looked in the direction she was staring but nothing was there."

"I'll find out...thanks Billie for driving tonight."

"Sure. She doesn't need any more stalkers, hope everything is okay."

Pete turned to go in the house.

Billie sat at the end of the gravel drive looking left, then right. Home was to the right, and Cal was at the station to the left. She made the decision to see Cal. Her little 4-banger buzzed over the bridge and pulled into the police station lot. She parked right in front and walked in.

Cal looked up from his desk and saw who had walked in. He knew Billie wasn't going to just pop in for a visit. "Billie, what's up?" He said coolly as he greeted her.

"Ah – Cal, Katie is acting weird." Billie wasn't sure what to say or if it was anything to really let him know; nevertheless she thought maybe it was important.

"Weird, how? Did something happen at work?"

"Not really, we had a great night, however when we left she stood outside the car staring like she had seen something. And when I brought her home she never said a word to Pete. Not even a 'hi'. Like I said...weird! I just thought you should know. Maybe she'll tell you what is going on."

"Thanks Billie, I'm just wrapping things up now, so I will head over and see if she'll tell me anything. Are you sure nobody bothered her at work?"

"No – work was good. She was fine until we got to the car."

"All right." Cal was puzzled.

"Well now that I told you about it – I feel better. Laters!" And out the door she went.

Cal went back into his office to put his files in his drawer and turned off the lights and left. Since he worked at the smaller secondary station, he could just lock up when he left.

Pete saw Cal drive up and let him in. Katie was still in the shower, so, Pete offered Cal something to drink.

"I'll take a Pepsi, if you have one."

Pete grabbed a Dew for himself then handed the Pepsi to Cal, and popped his open.

"How long has she been in there?"

"She has been in there since I came in from talking to Billie. Maybe 20 minutes give or take." Then he took a sip of soda.

"Billie stopped by to let me know she saw somebody in the parking lot after work and was acting strange about it. Did she say anything to you?"

"Nope!" Pete strolled over to the bathroom door and knocked. "Hey – did you fall in?"

There was no response, where usually she would yell a smart ass answer back. He spoke through the door again. "Katie, Cal is here, you coming out anytime soon?"

There was momentary silence, and then she hollered, "Yeah, I'll be right out."

Pete sat back down at the kitchen table with Cal, shaking his head. The two men talked while they waited.

"Cal, I was wondering if it would be possible for me to get some of my personal things from my truck tomorrow."

"Sure, Pete. Just give me a call when you want to go, and I will meet you at the city municipal yard."

Then they heard the door creak open. Katie emerged wearing a T-shirt and a pair of sleep pants. Her hair was wet but combed through. She had no makeup on and was flushed from the hot steamy shower.

Cal turned in his chair to greet her with open arms, and she came to him. He enfolded her in his caressing arms and drew her body close to him.

She returned the hug. It felt good. After a lengthy moment she released her hug.

Cal asked, "How did it go tonight?"

Katie padded over to the refrigerator and took out a soda for herself. Then shutting the door behind her, she pulled out the chair between the two men. "Good, we were busy. But I have to tell you; I think I'm losing my mind!"

"How so?" Cal asked.

"I know this isn't going to make any sense, but I could have sworn I saw Scott Warren tonight leaning against the wall outside, smoking a cigarette and watching me. Just as plainly as I used to."

Pete had a confused look on his face. "Kate, Scott's dead!" Then Pete looked over to Cal, "Right?"

Cal didn't say anything at first, he just sat there thinking. After a few seconds he reaffirmed what she already knew, "Katie, you know Scott is dead." Then he continued with his thought. "I have no doubt you did see someone watching you. You have guys at the bar who look at you all the time. However, because of all the stress from what has happened, you just noticed this guy and for whatever reason he gave you a bad vibe."

Pete agreed, "That makes sense."

"No - I know what I saw." She turned to Pete, "Pete, you know I don't get frazzled over nothing. This was different." Turning back to Cal, "He wanted me to see him! I just can't figure out why this guy wants to mess with me. While I was in the shower I started thinking about that. Do you remember when I told you I thought that there was something else going on, that we didn't know?"

Cal's expression changed.

Katie was only just beginning to read Cal, but the look on his face was easy to read.

"What is it, Cal? You made a connection didn't you?"

Pete was intently listening, trying to figure out what they were talking about.

"Katie, it's only a gut feeling, I wish I knew for sure."

"Well, whatever you're thinking, your gut is usually right?"

Cal sat back in his chair, looked directly at Katie, and asked, "Who would want to play games with you? I'm sure you know who it is."

Pete thought that Cal's directness was cold.

Katie was surprised not just with what he asked, but how he asked. "What?"

"Who rubs you the wrong way, Kate? Is there anyone you know that is upset you don't pay attention to them? Is there someone at work that gives you a bad vibe?"

Katie thought first about her co workers. "That's easy...Eddie. He's a creepy jerk who likes messing with me, all the time."

Cal asked, "How? What does he do?"

"He just does things. He'll sneak up behind me and scare the crap out of me. He'll block my path. I don't know, he just does things. I don't know how else to explain it."

Pete said, "Sounds more like a juvenile crush to me."

"Does he threaten you?"

"Well, no..."

"Has he ever asked you out?"

"No."

"Has he done anything or said anything that would warrant you to think this guy is dangerous?"

"Cal - no, but there is something about him that just bothers me."

"Like a pesky little brother or more like a juvenile crush?" Pete asked.

Katie shot back, "No - more like a pain in the butt 'big brother'. Really, none of the above...he's just different."

Cal was a little disappointed that she didn't get a dangerous vibe from Eddie. He didn't like the guy either and was hoping that his gut was right about him.

"Okay, how about any of your customers?"

Katie thought about the ones that really stood out. They didn't give her a bad vibe; they mostly just flirted with her or tried to ask her out. "Sorry, no-one really pops out at me...wait - there was this one guy, I've only seen a couple of times. I think he was looking for someone. I think his name was Charlie? He was big and creepy too, but like I said, I only saw him once."

"Then what makes him come to mind?" Cal asked.

"First of all, he gave me a $50 for a beer and told me to keep the change. He thought he was slick and then asked me out. When I told him no, he winked at me and said something under his breath. After that, one of my regular customers told me 'Charlie was bad news, and to stay away from him'."

Cal, sounding optimistic asked, "Would you know him if you saw him again?"

"Actually I think I would, but the guy from tonight wasn't him."

Cal sat back in his chair and sighed, letting all the air out of his lungs, almost sounding as if he'd been defeated. "Kate, I'd feel better if you let Erik walk you girls to your cars after work. Erik's presence alone should deter anyone from bothering you."

Kate smiled, "Well, that's a fact."

The three sat at the kitchen table discussing different possibilities, and Katie brought up her thoughts as well. Cal had come up with some of the same ideas. She seemed to be reading Cal's mind.

Pete didn't want to leave Katie alone now that this was going on. He didn't feel right about it.

"Pete, you have missed so much work already."

"It's just a job."

"Yeah, a job that isn't easy to come by."

"Pete, I wouldn't want to leave her either. But if I were the one to leave her with you, I'd know she'd be okay."

"Hey, I hear ya, but I'm not leaving until I know she's not in any danger from this guy."

"You know you're going to get sick of me."

"I'm already sick of you, Sis!" Of course he said that with a big grin.

Chapter 28

Katie had slept in. It had been a long night and she needed the sleep. Pete peeked in on her and then quietly closed her door. He gingerly walked down the stairs trying not to make too much noise. He started the coffee maker then stepped out for a smoke.

He stood there on the stoop realizing that he had quit. His hospital stay was the extra help he needed. So, he sat down waiting for the coffee to brew, thinking of all the things he needed to do before he left. Reminding himself to give Debbie a call. He'd have to wait until later this afternoon before her shift started. She had certainly made an impression on him. Pete liked women who could take teasing and give it right back, and Debbie was one of those women. He checked his watch; it was almost 10 o'clock in the morning. He decided to call Cal. It was still too early to call Debbie.

"Cal, its Pete."

"Hey Pete, what's up?"

"Any time you have this morning to go over there?"

"Sure. When are you coming?"

"I can come now. Katie's still sleeping."

"Okay, give me 20-minutes."

"See you then." And Pete hung up the phone. He stepped inside to check the coffee; it was ready.

Pete grabbed a travel mug off the drying rack and started to pour the hot steaming brew, when he heard Katie walking around above him. He hollered up to her, "Want some coffee, Sunshine?" He usually only called her 'Sunshine' when she was being stubborn or ornery.

She was already coming down the stairs when she answered him, "Yep, that's me, little Miss Sunshine!" She joked.

He filled a travel mug for her too, and handed it to her.

"Thanks!"

"I just called Cal, and I'm going to meet him in 20 to reclaim anything I had in my poor truck."

"Do you want me to go with?"

"Good then you can drive. Oh - and you might want to get dressed." He said, looking at her sleep pants and t-shirt.

Katie set her coffee down and started towards the stairs. Stopped, spun around and told Pete, "I am glad you're here. I can't tell you how much it means to me. But now that Scott is dead, I really don't think you need to lose your job to stay here and baby sit me. That isn't going to happen!"

"What-ever…" Pete busted out with a loud laugh and shook his head. "Just go get dressed."

***

Pete and Katie met Cal at the gate of the Municipal garage. Cal walked with them to the back. There Pete's Dodge was all smashed and cut up lying in a heap.

Pete had an affinity for that truck. He walked slowly towards her and placed a hand on the fender. He shook his head in disbelief. "My poor truck...I'm going to miss you girl."

Katie walked over to her grieving friend, and patted him on the back. "Pete, it'll be okay, she was a good truck while you had her. You'll get another truck." She said, placating him in a sarcastic tone.

"Not funny, Kate! I just set her up the way I like and now look at her. Just look at her!"

Pete turned to Cal and asked, "They had to cut me out?"

"Yeah, they did Pete. I have the pictures to prove it...if you really want to see."

"Actually I would."

"Sure, we can go back to my office when we're done here."

Pete searched his truck for anything that wasn't broken. He didn't have much in the glove box. Under his seat was one CD that was okay, it just happened to be Van Halen's '1984'. Pete got a kick out of that! Even Katie laughed. Cal figured it must be a private joke between them, because he didn't get it.

His keys, a flashlight, the CD and a jean jacket were all he could retrieve.

"So much for that!" Pete stated. "Were you serious about showing me the pictures?"

Cal never gave empty offers. "Sure let's go to the office."

They didn't need to drive far; the station was only around the corner from where they were. Once in Cal's office they were seated, and Cal shut the door behind him. He pulled out a file from his bottom desk drawer. "Pete, I know you want to see these, however I will warn you; they are startling." Then he placed some of the photos out for Pete and Katie to see.

Katie was the first to react to them, and she was shocked. "Pete, you are so lucky to be here! I am so surprised you lived through that!"

Pete sat there picking up each one and studying them.

Cal could tell by the intense look on Pete's face that Pete was trying to recall what happened.

Katie caught Cal's watchful gaze, and returned a wary smile.

Pete held a picture of himself lying upside down in his truck, bloody and unconscious. He stared at that picture for a long time. Then he finally said, "Whoever did this is very dangerous. He was trying to get me away from the house and away from Katie. This was his attempt at killing me, Cal. I think Katie's right. There is something we're missing. He isn't after the drugs. Druggies are stupid. This guy is smart." He glanced up from the photograph to Cal. "He wants Kate."

Katie gasped, "What?"

Cal chimed in, "I think so, too."

"Wait a minute! How do you come to that conclusion from a picture of you?"

Both Pete and Cal looked directly at Kate. A daunting truth stared her in the face.

Cal's rich velvet voice hardened, "Kate, a man who was entering your home turns up murdered not 300 yards from your house. Pete is hit in the head so hard that any normal man, no offense, would have died, and then he and his truck get driven off the deepest end of the quarry. Now you say there is a guy watching you, and he's making sure you see him."

She sat there absorbing it all in. Katie's spoke with vehemence, "But why? And who? What does he want from me?" Katie had a renewed strength; she was angry and that was a good thing.

Cal answered, "That, is what I've been working on. I wish I had the answers. I was hoping you felt Eddie Landers was dangerous."

"Yeah, this is why I'm not leaving!" Pete decisively told Katie. "If I have to sit at the Brick Yard and watch you work, and then escort you home every night, until this guy is caught - that's what I'm going to do!"

"No, Pete, you're not!" She was very firm in her response.

Cal broke in, "Kate, I know you don't like it, but Pete is right. You need someone to keep an eye on you until we catch the guy who did this."

"And how long is that going to take? I'm not trying to be flippant here, but realistically we don't have a clue who he is, do we? Or if we're dealing with the same guy; it's only a theory we have."

Cal understood her ominous questions and with good reason. She couldn't be guarded all the time, and so far he hadn't gotten any answers from any of his inquiries.

Chapter 29

Billie came by to pick up Katie for work. She never even got out of her car when Katie slammed the door behind her and marched to the car with purpose. She hopping in next to Billie and snapped, "Let's go!"

Billie could read Katie's mood and it wasn't good. She started up her little car and raced out onto the road. She refrained from asking Katie anything until they were at the stop sign past Fox's Liquor Store. "Okay – what's with the attitude?"

Katie glared at Billie for even asking.

"Oh no - you don't get to be like this and not expect me to ask why!"

Even though Kate's foul mood was tempestuous, she knew she couldn't take it out on Billie.

"To make a long story short - Pete and Cal have a theory on what's been going on; that there is a connection between who killed Scott and drove Pete over the edge in the quarry. Also they think that it might be the guy who I saw last night, and that he's playing games with me. Now Cal and Pete both think I need to be 'baby sat'! Can you believe that?"

Billie was stunned to hear that it may be all related, "If that *is* true Kate, then you do need someone to watch you."

"Et tu Brute?" At least Katie smiled when she said it.

They parked in the front of the bar. They weren't supposed to but Billie figured Bob and Erik wouldn't mind, considering there could be someone stalking Katie.

Erik waited for the girls to enter before commenting. "What's that, you ladies think you get 'car blanch'?" He winked at Billie and smiled. Cal had called Erik earlier in the day and asked him to keep an eye on 'Red'. Erik wasn't going to let anything happen while she was at work.

Steve and Tanya who were working the upstairs bar were joking with Eddie. Tanya was always such a big flirt. Just seeing Eddie having fun annoyed Erik. He thought anyone who was in the military should conduct themselves in a manner befitting a U.S. soldier and as much as Eddie bragged, he fell short in every category. He certainly wasn't a dedicated employee, especially when he would just disappear instead of working the door like he was supposed to. Eddie only seemed interested in bragging about being a Ranger when it benefited his cause. He was different people depending upon who he was with. Erik couldn't figure him out. Eddie would be the quiet shy guy, then turn around and be a want-to-be braggart. It was like working with "Sybil". If they could find another bouncer, Erik would love to get rid of him.

Feeling Erik's scrutinizing gaze Eddie decided it was time to take his place at the front door and actually do some work.

Downstairs Jessica and Jack were tending bar. Katie was retrieving a round of drinks for the band and Billie was standing at the end of the bar talking to her while she waited.

"You're in a better mood."

"I guess; I know they're right, I just don't like it is all."

Jack placed the drinks on Kate's tray, and then she left to deliver them to the band.

Jack asked Billie, "You looked worried. What's up?"

"I'm concerned." She replied as she watched Katie.

Jack knew what Billie was referring to and he couldn't understand why someone would want to hurt Katie.

Jack grew up in Burlington and loved it here. It was a laid back friendly place to live. The only trouble they ever really had was from a local biker gang, the "7-Sons of Sin". Now, the murder had everyone edgy.

The band was to go on at 10 o'clock. Erik would start letting people down around 9:30.

Pete wanted to be at the bar with Katie, but she put her foot down and wouldn't have it. He only wanted to see if he noticed anyone paying extra attention to her while she worked. Pete thought to himself, *"She told me I couldn't be in the bar, but she didn't say anything about me waiting for her outside."* Unfortunately, he was without a vehicle, and Katie's red Nova wasn't exactly low key. So, he called Cal.

"Cal, it's Pete; I was wondering if there was any way to get you to drop me off at the Brick Yard."

Cal laughed, "She told you to stay home, huh?"

"Kinda. But she didn't tell me I couldn't hang out in the parking lot and wait for her to get off of work."

"Kate's not going to be too happy that you're doing this."

"I really don't care. She'll be pissed, but she'll get over it. I need to see for myself if there is anyone who I find to be particularly interested in Kate; just to satisfy my own curiosity, I guess."

Cal agreed to give him a lift. Within 10-minutes Cal was picking Pete up. "You really want to do this?"

Pete gave Cal a sideways glance.

Cal drove Pete to the backside of the Brick Yard; police cars tend to attract attention. "Do me a favor while you're watching, keep an eye on Eddie. I don't trust him. Maybe it's his lack of social skills, but there is something about him that's been nagging me." Cal said, as he came to a stop letting Pete out.

"If I see anything I'll give you a call." Pete shut the door and Cal pulled away.

Pete walked between two buildings and stood on Pine Street surveying a spot to watch the bar from. Cal suspected the doorman, Eddie, so he strolled a crossed the street three businesses down making sure not to be seen by Eddie. He then walked through the back alley to the little bakery directly across from the Brick Yard. It was perfect. The street light didn't reach that side. The bushes on either side of the steps made a small nook in which Pete could sit in the shadows. A few minutes had past when he realized he didn't have any smokes. "Damn it! Fine time for me to quit smoking!"

He had a pack of gum with him, not as satisfying but it would have to do. He checked his watch; it was 1 o'clock, an hour and a half to go before the bar closed.

People started leaving the bar; only a few at first. A heated argument was brewing in the lot next door between a man and what appeared to be his girlfriend. She hauled off and slapped him so hard that Pete heard it all the way over to where he was sitting. "Make that his ex-girlfriend!" He thought to himself with a chuckle.

More people filtered out. A small group continued their party outside, congregating in the parking lot by their cars.

Pete glanced back to the front windows of the bar. Eddie was gone. Pete checked the time; it was 2 o'clock. Last call. Looking back up, he saw Eddie stepping outside. He was casually leaning against the front of the Brick Yard, with his hands in his front pockets, and his right foot propped up behind him on the wall. Pete almost felt Eddie watching him. *"He can't see me can he?"*

A squad car turned the corner and past by slowly. Ed nodded at the cop and the squad continued on its way. Eddie went back inside the bar. Pete still wasn't so sure if he could be seen. He checked his watch again; 2:15.

Erik and Eddie could be seen clearing out the bar. A group of young girls flocked around Eddie flirting with him. One of them handed him what looked like a piece of paper with their phone number on it. The girls left giggling. The one who had given him what seemed like a piece of paper looked back over her shoulder at Ed to see if he had been watching her walk away.

He was, and gave her a big smile and a thankful nod. That made her obviously happy.

Pete didn't feel Eddie was dangerous, although "chicks dig jerks" and "bad boys".

Pete's rear end was falling asleep. He had been sitting on the cement steps too long and needed to stretch. He stealthy got up and moved around to between the bakery and the insurance company. Still in shadow he stretched and cracked his back. Oh that felt good.

Needing a fresh piece of gum Pete unwrapped another stick and placed the stale chewed piece in the wrapper. He flicked the little silver ball he made into the trash can on the sidewalk. Now he only had 20 minutes before Billie and Katie would leave the bar. He never saw anyone who fit Katie's description.

It was now 10 minutes to 3 o'clock. Erik held the front door open for Billie and Katie. They looked to be in a jovial mood. Jack followed them out. While Katie waited for Billie to unlock her door, Jack took Billie aside whispered in her ear and gave her a quick kiss.

Pete noticed Tanya's reaction to this. She was very unhappy, slamming her car door and gunned the engine before she took off. Katie and Billie noticed too, since Tanya was parked right across from them. Pete caught Eddie also watching them from the front window of the bar. Billie drove off taking Katie home. Without anything else to see, Pete took out his cell to call Cal for a ride back to the house.

Pete walked to the next block over so no one would know he was across the street. Cal picked him up there.

"Thanks, Cal."

"Sure! Did you see anyone who might fit the description Katie gave?"

"Nope! I had some entertainment, but I didn't see anyone suspicious. Even Eddie seemed normal." Pete could tell Cal was disappointed.

Hesitantly, Cal asked, "Would you mind doing this again when she works? Maybe he only comes on certain nights."

"Yeah, I can do that."

Cal pulled into Kate's driveway and with a smile sneaking across his face asked, "So, what's your story?"

Pete laughed. "I don't have one."

Cal suggested, "You could always say you were hanging out with me. The station is within walking distance from here."

"Katie will know I'm lying. She can tell when I am less than truthful."

Cal smiled, "Well good luck with that!"

Pete offered, "What - aren't you coming in?"

"Oh, no! You can tell me how it goes later."

Pete leaned in and said, "Chicken shit!"

Cal replied with a little laugh. Then Pete shut the car door. He almost made it to the front stoop before Katie met him at the door.

She saw it was Cal who was leaving, already pulling out onto the highway.

All Pete could say was, "Hey, how was work?"

Katie had the same disapproving look his mother gave him when he would come home after curfew. He had to chuckle. He couldn't help himself. "What?"

She glared at him and asked, "Why were you at the bar?"

"You saw me?" He asked.

"I didn't have to, you just admitted it."

"Like you actually thought I was going to just sit here?"

"Cal brought you home, was he in on this, too?"

Pete straight faced told her flat out, "No." Then he said with a grin, "But he did bring me home."

Katie gave Pete another one of her probing looks, and then let him enter the house.

"Sis, why are you being so difficult about this? You need to look at this differently. We care about you and don't want anything to happen to you. If this guy who's watching you is the same one who did this to me…"

"I know, Pete! I'm not upset with you. I'm upset with the situation. I don't like feeling, like I'm not in control of my life. What did I do to this guy? Did I see or over hear something I wasn't supposed to? What do I have that he wants? The drugs and money are gone. I just don't get it Pete!"

It didn't make any sense to Pete either. But he knew he got in the way of whatever this guy wanted and almost lost more than his truck. He had an epiphany. "Katie, I think I know how we can get this guy to show himself."

"How's that?"

"Let me sleep on it." Pete pulled out his cell phone and started dialing. "I'm calling Cal, we'll all have breakfast in the morning, and I'll tell ya then. Cal, its

Pete. Are you able to meet us for breakfast in the morning? I have an idea."

"She didn't ground you did she?" Cal probed half way joking.

"Ha-ha, no it's all good." Pete smiled and winked at Katie.

"I don't have to be in until noon tomorrow so breakfast sounds great. Where?"

Pete shrugged his shoulders, not that Cal would see but Pete's a pretty animated guy. "Kate, where do you want to go for breakfast?" Pete asked.

"Sonny's isn't too far."

Cal heard her over the line, "That's fine. Can we make it 9 o'clock?"

Pete agreed.

Chapter 30

Sunday morning Cal met Pete and Katie at Sonny's. Sonny's Diner was a little greasy spoon on the out skirts of town in Bohner's Lake. A small Mom-and-Pop joint that didn't look like much, but the food was terrific.

A shriveled up, overly tanned waitress gave them menus, and poured coffee in brightly colored cups of coral, ocean blue and lime green.

A table of old retired gents in the middle of the room shot the bull and joked with their waitress.

Katie already knew what she wanted this morning so she needn't bother looking at the menu. When the waitress came back for their orders. Katie ordered a country skillet and a tomato juice. Pete ordered the Eggs Benedict with American fries and Cal ordered the short stack pancakes with bacon and sausage, with a tall orange juice.

Cal took Kate's hand under the table and held it.

Katie was eager to hear what Pete came up with. "Alright, spill. Tell us your idea."

Pete paused and looked at Katie for a long time before he spoke. Then turning to Cal he said, "I think I should leave."

"What?" Cal and Katie were both puzzled.

"Now listen." He said as he turned his attention back to Katie. "This guy only needs to think I left. Then, he'll make a bolder move, and that's when we'll catch him."

Kate searched deeply into Pete's eyes, and then spoke clearly, "You want to use me as bait!"

"Oh no, that's a bad idea!" Cal almost growled.

Pete put his one good hand up, "Hold on, just hear me out. He wanted me gone so I'm going. Not really but he won't know that. He's bound to come out of the woodwork to get to you Katie. We won't let it get that far but we're going to make it easier on him is all."

Cal clenched his teeth. His steely-grey eyes seared into Pete.

Katie spoke up, "You're right!"

"I am? Can I get that in writing; cuz' it doesn't happen too often?" Pete said with some surprise in his voice.

Cal barked, "No, he's not!"

"I think this could work." Katie chimed.

"What? Kate, you can't be serious?" Cal was baffled.

"Cal, if he thinks I'm alone, he'll make a mistake and come after whatever he's looking for. With Pete at the house it just delays the inevitable."

"Do you hear yourself?"

"Think about it, Cal. You could put surveillance back on my house and see who shows. When he does, you grab him."

"Kate, I want to get this guy too, but not by putting you in jeopardy."

"Cal, she won't be. We'll be there or at least you will be. I can watch the bar from the outside the nights she works to make sure no one bothers her in the parking lot."

Cal didn't like the idea and had no qualms about expressing that. "Would you listen to yourselves? This isn't some game! I won't put you in harm's way. We don't have any idea what he's after. What if it's you he wants? Look at what he did to Pete!"

Cal took Katie's hand again, and looking into her bright eyes said, "I can't use you as bait. I won't." His smoky voice was strong yet tender.

Katie could feel how much she meant to Cal. But she felt this was the best way to get it over and done with, faster. She had lived with someone stalking her for months now. She wanted it to stop. She met Cal's gaze and in a reassuring voice said, "Its okay, Cal."

"No, its not!"

That sharp remark got Katie's haunches up. "Well, I don't like having to be baby sat! And for who knows how long? If we try what Pete suggested it could be over sooner than later. I don't necessarily like being used for bait, either but I trust you, and I'll be fine."

Pete was sitting on the edge of his seat. He knew Katie all too well, and her tone was one that said she was doing what she wanted - regardless. He thought to himself, *"She's back..."* Pete certainly didn't mean to stir up any conflict between Katie and Cal. That wasn't his intention.

Cal's voice hardened. "You two are nuts! What if something goes terribly wrong? Like I said before, what if it's not something that he wants - but you, Kate? Have you thought of that? Anything could happen with you alone in that house."

Katie, who was still holding Cal's hand, gave an extra reassuring squeeze. "I want to do this, Cal. I want this to be over." She said looking directly into his troubled grey eyes.

Cal softened his tone. "I don't like it."

Katie said, "I'm doing this."

With infliction in his voice Cal stated, "You are the most stubborn..."

Pete who had been sipping is hot coffee chuckled. "You're just figuring that out are ya?"

Katie shot Pete a look of sibling disdain.

Their waitress brought them their food, and then topped off their coffee.

There was obvious tension at the table. Pete was starving ,so he wasn't going to let it disrupt his meal. Katie's skillet was extremely hot so she poked at it with her fork to release some steam and let it cool down before she attempted to eat it. Cal who lost his appetite took his time buttering his pancakes.

The silence was deafening. Cal had been mulling everything over in his head; decided he wasn't going to let this get in the way of any future he might have with Kate. She was definitely head - strong. And considering what she had been through in the past, he could understand why she wanted this to be over. He just couldn't stand the thought of her getting hurt. Changing his tone with her he said, "Kate, I know you think this is the best way to get this guy to come out, but I'm not entirely convinced. I also know that you have your mind made-up, and whether I agree to this or not you're going forth with it." Cal then turned his attentions to Pete who was enjoying his Eggs Benedict. "Pete, I hope you're right."

Katie was picking at her skillet. She wasn't very hungry any more either.

Cal took a long drink of his coffee. Then broke off a piece of sausage with his fork and ate it. "So, when were you planning on 'leaving'?"

Katie looked up from her skillet to Cal. Pete stopped chewing for a moment. Swallowed, and then took a sip of coffee to wash it down. "If we can, I'd like to pack today and 'leave' first thing in the morning. But here's the thing; I would kind of need to stay with you if I could. It's within walking distance from the bar, and I'm still without wheels."

Cal smiled. "I figured as much."

The tension lightened up, and they ate their breakfasts mixed with lighter conversation.

Cal picked up the tab. He walked Katie and Pete out to her car. Pete gingerly got in the passenger side, carefully shutting the door. He knew how particular Katie was when it came to her car. There was no slamming these doors.

Cal reached around Kate and placed his hand on the small of her back bringing her close to him. "You know how much you mean to me?" He asked her.

Katie's eyes locked on his. She was on her tip toes looking up at him, practically nose to nose. He met her the rest of the way, and kissed her hard. When their lips finally unlocked, Katie felt like she was floating on air. She loved his kisses. They all seemed to have different meanings and emotions behind them. This one told her he loved her without him saying it.

"I have to get to work. I'll call you later."

"Sure..."

He gave her another quick kiss, this time on the cheek, before she got in the car. He carefully closed her door tight. She started up the small block 350 and it rumbled to life. The horse power in that little Nova made the car shake. She idled out on to the road and eased into the accelerator. It quickly stopped the idle shaking, and soundly disappeared down the highway. Cal watched her go, and then turned to get into his car which had been parked right alongside of Kate's. He was being plagued by his emotions, and the weight of this case was starting to take a toll on him. A million things were going through his mind. Before he knew it he was pulling into the station. Sgt. Nelsen and Gentry were already working at their desks when he came in.

Cal walked through to his office. He sat down at his desk and pulled out the case file; which was slowly growing. He checked messages; nothing important. At least not the message he had been waiting for from the C.I.D.

Cal was troubled. He went back over all his notes. *There has to be something here that we overlooked. Something that will tell us who this guy is.*

Nelsen knocked on the door interrupting Cal deep in thought.

Cal looked up and motioned for Nelsen to enter.

"Chapman?"

"Yeah, what's up, Sergeant?"

"Can I have a private word with you?"

"Sure, close the door behind you. Have a seat."

"Cal, you and I have been friends for a while...I don't want you to take this the wrong way..."

"Just say it, Jim." Cal was blunt and appreciated directness from his friends as well.

"Cal I know you've been seeing Katie McGuire. And I know this can't be easy. But are you sure you aren't too close to this case?"

Cal's steely-grey eyes turned cold. Questioning where that came from, he raised an eyebrow to Nelsen.

"I just need to know that you can keep it together if something happens."

"My personnel life is none of your business, Jim."

"It is, if you're too close to the subject."

"Kate is not the subject. Kate's the victim here."

"Could be? But don't you think that your feelings could be enhanced because she needs saving? Cops can't get emotionally attached to those we're trying to help!"

Cal cut Jim off, "I met her before any of this happened. My feelings for her are not because she needs saving!"

"Look – all I'm saying is someone took out her overly protective friend and almost killed him. Considering all the cash and pot we took from her house and the body that was found not more than 300-yards from her. I'd say I have right to ask if you can handle it."

Cal sat back in his chair strongly considering Jim's request. "Do you honestly believe I can't?"

Jim had been a cop for a long time and was about ready to retire. He and Cal were friends, but as a friend he needed to know where Cal's head was. "I have no doubts that you can work this case. You are a great cop and good at your job. I am only questioning because of all the hours you've been putting in. And you know if this were anywhere else, you'd be off this case."

"I do."

"This can't be easy on you Cal. But you can't continue to put in the hours you have been, and what happens when this guy who murdered one guy and almost killed another - gets Kate?"

Those words struck home. Cal had already been thinking the same thing on his way in to work. "Jim, I need all the help I can get here. This guy is going to make a mistake and when he does we need to be there. Pete is leaving tomorrow, so Katie will be all alone in that house. I want to put surveillance on her house."

"With what? Cal you know we can't put anymore guys on this; we don't have the man power nor the funds. We're a small department and what you want can't happen!" Nelsen sighed, "But, we will do what we can. Okay?"

"I know Jim, and thanks...By the way, the day I feel I can't handle a case - is the day I turn it all over to you."

Jim snickered. "Yeah, you only have 18-months to rely on me you know?"

"That many, huh?" Cal smiled.

There were no hard feelings. Jim just wanted reassurance that Cal was focused.

Chapter 31

Pete didn't have much to pack. Katie sat on the edge of his bed swinging her feet. "I'm gonna miss you, Pete."

"Yeah, I'm going to miss you, too."

"It sure will be quiet around here!"

He shot her a dirty look even though he knew she was teasing.

"Do you really think this is going to work?"

Pete pulled the tie shut on his duffle bag and then set it on the floor. He stepped up in front of Katie and very somberly said, "Sweetie, I really do. I have this feeling he's a predator. He's been hunting you and he'll have a chance to make his move once I'm gone."

"Cal isn't very happy about this."

"I know it."

They headed downstairs.

Pete didn't like using Katie to catch this guy either, especially considering all she'd been through.

Pete set his bag down by the front door.

Katie had a roast cooking in the oven and the heavenly smells wafted through the entire house making Pete hungry.

"Damn that smells good! When's dinner?"

"In about an hour. I've invited Billie and Jack over too."

"I didn't know we were having a dinner party." He said raising an eye brow at her.

"Consider it your going away party."

"Gotch ya!"

Only Pete, Cal and Kate knew he really wasn't going anywhere.

Cal had been staring at the autopsy report, along with his notes for hours. He knew he had to be looking for someone with military experience, most likely Special Forces training, but whom? Eddie Landers was the one he would bet money on but nothing at either crime scene could be tied directly to him. It just didn't make any sense; how was he tied to all of this? However Ed's trademark boots and his sore leg kept him as Cal's number one. That and the way he looked at Kate like she was prey. He kept telling himself it wasn't jealousy, it was something else. Cal had been staring at the case file so long that his eyes were giving him a headache. He put his thumb and fore-finger to his eye lids and rubbed, relieving some pressure. He then opened his top desk drawer to find a bottle of Excedrin. He took two and reached for his water when he realized what time it was. *Shoot! I'm supposed to be going to Katie's for dinner.* He thought to himself.

It was getting late and he needed to pack it in for the day when the phone rang.

"Detective Chapman," he answered.

The familiar voice on the other end was a woman. "Stacey?"

"So, you do remember?"

"What can I do for you Stacey?" Cal's tone was straight forward and lacked any warmth.

"That's right, you always were all business…I'm returning your call."

"My call? What are you talking about?"

"Aren't you looking for a murder suspect?"

"I am."

"Well your father helped me out so I'm with CID now."

"So, this is business?"

"I'd like to think both…but I know that ship has sailed."

"Stacey – do you have something for me or not?"

"Okay…" She gave a subtle sigh and got right to the point. "Based on the criteria you gave us, I have three men that fit your profile. One is in the Janesville area; one is in the LaCrosse area. But the one in the Milwaukee area stands out as your number one. Edward C. Landers; kicked out of Special Forces training because of personality traits. Drill instructor caught him doing something disturbing and sent him to a military psychologist team. They discharged him other than honorable. According to this he's in your area."

Finally the CID comes through with the information of the century. Cal couldn't believe it. He always had a feeling about Eddie; his gut was right.

"Stacey I'm going to need you to send me everything you have. I need the details of the psychiatric diagnosis."

"*That* is privileged! You know how this works Calvin. You're going to have to ask for it through proper channels."

Cal caught on to the discontent in Stacey's tone, "Well then, you can expect on receiving that warrant for his psych records. Thanks for the call Stacey." Cal hung up. He was excited about the information, but now he had real concern for Kate's well being. Now there wasn't much he could do until morning, and left for Kate's.

By the time Cal arrived, dinner had been placed on the table. He could smell the wonderful meal Kate had prepared from outside.

He let himself in, "Sorry I'm late. I had something to tie up at the office."

Katie greeted Cal with a peck on the cheek. She was happy to see him.

Both Katie and Pete caught a change in Cal's mood from this morning.

She poured a glass of red wine and Cal joined them at the table.

Chapter 32

Cal was in bright and early. There was so much to do. He grabbed a cup of hot coffee and sat down to start making his first of many phone calls this morning when Nelsen strolled in. Cal waved him into his office.

Nelsen also grabbed a cup of coffee on the way in. "What's up, Chapman?"

"Come in, I want you to hear this." Cal said as he finished dialing the phone. The call was to the County State's Attorney's Office. Cal was making an appointment to see them - then faxed the warrant fact sheet over. When he got off the phone Jim had the strangest look on his face. "What did I miss?"

"CID called last night. All we have to do now is go through all the bullshit bureaucracy to make sure when we get Eddie - it sticks."

"Eddie? You mean the bouncer at the Brick Yard?"

"One in the same."

"You always had a bad feeling about him. Are you sure?"

"That's why I have to get the County State's Attorney to get a subpoena from the U.S. States Attorney to get Edward C. Landers' psych records from JAG. It's a lot of paper work, and we need to get started right away if I'm going to get Eddie in here for questioning. I don't have any doubt he killed Scott Warren, nor do I have any doubt he tried to kill Pete. We just need to prove it. And when we do, I don't want the bastard walking."

Jim wasn't too surprised that Cal thought it was Eddie. Eddie was different. Kind of quirky, and when Cal didn't like somebody it was for good reason. Jim trusted Cal's instincts about people because he was usually right about them. Now that Cal was more than certain that it was Eddie they were interested in as a murder suspect, it was going to be easier to keep an eye on Katie. Except for the fact that Eddie and Kate worked together. In Jim's long experience you never wanted to let them know you were coming. They didn't want Eddie to spook and do something crazy to Katie.

* * *

At Cal's meeting he added a copy of the medical examiner's full report as part of his own. His summation of all the information leads to narrow his investigation down to Edward C. Landers, as their number one suspect.

Cal strongly urged the State's Attorney, "This suspect is likely the murderer, and based on these facts they point to probable cause prima-facie case of proof at first glance."

Cal was given his subpoena for military psych records for Edward C. Landers, by the U.S. Attorney and served the JAG office in Fort Brag, N.C.

Cal was thrilled things were finally moving in the right direction.

Chapter 33

As Katie and Pete were walking out the door Katie saw the empty hook when she reached for her keys.

"Pete, do you still have a key?"

"Key - what key?"

"I'm missing the extra house key and thought you had it."

Pete pulled out his key chain, "Nope! Wait...I did take a key that night...I...I forgot all about it. But, I had it in my pocket and I haven't come across it. Maybe it's in the heap that used to be my truck?" Pete felt a sudden dread, that now, who ever tried to kill him had to have taken it when he took his truck keys. The look on his face said it all.

"Pete? He's got my house key, doesn't he?" She asked feeling like the wind was just knocked out of her.

"I think he might. Let's forget this. It's too easy for him to just walk in here. I'll tell Cal we're not doing this. He'll be happy about that."

Katie shook it off. "No, I still want to catch this guy. I'm just not feeling as brave about it as I was 30-seconds ago", as she locked the door behind her.

After they drove around for a while, she drove past Cal's and slowed to a stop a few houses down. Pete had to walk through the backyards and sneak in Cal's back door. Just in case someone would see that Pete didn't really leave.

"Hey, you be careful, okay, Sis?"

***

Both Eddie and Erik were at the door when Katie came into work that night.

Erik gave Katie a wink, "Hey, sweetheart! You're looking fine!"

Katie gave Erik one of her beautiful thankful smiles. She felt good too. Wearing a form fitted denim skirt that showed off her curvy legs with a black clingy cap sleeve shirt. "Thanks, Erik!"

"I heard your friend Pete went back home?" Erik asked.

This caught Eddie's attention.

"He did. He couldn't miss any more work." Katie turned to go down stairs, "Well, I'll talk to you guys later."

Eddie couldn't help but stare at her; thinking about how sexy she was, the way her wavy red-hair flowed over her shoulders, and how he wanted to feel her curvy legs wrapped around him.

Erik noticed Eddie was looking too long and elbowed him. "Hey, pay attention to the door."

Downstairs Jack was whispering sweet nothings in Billie's ear.

"I see how you are! The first good looking guy comes along, and you dump your friend like an old wet newspaper!" Katie said teasingly.

Jack winked at her.

Billie was happy to see Katie kidding around again. "So you took Pete back today?"

"I did, it sure is quiet now that he's gone." She smiled.

"Do you think we're going to be busy tonight?" BJ asked no one in particular.

Jack shrugged and continued setting up the bar the way he liked it.

Katie set up her serving tray; cash in the pocket and quarters in the rocks glass on top of a few napkins. She asked for a bottle of water from Jack.

"Sure, Red."

Billie was glad to find a guy that Katie not only liked but also got along with. Katie usually never approved of the guys Billie dated; although they really never stayed around too long any way. Jack was different. They weren't technically dating, just "hanging out". It was frustrating for BJ, but she'd take whatever time Jack was willing to give her.

By 11 o'clock Katie figured everyone would know Pete was gone and she'd be alone again. News traveled fast.

Pete, who was camped out at Cal's was edgy and apprehensive. If he had to sit there any longer, it would surely drive him nuts.

Cal, never liked the idea in the first place, and was following up on any and all information he had on Eddie. He was right about the suspect having military training. The focus was all on Eddie now. He called Pete before he left for the bar. Pete had to be extra careful not to let Eddie suspect he's being watched.

Pete jumped up out of the chair he was sitting in. "She knew all along that Eddie was a creep! So, he's the ass that did this to me?"

"I believe so, Pete. That's why we can't let him know we're watching him. He has had Special Forces training, and probably already senses we're onto him. He's very dangerous, and we have to be careful not to spook him. My men and I will keep a close eye on Kate's."

When they hung up, Pete's adrenaline was pumping so hard he could have flown to the Brick Yard. Pete was extra careful when crossing the street to the south, then headed up the back alley to the little bakery across the street from the bar. Pete glared at Eddie through the glass doors. Staying in the shadows, Pete was fully aware of every move Eddie made, until he took a break. Then he was out of sight. Pete timed the 15-minute breaks like clockwork. Eddie, if anything, was precise about his breaks. Around closing Pete observed how Eddie interacted with a few young women who approached him. He'd smile, but not really talk to any of them.

Not much of a talker, Pete noticed.

A squad car made its rounds, doing a sweep of the lot next door and then passed on by.

Soon, Erik walked Katie out to her car along with Jack and Billie. Pete just kept his eye on Eddie.

Eddie had no real response to Katie. Just a nod and 'have a good night.'

After Eddie and Erik were locked up they went their separate ways. Erik was parked around the corner, but Eddie was parked behind the Brick Yard. Pete could barely see the back lot from where he was standing. He waited, and watched for head lights to go on. Then, he saw movement of a vehicle leaving the back lot.

So much for any excitement. Keeping to the shadows, Pete moseyed back to Cal's. Not much happened here in town after hours, so he walked in the dark without anyone seeing.

It had been a good night at work for Katie. Not super busy but steady. She didn't notice anyone watching her tonight and didn't feel anyone staring either.

Billie left with Jack. Katie figured things had progressed nicely between them, and, she was happy for Billie.

Her house was dark except for the front porch light. She closed the door and locked it behind her, thinking how ironic. If he has the key, he'll let himself in so why am I locking the door? Just to slow him down? Katie set her purse down on the antique flour bin and hung up her keys. "Damn – I wish I knew for sure where my key was." She was in a good mood despite the weight of knowing someone out there, was after her and might have the key to the house.

Katie showered and got ready for bed. The house was too quiet, now that Pete wasn't there anymore. She was just about to crawl into bed when the phone rang. It was Pete calling, "Hello!"

"Hey, Sis! How did it go tonight?"

"It was good..."

Pete was reluctant to let her go but didn't want her to worry needlessly. "Okay, then, I was just checking on ya."

"I know."

"G'night Sis, sleep tight!"

"Good night, Pete."

Katie assumed Cal or one of the officers would be driving through soon. She closed her phone and laid it on the small night stand by her bed. Then covered herself up and stretched out. It felt good. In no time at all she was falling asleep.

***

Gloved hands cautiously turned the key, unlocking and slowly opening the door to Katie's home. The stranger found his way to the staircase. He recalled how the old stairs could give him away. So, he climbed the wooded steps with vigilance, and crept stealthily up to Katie's bedroom. He stood in her doorway for a moment just watching her sleep. He was about to step in to get closer, but suddenly stopped when she turned over. He waited a few seconds then proceeded to the right side of her bed. However, he inadvertently stepped down on a creaky floorboard, which gave him away. He paused, waiting for a response from Katie.

She heard it. Although she didn't respond, all of her senses were now heightened. Lying perfectly still, she carefully moved her hand under her pillow and wrapped her fingers around the knife she concealed. She was terrified to move. Katie intently listened to the dark.

When she gave no signs acknowledging his presence, the stranger came even closer to her. His low steady breathing was faint but she could hear him. She was so anxious, a wave of panic pushed through, and she tried hard not to tremble. *"Just play dead girl."* She thought to herself. Her heart was thumping so hard in her chest - she was afraid the intruder might hear it as loudly as she did. As he reached the side of her bed, his cologne hit her nostrils. She did know who it was. A chill ran through her.

He reached out to her, touching her silky hair. She barely flinched closing her fingers more tightly around the handle of her knife. He inhaled deeply, breathing in her scent. She smelled like spring. So fresh and beautiful, he couldn't stand to watch her from a distance any more. This was the night he was going to have her. The thought of taking this beautiful woman made his organ begin to swell. Although, before he could do anything, the sound of a car rolling down the gravel in front of the house distracted him. The stranger swiftly went to look out the window.

Now was Katie's chance. Flooded with adrenaline, she jumped up out of bed just as he carefully parted the curtains to peer out.

He was completely taken by surprise and bolted from her bedroom, taking the stairs 3 and 4 at a time. He didn't have any other choice but to leave by the front door. It was a squad car that had pulled in and was circling in the implement lot. He bolted out the door and ran north past the large tractors and over the highway to the farm across the way. Katie came running out of her house and then cop saw her and quickly drove over as she was flagging him down.

Her heart was racing, Katie yelled, "There was a man in my house! He just ran out, didn't you see him?"

The officer hadn't seen anything. He must have been turning the squad around as the stranger escaped exiting through the front. He immediately called for backup.

Chapman heard the call go out and in no time Cal was pulling into Katie's driveway.

A Stranger in the Night

He barely parked the cruiser before racing over to her side. Katie was shaking so hard that her body seemed to be convulsing. She wasn't crying but she could hardly catch her breath, and everything seemed surreal to her at the moment.

Once Cal was with her the other officer stepped aside. He put his arm around her and pulled her close to him. In a soft gentle caring voice Cal asked, "Are you alright? Did he hurt you?"

Katie's eyes were blank and far away. Her body shook uncontrollably. Cal just held her for a few moments while the other officers searched the perimeter.

"This is what I was afraid of." Cal thought to himself. The anger was building from deep inside him. He had to do something. Eddie needed to be stopped before anyone else got hurt.

Sgt. Nelsen drove up from the quarry and came back to the house. There was no sign of another vehicle. However, if this was Eddie, he was probably hoofing it down the tracks and was long gone by now.

Katie was slowly getting a handle on her uncontrollable shaking. Cal thought she could have had a break down the way she was trembling so badly.

"Kate, honey...I need to know if you're okay."

Katie nodded her head 'yes'.

"I don't want you to be alone tonight. I'd like you to stay with me at my house in town. Would that be alright with you?" Cal's even soft tone was sincere and reassuring to Katie.

Once again she nodded 'yes', with her body still shaking.

"Nelsen, can you take care of this? I am going to take her to my place, where I know she'll be safe and get some rest."

Jim agreed, "No worries, we'll check everything out and get back to you."

Jim helped Katie into the front seat of Cal's Crown Vic and stayed with her while Cal ran inside to grab a change of clothes. He was careful not to disrupt anything and noticed at a glance that nothing seemed out of place. The front door wasn't damaged, and the basement door was still latched. Katie had a laundry basket of clean clothes sitting on the floor by the couch. Cal grabbed a sweater and pair of jeans, socks and her shoes on the way out. He knew if there was anything to find Nelsen would find it.

Cal shut his door, "Thanks, Jim. You know where to find us."

Jim tapped the roof of the car in response. He then watched as Cal pulled out and drove out over the bridge to home. *"That poor girl can't catch a break."* He said to himself shaking his head.

In minutes Cal was pulling into his driveway. He parked alongside the walkway, and then got out to help Katie, who had been silent on the ride over. He opened her door while holding her bundle of clothes. Then coaxing Katie out of the squad, "Sweetie, let's go inside." His words prompted her to go with him.

Pete, who had been on the phone with Debbie, while sitting in the dark, channel-surfing, heard Cal unlock the front door. "I have to go, we'll talk soon." Then Pete hung up as he stepped out to greet Cal. Only to find a shaking and distant Katie standing there wrapped in a blanket.

Cal had a worried expression on his face. He set her change of clothes on the bench in the front hall and gently guided Katie to the living room where Cal turned on a lamp with soft light so they weren't totally in the dark.

The dread that Pete was feeling seemed to be coming true. "What the 'hell' just happened?"

Cal shot back, "Not now!" and motioned for him to hold his thoughts. He then sat Katie on one of the large leather sofas and took a throw off the arm chair to cover her up in.

"Kate, Sweetie, would you like some water?" Cal asked calmly.

Katie looked up at him. "Yes, please." She managed to say. Her shaking had slowed considerably, now just a shiver like she was cold.

Cal motioned for Pete to follow him into the kitchen. In hushed tones Cal quickly gave Pete the complete run down about what happened.

Pete felt awful. But right now it wasn't about him it was about Katie.

Cal asked for Pete's patience in the matter and for him not to push anything. Pete agreed, even though he'd never been one to be patient when his friends were in trouble. He wanted to 'find Eddie and kill the son of a bitch'.

Pete thought Katie looked cold, "Do you have any tea in this place?"

"Aah...yeah. There is a tin in the cupboard above the coffee maker."

"I'll make Katie some tea; she likes hot tea to unwind, it'll help."

Cal pulled out his tea pot that he only used when his mother visited, filled it with water and put it on the stove.

Pete searched the cabinet and found the tin with tea.

They came back into the living room and found Katie deep in thought - staring out into space. Cal handed her the glass of water.

She took a sip; then another. Cal sat on the couch next to her but gave her space. Whatever she'd just gone through he didn't want to smother her only give her support. He needed her to trust him.

Pete sat opposite the two, bouncing his leg with irritation.

The color had come back in her face; she seemed calm and was breathing steadier, now. Katie looked over at Pete, then to Cal.

"It's Eddie." She stated without any expression. "I know it with every fiber of my being, it's Eddie."

Cal kept a calm even tone in his voice and asked, "Did you see him in your house?"

Pete was quite impressed. There was no way he could have kept the anger out of his voice.

Katie shook her head no, "No, it was dark, but I could smell him."

Pete chimed in, "What do you mean, smell him?"

Katie looked at Pete, "He has a very musky odor. I don't know any other way to describe it. It's earthy, but it's very distinct. He was the man in my room tonight. I know he was!"

Cal knew it was Eddie also, but he had to prove it. Now there was no way in hell he was going to let Kate go back to that house.

Katie was watching Cal, who was deep in thought. "You don't want me to go back to the house do you?" She was reading his mind again.

"No, I don't! I want you to stay here, where Pete and I can make sure no one can get to you."

"I have to go to work tomorrow night. If I don't, Eddie will know I know. I don't want to work with him, or be anywhere around him. But I don't want to have to keep looking over my shoulder if he runs. Besides, I am very safe at work. Erik will keep him away from me. Jack is down stairs with me. I'll be fine at work."

Pete and Cal exchanged looks of disbelief. "You are incorrigible!" Cal stated.

Katie knew they weren't happy she wanted to go back. "If I go back to work, he will trust that we don't know it was him.   We'll spread the word that I was attacked in my home, but that 'I didn't see anything'. Besides you know Steve probably already knows anyway."

Pete shook his head in amazement, "You, my friend, are nuts! What the hell are you thinking? I was wrong to suggest using you as bait in the first place. If it wasn't for that cop checking up on you...well you could have been hurt or killed or worse!"

"Worse? What's worse than dead?" She gave pause.

The sound of a high pitch whistle went off in the kitchen, breaking the pace of the conversation.

Pete got up to make her a cup of tea. "Does anyone want anything while I'm up?"

Pete looked to Cal who was deep in thought again. "No? Okay then." Pete said with attitude as he left the room.

Cal was making a mental list of all the things that needed to happen. He didn't want to jump the gun and blow it. Before Eddie skips town he needs to bring him in for questioning.

Nelsen called, so Cal took it in the other room. Pete took his seat beside Katie, handing her a cup of tea. "You okay, Sis? He didn't hurt you did he?"

Katie shook her head 'no'.

"You had us worried there. Where did you drift off to?"

"Pete, I could have killed him...I think I wanted to." Katie's eyes weld up. "I was so scared, and angry. I had my knife and I wanted to stab him with it."

Pete offered a hug and she leaned into him, resting her head on his shoulder; her legs were curled up underneath her. Now that her shaking had subsided she was feeling better. She needed a release and that was her body's way of dealing with all the stress. Katie had been on a terrifying roller coaster of emotions. Pete couldn't believe all that Katie was dealing with.

They could hear muffled tones coming from the front room. Cal sounded all business.

Nelsen told Cal, "Whoever it was, let them-selves in. No break-in and nothing was disturbed. Cal would have to question Kate as to what she remembered. "Jim I know it's late and you are off tomorrow, but I could really use your help."

"Yeah, I'll be in. How early do you need me?"

"Get some sleep. I don't think we can get the FBI in before noon anyway."

"See you then."

Cal's conversation had piqued Pete's interest. Cal turned around to find Pete standing in the doorway eaves dropping.

"He used a key to get in didn't he?" Pete asked.

"How did you know that?"

"He took it out of my pocket when he took my truck keys and then dropped my ass off the cliff." Pete sounded pissy.

"You're only just telling me this now?"

"Hey – we only just found out about it today."

Cal was visibly upset, "We? She knew this guy had her house key, and she stayed anyway?"

Pete was upset, "What do you want me to say?"

Cal was angry, but didn't want Pete to blame himself for this. "Pete, he would have found another way to get at Kate. So now, if we find him with her key...we're nailing his ass to the wall."

Then Cal said, "Let's get her up to my room. She needs to get some rest."

Pete wasn't able to do much with one arm. Cal had to be the one to get her up off the couch, and they slowly made their way up the stairs.

Katie remembered the first time she'd been shown Cal's house. The master bedroom suite was only in the tear down stage. Now, when he opened the doors for her, it was a large open canvas waiting for a woman's touch. And he had an enormous bed with a big beautifully carved headboard. The feather down comforter looked so cozy.

Pete turned down the covers for Katie and she got in. Pete gave her a big hug and said 'night, Sis'.

"Thanks, Pete!"

Pete knew Cal wanted to talk to her, and left to mull things over in his own room closing the door behind him.

Katie reached out for Cal. He took her hand, which was still a little cold, and sat down on the edge of the bed. "I'm sorry," she said.

"Sorry? For what do you have to be sorry about?"

"You were right, I was wrong. I never should have allowed myself to be alone right now."

Cal couldn't believe his ears. He sat there quietly, searching her face, and then asked, "Are you sure you're going to be all right? Do you want to talk to someone about what happened?"

"He didn't hurt me, and the only one I want to talk to right now, is you. Could you stay with me?"

Cal wanted nothing more than to be here with Kate in his arms, but didn't feel it was right. "I'll stay for a little while. You talk about whatever you want to, okay?"

Katie gave Cal her best smile, even though he could see how tired she was.

Cal kicked off his shoes, removed his tie, and then unbuttoned his shirt to get somewhat comfortable. He crawled up on the bed beside her but stayed on top of the covers. She shifted her body so she could snuggle up to Cal and began to unload. He knew she was a strong woman, but he couldn't believe how strong she was until now. Katie amazed him on a daily basis. Knowing what she had been through less than two years ago, and then to have this stalker, someone in her house, in her room about to do Lord knows what. And yet, she has the courage to go back and work with this guy, so they can arrest him. This was truly remarkable by anyone's standards.

Katie was driven by anger now. She was determined to see this through.

Cal finally had to ask, "Sweetie, what do you remember happening, tonight?"

"I got home from work, showered and got ready for bed. Pete called, checking up on me, just as I was getting into bed. I remember looking at the clock thinking you or one of the other officers would be driving by shortly. I laid down and must have dozed off a little, when I heard the floor boards next to my bed creak. I froze. My hand was already under my pillow where I keep a knife, and I grabbed it but made sure I lay perfectly still. I was so scared. That's when he touched me."

Cal hearing those words clenched his jaw tight.

"I couldn't breathe at that point. I froze, and I couldn't move. But I could smell him. His musk burned the inside of my nose. That's when I knew it was Eddie.

He is the only one I know that wears that musk. It's horrible, it really is. I remember hearing a car, and then he walked over to look out my window. That's when I couldn't take it any longer and jumped out of bed with my knife. I think I startled him, 'cuz he took off so fast, bounding down the stairs and rushed out the front door. There was no way I could keep up with him. The cop that drove through never saw a thing, just me with my knife. I was fine until I had to sit down. Then this wave hit me and I just couldn't keep myself from shaking. I was so cold, and I felt like everything I went through before was happening to me all over again. Everything rushed me all at once and I couldn't focus. I didn't mean to scare you. I don't know...I just went inside myself for a little bit to collect my thoughts. I guess...it was just too much. But you were right. And I am so sorry I didn't listen to you."

Cal didn't know what to say. He was relieved Kate wasn't physically hurt. He just held her close in his arms and kissed her. "I love you, Kate. I don't know what I would have done if something happened to you tonight."

His words took her off guard.

Nothing more was said. Katie felt safe in Cal's arms and could relax enough to finally fall asleep. Cal was going over everything in his head on how he was going to proceed. He certainly didn't want her to go back to work with Eddie. He had to stop him, now.

Pete lay wide awake. And as apprehensive as he was there was no way he'd get any sleep tonight. His only thought right now was that he wasn't going to let anything happen to Katie.

Chapter 34

It was 8:30 a.m.; Cal barely rested his eyes when he was up and in the shower. Katie was sound asleep when he left the room. Pete was down stairs making coffee. He didn't sleep much either.

"Pete."

"Coffee?"

"Thanks, I'll take it to go. I have a lot to get done this morning before I get Eddie to come in for questioning."

He noticed Pete had *that look* then said, "And Pete - please, whatever you are thinking – don't!"

Pete got a smirk on his face. "I don't know what you mean," he said, coyly.

"Pete, I'm as serious as a heart attack...let me do this the right way."

Cal empathized with Pete and wanted to take Eddie out too, but he couldn't. He needed Eddie to be put away for good and not have this come back and bite them in the ass.

Pete knew Cal was right but his emotions were running high and didn't like to hear it.

"Just stay with Katie, Pete. I need to know she's safe. I promise you, I will get this son of a bitch!"

***

Once Cal was in his office he immediately started making phone calls. First, to Bob, the owner of the Brick Yard, and told him about what happened at Katie's last night. He wanted everyone who worked there last night to come in to the station for an interview today. Steve had already told Bob about the break-in and that everyone was going to be called down to the station. Erik would see to it that Eddie would come in with him. If there was any trouble Cal would have a police escort waiting. But he didn't want Eddie to be suspicious that he was their main suspect.

Eddie was so cocky and sure of himself that when Erik called to give him a heads up, he never even thought about bolting. When Cal made the same call to Eddie, he told Cal he'd be in. He even asked if 'Katie was all right'.

"You smug son of a bitch - your ass is mine!" Cal thought to himself, as he hung up the phone.

A courier had brought over Edward's military records bright and early, so Cal was reviewing them when Jim came in. The two worked together getting all their 'ducks in a row' before the forensic psychologist from the FBI reviews the entire report. They didn't need to wait long. The woman from the FBI came in around 11 a.m. She went over everything and agreed, "Yes, call him in."

This was new territory for Nelsen. It was almost exciting to finally work a case like this if it weren't for the people involved.

One by one the employees from the Brick Yard came in for questioning. Bob, Tanya and Erik, then Jack and Billie were interviewed. When Eddie came in, Jessica was just leaving and so was Steve. This put Eddie at ease. He figured they were going to just give their typical lame interview that didn't amount to much, but go through the motions of 'did you see anyone pay particular interest to Katie?' Blah, Blah, Blah. He smirked to himself.

Cal was in the conference room mentally preparing. As badly as he wanted to rip Eddie's head off he needed to gain the bastard's trust to get a confession out of him; at least for the murder of Scott Warren, if he was going to put him away for good.

Nelsen called Eddie's name, and brings him to the back conference room. Cal was sitting at the large wooden table with a few files in front of him, with a note pad, and pen in hand. He barely looks up to acknowledge Eddie. "Come in, have a seat."

Eddie felt even more confident, thinking that they don't have a clue, who was in Katie's house. He pulls out a chair and sits next to Cal.

Cal proceeds. "My name is Detective Cal Chapman. I will be interviewing you today. For the record your name is," He looked down at Ed's file and read aloud, "Edward C. Landers. Is that correct?"

"Yes, Sir."

Cal continued to ask all the usual questions taking his time, but then goes off course and starts to ask Ed about his military experience. "Weren't you an Army Ranger?"

Eddie cocked his head slightly to one side. "I was."

Cal continued, "That had to be something. Feeling strong, invincible, and being in the best shape of your life. Looks like you still work out. I bet it's hard to give up?"

"I don't know what you mean, Sir."

"You know, give up the honor and respect of wearing the uniform."

Eddie thought this was a strange question. But he was proud to be a member of the U.S. military. As soon as Eddie started talking about being in the Rangers, Cal had him. He knew he was lying.

Cal was carefully guiding their conversation from the case at hand to Eddie's military training and back to Katie. Cal was laid back for most of the interview, allowing Eddie to get comfortable.

Before Cal could ask him about Scott's murder, he decided to shift directions on Eddie. "Say, have you eaten yet? I'm starving! It was late last night, and in early this morning, now they have me doing all these interviews. How about we take a break?"

Eddie wasn't sure where Chapman was going with this, but he was curious. Cal seemed relaxed and this didn't give Eddie any indication that he was a suspect. "No, Sir. I haven't eaten."

Cal hollered out the door, "Nelsen! Can you come in here please?"

"Can we get a couple of bar burgers in here?" He looks to Eddie. "Want a beer?"

Eddie couldn't believe this interview. It was more of a social thing. He shrugged his shoulders, "Sure, sounds good."

"And a beer for Eddie; I guess I'll just have a cola."

Cal didn't want Eddie to lawyer up and this 20-minute casual lunch break was the perfect time to set Ed off his game.

Cal excused himself, meeting Nelsen out in a front office out of sight from the conference room. "Did you get it?"

"We did."

Cal stepped back into the conference room with fresh hot bar burgers. He hands Eddie the can of beer. "Sorry, they won't allow a bottle in here. Best I could do."

Eddie was carefully watching Cal's body language for any signs that he was the one they were looking for.

Cal opens his can of soda and takes a sip, then sets it down. Cal's body language is low key and relaxed. The two men start to eat their lunch, casually talking with a joke here and there. Cal dwells on Eddie's military life and gets him to open up. "It's a 6-year enlistment to be a Ranger. That's impressive. You have to be smart too. They only let the elite join Special Forces."

This brings a smile to Eddie's face.

"I bet you're smart as hell Eddie."

Eddie can't help but to brag about what he got to do in the Rangers. Flamboyantly boasting about how great he was.

"So, why did you quit Eddie?"

Cal continued to boost Eddie's ego then tear it down. Wearing him down was key.

"You know that kid, Scott Warren we found under the bridge, just down the road from here? We think he was killed by someone with your military training."

Eddie's body language suddenly changed. Now, he sat back in his chair on guard with the direction of this questioning.

"What does that have to do with me, Sir? The papers say it was drug related."

"I'm just sayin' that the one, who murdered Scott, had your particular set of skills. Maybe you can help us?"

"How is that, Sir?"

"Well, you would know a lot about the individual we are looking for. You both have had the same kind of military training for instance."

That comment started to ease Eddie a little bit.

Now, Cal pulls in his chair really close to Eddie so that they are knee to knee. This puts Eddie on alert once again.

"Is there any reason to believe I would have any evidence to connect you to the scene of this crime or witnesses to this crime?"

Eddie tried very hard to play it cool, "No, Sir!" But his body language betrays him. His foot starts to tap, and he shifts in his chair.

"Did you know Scott Warren?"

"Forgive me Sir, but you already questioned me about that when it happened. Like I told you then, no Sir, I did not know Scott Warren."

"Are you sure you never met this guy." Cal had placed the photo of Scott in front of Eddie. "He frequented the very bar you work."

Eddie looked at the photo. Cal notices no response.

"Maybe I've seen him, probably but nothing that stands out."

Cal takes him at his word.

"You said you were in the Gulf War. How did it feel when you killed someone?"

Eddie began to lean forward again and rubbed his jaw. "Kill? Killing is what I do best...I loved to kill."

"How many did you kill?"

"I don't know..."

"Sure you do. I know everyone of my kills."

Eddie sat there trying to figure out what Cal was asking then fired back, "Man, I killed at least 10. I was the best!"

Cal notices that Eddie uncrosses his arms and relaxes a bit more. His eyes now looked up and to the left, and Cal realizes he's gaining his trust again. Ed had an unnatural comfort when it came to killing. Cal knows this is their guy.

Nelsen comes into the conference room. Eddie wasn't so sure about this now. Sgt. Nelsen made him feel a bit uncomfortable.

"So Eddie, tell Jim here about your Special Forces training, like you told me. This is great Jim, you have to hear this."

Jim pulls up a chair across the table from Edward, portraying interest.

Cal prods Eddie into talking more about what kind of training he got. "Rangers live in a forest out in the elements right?"

Eddie concurred that they did and added some interesting tales.

Nelsen pulls out a bagged and tagged survival knife, and then hands it over to Cal in front of Eddie.

Eddie pushes himself back into his seat. His leg starts bouncing up and down in a nervous manor.

Cal looks at the knife then up into Eddie's eyes. "I have to ask you something Ed. Is this the knife issued to you by the U.S. Special Forces?"

"Why would you ask me that?"

"I'm the one asking the questions Edward. But since you asked, I'll tell you. We believe our victim was killed with a knife just like this. This is the same type of weapon used to kill Scott Warren. Long blade, serrated edge. Didn't you have to train with this type of knife? Survival teams are dropped and left to find their way back using only this knife. You said so yourself."

"Yes, Sir."

"Did you ever kill anyone with a knife like this?"

Ed hesitated, then answered, "Yes, Sir."

"Tell me about that."

This line of questioning was helter skelter. It confused Eddie as to what was going on, but he was too curious to stop now. "I had an assignment one night; in quiet – out quiet."

"Well, do you own a knife like this? Did you procure one when you left the Army?"

Now, Eddie was sure he was a suspect. "No, Sir. I don't have a knife like that?"

"Would there be any reason anyone would have seen you with one, or lie about seeing you with one?"

A bead of sweat started to form on the side of his left temple. "I guess someone could lie."

"Who? Who would lie about that Eddie?"

Eddie suddenly got cocky, "Don't know Sir, I'm a bouncer at a popular bar, I piss people off."

"I hear you've bragged about being an Army Ranger. Some think you're full of yourself. Is that true or are you lying?" Cal stared directly at him with attentive silence.

"They are lying, Sir. I was an Army Ranger."

"You don't own a knife like this and you didn't know Scott Warren?"

"No, Sir."

"Can I have your written permission to search your apartment?"

"No"

"No? You could prove you're not a suspect. We know our vic was a drug dealer."

Eddie was annoyed, "No."

Cal continued to badger, "I have some problems with the information you have given me. I have some real problems...matter of fact you're lying to me. I know it."

"When was I lying?"

"Well Eddie, you're lying about the knife. I believe you own one. You do know the vic. And let's look at the way the vic was killed. You know how to kill like that; in an upward thrust. They trained you to kill and you said it yourself you were good at it."

Eddie didn't realize it but he had a smile on his face when Cal was telling him he was good at killing.

"I don't think you are coming clean with me. I think you know something about the murder. You're not telling me everything. I think you know more about this, and you're involved, in some way Eddie."

There was silence. Nelsen sat quietly observing as this unfolds before his eyes. Even he didn't know where Cal was going with this.

Cal encourages a response from Eddie. He really leans into him and says in a low strong voice, "You are a very dangerous person Edward. I think a very dangerous person did this crime. You are capable of something like this. I don't' know why someone would murder this happy dope like that. The person who killed this guy likes to kill. He likes to feel the weight of the person dying."

Silence, but Cal could see Eddie recalling the act in his head.

"I want to ask you something Edward. Is there any reason you would think I would be looking at you as the perpetrator of this crime?"

There was a period of attentive silence.

Eddie started to squirm. "No, tell me Sir."

Cal repeated what was just said. "You told me you enjoyed doing your job." Cal listed everything all over again. "You had military sanction; you told me you like to kill."

Cal intently glared at Eddie then said, "You know what Edward? I have friends who are in Special Forces too. The difference is they didn't enjoy killing. They did the job they were ordered to do. They were good at it, but they didn't enjoy doing it like you did. And you did enjoy it didn't you?"

Eddie finally responded with, "Maybe - I didn't so much."

"It doesn't appear you're so sure of yourself, now you're changing your story? Edward, I know you're lying to me and I can prove it."

Cal reaches down into a briefcase set on the chair between Jim and himself. Then he places a very thick file on the table in front of him. Cal taps it with his fingers. "You know I have a lot of evidence and information in here. I believe everything you have said in the past 3-hours has been a lie. Not only are you lying, you refused to let me search your apartment. What are you afraid of Edward? Drugs? I don't think you have drugs. But we'd find physical evidence like this knife. Look at this knife. See this blade – its teeth; hard cold steel. Look how sharp it is. What it does to a human body – or bone..."

Cal waved the knife in Eddie's face, back and forth, watching his body language.

"Are you sure Eddie, you don't own one?"

"I want to go home now."

Cal's calm tone changed to one which was still a low set demeanor but over bearing, "Not yet! I told you, I know you are lying to me. Do you want to know what the biggest lie was? Do you remember when you left the service? Gulf War experience? Eddie, you were discharged after only 2 ½ years, and you were washed out of Special Forces school after only 3-months." Cal continued tapping the thick folder before him.

"Just so you know, this has been read by the FBI, the US Attorney, and reviewed by a forensic psychologist. They all say you're a pretty sick guy. You like to kill, but you don't need anyone to tell you that. How do you explain to me the lies? Bragging about your service; about your knife...are you sure they made that all up?"

Silence.

Eddie's foot was tapping faster now.

"You've been lying to me this whole time Edward. Do you think I'm stupid? Did you honestly think that I wouldn't follow up? I ruled out all the other suspects. Why?"

More attentive silence.

"Tell me why, Eddie?" Cal asked as he lightly touched him on the knee. Eddie protests.

"I don't want to hear any more lies Eddie. I know you killed Scott. Don't insult my intelligence. I know you did this, and this file proves it. Don't even try to deny it. Everyone knows you did it."

Eddie started to speak but Cal raised a hand to stop him. "Nope! No more lies, Edward. What I really want to know is why. Please tell me why?" Then Cal pounded the table, "I know you did it!"

That not only startled Eddie but Jim too.

"The only thing I don't know, is why? By the way, is the knife in your apartment? I want to search for the clothes you wore, anything with blood on them, and your boots. I see you're wearing boots with a thick tread."

This badgering went on for another 2-hours, back and forth. Nothing to drink or bathroom breaks. Cal continuously rides Edward and won't let him relax.

"Am I under arrest?"

"I didn't' say you were under arrest. Should I put you under arrest? I just need to know why you did it. It's plausible you had a good reason. This was a brutal murder. You must have been really pissed! What did he do to you?"

Eddie sat not sure of what to say or do. Cal was relentless.

"Maybe it was an irresistible impulse?"

Now, Cal got his attention, "What's that?"

"Irresistible impulse is a defense. It means you were driven into such a rage you lost control; an involuntary act. This guy really made you mad."

Eddie thought about that for a moment but then Cal came back strong.

"I know you did it, how about you tell me why?"

Eddie couldn't take much more of Cal's pounding. He finally starts to break down. "Tell me more about that irresistible impulse."

"Well Eddie, maybe they will go for a lesser charge so you won't spend the rest of your life in prison. What was the reason you killed Scott Warren? He was just a lowly drug dealer."

"He was getting in my way!"

"In your way? In your way for what?"

"You Chapman, of all people should be thanking me!"

"Thanking you? Why is that?"

"You know about the drugs in Katie's attic. Who do you think would sneak into her house late at night and visit her?"

Cal wasn't going to fall for any emotional game play. But he inquisitively had to use any avenue Eddie gave him. Cal let Edward continue.

"So you're saying you killed Scott to keep Katie safe? You knew he was a threat to her? You work with her as a bouncer and you protect the women at that bar. You're intentions were honorable."

Edward liked the sound of that. After all he loved Katie, he'd never hurt her. "I wouldn't hurt Katie - I couldn't." In his own perverted mind he truly believed that.

It was a very chilling statement, and Cal didn't let on that it struck a chord with him.

"But you did kill Scott to protect her? You gave him what he deserved; you did what you had to, to protect Katie. This Scott was a 'Peeping Tom', a dangerous drug dealer breaking into Katie's home. The law, me, Pete we didn't protect her, so you took it upon yourself to right a terrible wrong. Ed there is another defense for what you did to Scott, for Katie's sake. It's called the 'defense of necessity'. Did you know that under the law, that defense justifies the commission of a certain crime, because it is extremely necessary to remove certain danger; danger of rape; bodily harm; danger from a serious crime about to be committed? So you stopped him from hurting Katie, by killing him."

Cal was setting the themes for Eddie. Eddie was eating it up. Cal made him feel like he did right by killing Scott. Cal was sounding almost grateful to Eddie. However, Cal needed his written admission.

Nelsen knew there was a catch in what Cal had told Eddie, which was that the crime being stopped has to be an imminent act, about to happen in the next instance, of course that wasn't the case with Eddie, but he doesn't know that.

Cal creates an aura now that he is trying to help Eddie out of a 1st degree murder charge, by allowing two defenses, giving Ed hope that he will not do much time in prison.

Still toying with Eddie, Cal now provokes him, "I have to say, I'd have done the same thing to protect Katie; so would Pete, that it was 'necessary' to take action now and not wait for it to happen."

Eddie now believes that what he did was logical, even a self-sacrificing act.

Cal tells him, "A kind jury will believe you, I need you to write that down, and definitely include in your confession both alibis, two well-intentioned reasons for your actions. The safety and well being of a woman and the protection of society from a terrible drug dealing sex deviate."

Cal pushed his legal pad over to Eddie and had him start writing.

Cal had worn Eddie down. Eddie's ego and curiosity got the better of him. It was one of the longest days in Chapman's police career.

Jim was amazed and in awe of how it played out. It felt good to close Scott Warren's murder case and know they got Katie's stalker, Edward C. Landers. It was now only a matter of forensics to link Eddie to Pete's accident. Cal was feeling great.

Chapter 35

It was dark and beginning to rain by the time Cal left the station. A heavy weight was finally lifted. Cal couldn't feel any better than he already did tonight. Opening the door to his Victorian home the warm smells of home cooking hit him. Pete and Katie had busied themselves in the kitchen all day baking anything and everything.

Pete and Katie had the music so loud they hadn't heard Cal come home. He stood in the doorway observing what used to be his kitchen and was now a bake shop. Katie had just taken a pan of some chocolate-chip cookies out of the oven. Pete was one-handedly prying them off the pan with a spatula and putting them on to a rack to cool, when Katie looked up to find Cal standing there. Her heart stopped. She wiped off her hands on the apron she was wearing and quickly came over to greet him.

He smiled, thinking how cute she was with a dusting of flour on her cheek. He dropped everything right there and swooped her into his arms and gave her a kiss she'd never forget. She felt so good in his arms. He looked over to Pete and winked. With that, Pete knew they got Eddie.

"We have him locked up, Kate. He's going to prison for the murder of Scott Warren. He confessed."

Katie was so relieved. "What about what he did to Pete?"

"We will have a match to the print we found in the quarry as well as the one by Scott's body. Forensics will tie up any loose ends. I don't want to jinx it. I want to enjoy this..." He said as he looked around the messy kitchen and smiled.

Katie realized what a mess she and Pete had made and wrinkled her button nose. "Sorry about the mess, we'll clean it up."

Pete jumped in, "Who's we, freckles?"

Cal could care less right now. "I smell something else? What are you making now?"

"Oh, I made dinner. I didn't know how late you'd be so I made beef stroganoff. I hope you like it?"

Cal hugged her again. "Sounds wonderful let me clean-up and we'll eat."

After dinner Pete was eager to call Debbie, so he excused himself going straight to bed. He could finally relax knowing Katie was safe from Eddie.

Cal helped Katie with dishes and packaged up the cookies and breads she and Pete had made. "Looks like the guys at work are going to have a real treat with their coffee tomorrow."

Katie laughed, "I guess I did go overboard. I just didn't know what to do with myself today. I knew I couldn't call you to find out what was going on, and the boredom was driving me crazy."

"Well at least now I know you can cook and bake." He said teasing her.

Once they had his kitchen back in order there came an awkward moment between them.

Cal asked, "You have been through so much already; I don't want to assume anything between us. But I would really like it if you would stay."

Katie had been through a bombardment of emotions in the last 24-hours. But only one thing kept her from losing it, and that was the thought of being in Cal's arms. She took his hand and led him up the stairs to his master bedroom suite.

He turned on the lamp that was on the nightstand, which gave a soft glow to the room.

Katie took one look at herself in the mirror and couldn't help but laugh aloud. "Don't I look sexy? Why didn't you tell me I was such a mess?"

"You look beautiful to me, Kate." Then taking her face in his hands, Cal kissed her on the nose.

"If I am going to stay the night...I'll be right back."

Once the bathroom door closed, Cal picked up his book and sat in his over sized tufted leather chair. The rain slanted against the windows making a soft rhythmic music. It wasn't long before Katie emerged from the bathroom wrapped in a towel. Her long red-hair was dark and wet. Her fresh face had an angelic glow. Katie's beautiful hazel green eyes twinkled back with the flash of lightning. She walked slowly over to Cal, who was in awe of her feminine beauty. The only thing holding up her over sized fluffy bath towel was the little tuck of the end she had over her left breast.

He was finally going to be with this woman who he kept falling in love with over and over again. Katie sensed he was just as nervous as she was. She liked that he was so much more than what people saw. Not only a tough guy, but vulnerable too.

Cal closed up his book, setting it down on the table next to the chair. He rose, standing in front of Kate. The lightning silently flashed and the rain began to hit the window panes with more force as the wind picked up.

He bent down to kiss Kate as she tip toed to meet his lips. His large strong hands firmly holding her body to him.

They kissed with such passion, eagerly wanting more of each other. Moving ever closer to his enormous bed, lip locked. Katie ran her hands up underneath Cal's t-shirt, reading every muscle from his sides to his back like brail, and softly raking her nails across his broad shoulder blades.

This sent electricity through Cal that would have driven any man insane. He pulled off his shirt, while she dropped his jogging pants. He took her towel, releasing it to the floor. They fell on to the bed with a jolt of desire. She was full of surprises, and he wanted to discover them all. Her taut nipples pressed in to his chest and she could feel his erection growing against her inner thigh. Katie gives in to her passion arching her back and tilting her pelvis allowing Cal to enter her. Slowly accepting all of him an electric current ran through her, giving way for a pleasure she'd yet to experience. Their bodies coming together in a heated rhythm in time with the pouring rain beating on the windows; driving them to ecstasy. She collapsed on to his heaving chest writhing against him. They lay there together in each other's arms for a while as she felt his heart beating heavily. She looks up at his handsome face with a satisfied grin and her bewitching eyes sparkled. Cal gazes into Kate's beautiful eyes and flashes a charming smile back.

She props herself up on one elbow looking down at him and traces his face with her fingers, then kisses him deeply. Her hair cascades over her shoulders. She likes seeing the effect her touch has on him.

They were in love and this is where they were meant to be.

Taken

Cal walked into the substation and could feel the tensions. There was a quiet buzz of conversations going on, and a few disgruntled looks. Cal found Sgt. Nelsen mumbling to himself typing a report at his desk. He paused in front of him, "Serge – what did I miss?"

Jim didn't even bother to look up from his "hen-pecking" before he started to unload. "That f'n chief we got! Son of a mother f'n bitch!" When Nelsen finally did look up, his jaw was clenched and his muscles pulsed in rage.

"Hey, Jim...let's take it into my office."

Nelsen stood up pushing back hard in his chair - making it slam into the wall behind him. He marched into Cal's office.

Cal followed, shutting the door behind him. Before Cal could sit down behind his desk - Jim just erupted.

"He's fuckin' with me Cal! The son of a bitch is screwing with me. I had less than two years to go! Now Kristine is begging for me to stay on another 3-5 years; so now he's fuckin' with me!"

"What the hell are you talking about?"

"That weasel bastard - Perry!"

"What did he do, now?"

"He has this way of showing obvious disgust for me! You know, all that body language interrogation technique bullshit – dressing down! He does that! On purpose – he does it to insult me! Rude, insulting, bastard! He criticizes everything I do, every decision I make!"

Cal tried to calm his friend down. "Jim, now slow down. Can you give me a for instance?"

"Okay – remember I had a disorderly conduct against that 75 year old woman with alcohol psychosis and schizophrenia? We've arrested her before – three times!"

"Yeah, Judy?"

"Right - and the States Attorney "says" she can't be prosecuted due to insanity. They told us not to arrest her any more, but to call the family...so that Son of a Bitch turned it on me and is giving *me* a 3-day suspension for dereliction of duty! Can you believe that shit?"

"I would have to investigate that...I never received anything on this."

"Of course not, Cal, he gave it to "Deputy Dog" to handle."

"So, now he's using the Deputy Chief as "internal affairs"?"

"Dogget couldn't find his ass from a hole in the ground! The handwriting is on the wall, Cal! I'm tellin' you!"

"Has he done anything else?"

The more he told Cal about what was going on, Nelsen's demeanor turned almost manic. "Cal, you won't believe this shit! He ordered a second I.A.

(Internal Affairs) complaint against me with the Dean of Students at the high school. There was a minor P.I. (personal injury) hit and run in their parking lot, that occurred right at shift change. The Chief took *three* of my officers from my shift and put them on a radar detail. He left me with one damn officer. So, that left me to cover the entire west side of town, and Gentry to cover the east side! Now, the dispatcher didn't say the high school had the offender cornered. It was given to me as just a report of leaving the scene. Of course, then the Dean wasn't happy because their CSO wasn't on duty, and had no one to handle the accident. The 3rd time they called us was when we learned they had the offender in custody. Apparently the high school failed to communicate that to dispatch, until the Dean was fit to be tied. So, I showed up, and the Dean was upset that it took so long for us to respond, there was no officer on campus and whose fault was that? The damn Chief! That's who! *He* pulled their CSO!"

Nelsen paused, only long enough to breathe. "When I was finally able to get this taken care of, I arrested the kid, charging him with three serious traffic offences and gave the Dean copies of the reports and charging documents. Which is the minimum he needed to bring an expulsion hearing on this punk, and I was able to put all this on his desk by 7:30 that night. The Dean was happier than hell! But that ass- hole Perry accused me of poor quality service and sent out his carbon copy to the school for the I.A. investigation."

Cal sat behind his desk absorbing it all in. He couldn't believe he didn't have a clue his friend was going through all of this, and he knew nothing about it, until now. He knew Chief Perry wasn't liked by the other officers, but he didn't realize the extent of deceit.

"Cal, do you know what the Dean told the Deputy Chief? 'I don't want to force a complaint against Sgt. Nelsen. He gave me everything I asked for and quickly. It appears to me *you* were the ones at fault for pulling the CSO to help with your radar detail!' That SOB suspended me for three days! He goofed, and I get suspended!"

"Jim, I don't see how he can do that." Cal said, still in disbelief. It wasn't that he didn't believe Jim, but to think that the Chief would orchestrate such blatant injustice.

"Don't you see what Perry is doing? He's fabricating complaints against me just so he can administer punishment. He is blackening my personnel file making me look bad in front of my men, and the entire department!"

Cal watched his friend as he unloaded. The Jim Nelsen, who had been his friend for years, was being turned into an angry disgruntled mess of a man.

"And another thing - I know he's only doing this because I told them that I was thinking about staying the full 25 years. He's making my life a living hell so I won't stay. He wants to force me into early retirement, Cal!"

"I'm surprised he hasn't nailed me then for not breaking up the biker party in the cemetery."

Jim gave Cal a gloomy shake of his head. His eyes appeared to be hollow and empty. "Cal, why don't you check your messages?"

Cal looked down at the phone and saw the little red light blinking, letting him know there were messages waiting.

Made in the USA
Monee, IL
18 March 2024

55137599R00184